Traegonia
The Ember Rune

Written by
K.S. Krueger

Illustrated by
Dino C. Crisanti

Outskirts Press, Inc.
Denver, Colorado

Traegonia
The Ember Rune
All Rights Reserved.
Copyright © 2011 Traegonia Inc.
v2.0
Written by K.S. Krueger
Illustrations by Dino C. Crisanti

Second Book in the Traegonia Series, First Edition
Ages 8 and up
Fantasy Fiction, Middle Grade Fantasy, All ages Rural Fantasy

Outskirts Press, Inc.
http://www.outskirtspress.com

ISBN PB: 978-1-4327-7604-6
ISBN HB: 978-1-4327-7718-0

Library of Congress Control Number: 2011933284

Outskirts Press and the "OP" logo are trademarks belonging to Outskirts Press, Inc.

PRINTED IN THE UNITED STATES OF AMERICA

Dedicated to our Spouses, Children, Family and Friends who have helped, encouraged and supported our dream; and for being a source of the Extraordinary in our Ordinary lives.

Thanks for Believing!

To Rita,

Always find something
extraordinary within
everything ordinary!

Thanks for
    Believeing!

2011

Contents

Prologue

Sometimes there are moments in our lives that can take us from an ordinary existence and propel us into an extraordinary series of events that will alter our lives forever. This is my story of one of those moments. Many years ago, I was just an average, ordinary kid. I had a best friend from school named Quinn. I lived in an average, ordinary, rural Midwest town with my mom and dad. My life was pretty ordinary, too, until I met Karia and Juna. They were not your average, ordinary friends; they are Traegons—young at the time like I was, and brother and sister to each other.

Traegons are mystical creatures of the forest. The first time I saw them, I thought they resembled what I would imagine a cross between a troll and a wingless dragon might look like. Some might say Traegons are strange looking, maybe even fearsome. I guess I might have thought that, too, at first, but now that I have gotten to know them, to me they are nothing short of awesome. They are small, only about a foot and a half to two foot tall when they are full grown. They walk upright like us, but their skin is not at all like ours. It is light brown and looks somewhat like the bark of a tree. Some have many lines with deep grooves, while others are more like that of a smooth young tree. Their knuckles look a little like raised, round knots. The males have a long muzzle with a square jaw and a single, long, fang-like dark tooth that protrudes upward, from one side of their bottom jaw. They have pointed ears that stand up, curving slightly forward. Some, like Juna, have wavy white hair, and others have none. They have large hands with only three fingers and an opposable thumb. They also have broad feet with three toes. The females have much softer-looking faces, still long but with more of a pointed muzzle. Their ears are also large but lie down at the sides of their heads. They have feathers for hair, and their hands are slightly smaller than the males', but with long, slender fingers.

Their clothing looks to be handmade. It is natural in color, so they are able to blend into their surroundings rather easily. They wear pouches, jewelry, and other embellishments, many of which they make themselves from found items or trade for with others within their community. They are skilled and civilized. Some might even say they are more civilized than we humans are, or at least some of us. They live at peace with the Earth, each other, and all of nature. They have families just like humans do, with a mother, father, and children. They are hunters, gatherers, carpenters, artisans, herbalists, and inventors. They live in trees, underground, or anywhere they can hide and remain undiscovered. They are incredible creatures, and since I have a gift for drawing, I have filled journals with sketches of them over the years. I started the first journal on the very first day I met them. Of course I have kept all of it hidden—the journals and the Traegons—and I only share this with you now because they have given me permission to tell our story.

There are Traegon villages out there, everywhere. I have only seen Karia and Juna's village on a few occasions, and it was only when I was taken there by Karia through a process they call *summoning*. These incredible creatures do not make themselves known to everyone, so I consider myself lucky that I was one of the chosen ones.

The first year that I met them, their village, which is located somewhere in a forest near where my family often went for picnics and weekend fishing trips, was nearly destroyed by an unscrupulous developer. He wanted to bulldoze the forest, all of it, for his own selfish reasons. We came to learn of an old Traegon prophecy which is why we were brought together. I believe it was fate, really. That was when my ordinary world became extraordinary because we realized then that we can do anything we put our hearts and minds to. We just have to believe in ourselves, in each other, and in what we wish to accomplish.

That was just the beginning of many adventures we would have. Since then, we have become great friends. Herein is the tale of another of our amazing adventures. You may or may not believe my story, but that's okay. Just open your mind to the possibility and decide for yourself...

Chapter 1
Our First Year

S hortly after our first amazing adventure, my family and I moved into a house that was close to the forest where the Traegons lived. That first year in our new house was everything I hoped it would be and more. The forest that bordered the property around our house was thick and teeming with all kinds of wildlife. The summer days were long and filled with many new experiences. Karia, Juna, and I spent lots of time exploring the woods, learning more about each other and our different worlds, worlds that exist side by side.

The more we learned about each other, the more we found that we had in common. We taught each other about how we live in our own worlds. They showed me how to identify the tracks of different animals in the mud along the river bank and throughout the forest. They also disclosed to me the important roles that each of these creatures plays in their world as well as in mine.

I showed them different games we could play and even taught them how to read and draw a little. Many times we found ourselves just having fun, as any kids would. Our physical differences, in our minds, faded day by day as we saw each other only as friends. I could not share their existence with anyone—not even Quinn, my best friend since preschool. They were so incredible, though, I just had to share them in some way so since I couldn't directly introduce him to Karia and Juna, I found a way introduced them indirectly.

There were many days when we would play a game we called *Track 20*, kind of a cross between hide-and-seek and Marco Polo. Quinn would run off in one direction and I in the other; we would go as far as we could to the count of twenty. We each had chosen a call, like a bird or coyote. Once we reached the count of twenty, we would turn back and announce ourselves with our call. Then we would work our way back toward each other. The goal was to track each other by the sound of our movement and our occasional animal-like calls. When one of us spotted the other, we would quietly get as close as possible and then call out "Tracked you!" It was fun when it was just Quinn and me, but once Karia and Juna got involved, it was a blast.

Karia and Juna were great at Track 20 because of their small size and their ability to be up in the trees where they could get a birds-eye view (or a Traegon-eye view, rather) of both of us at the same time or on the ground hidden in the brush. This would have been Quinn's game for sure, since he was so good at sneaking up on me, but with Karia's and Juna's help, I had a definite advantage. By the end of the summer, unbeknownst to Quinn or me, he had a partner of his own, for Juna eventually began helping him find his way back to me without either of us knowing. Once the playing field was leveled, Quinn started winning a lot more.

As fall set in, Karia and Juna had to spend more time helping Mim and Sire Argus, their parents, prepare for the cold weather. They spent less time with me then, but I had my own autumn responsibilities. I was back in school and had homework and chores. The days became shorter, and our time was pretty much limited to the weekends. I thought about Karia and Juna and the other Traegons, as the trees began to lose their brightly colored leaves. I found myself wanting to help them get through the cool days and even colder nights that were soon to come. One afternoon I was helping my mom go through some boxes in the basement. We found a whole box of old blankets.

"Dino, will you help me sort these blankets?" she asked me. "I want to take them to the shelter this afternoon."

"No problem," I told her, "but can I have a couple?"

"Sure, but what do you need blankets for?" she asked, puzzled by my request.

I had to come up with a quick and reasonable excuse, because I couldn't tell her what I was really going to do with them. "Um...well, uh...Quinn and I can use them outside when we are exploring this winter," I responded, hoping she'd buy it.

"Right. I should have known it would have something to do with you, Quinn, and those woods. How silly of me to ask." She smiled and tossed me a gray woolen blanket.

I set aside a couple more and took them to my room. I later cut them into smaller pieces, rolled them, and tied them with ribbons and twine. I gave them to Karia and Juna the next time we met in the woods, they took them to Mim and Sire Argus, who took only what they could use and delivered the rest to the main village, where they were shared among the entire Traegon community. Karia told me later that many of the Traegon families who received blankets were very grateful, and that made me happy.

When spring returned, we began spending more time together again. None of us could wait for summer. The days were getting longer; the trees and other plants were beginning to bud. It would only be a short while before the trees were full and green again. Karia and Juna were always no further than a holler away, and we no longer had to wait for the weekends to be together. I filled my first journal with drawings and was starting on a new one. Even though Karia and Juna had seen me draw many times before, they were still amazed by each new picture I created.

My mom had started working at the Department of Natural Resources office several days a week. She focused most her work on research and protection of native plants and animals. After spending so much time last year working to save this house and the forest around it, she decided she wanted to do more of that kind of work. She really seems to love what she does.

My dad also really came to like the house. I know he wasn't crazy about moving from our old house, but I also know he would do anything for my mom, and she really wanted this house. Moving close to the river helped, since Dad loves fishing. Now he can fish anytime he wants and doesn't have to wait to go just on the weekends like he did before we moved.

Chapter 2
Sleep Tale

K aria woke to a low roar and crackling sound in the distance. She sat up in her dark room and listened. Immediately she noticed feeling sweltering warmth. She wiped away the perspiration that settled on her brow. The entire room seemed to be baking, as if someone had left a fire hole burning strong all night. She knew, though, there was no fire hole in her room, which was situated deep in the ground beneath the old willow. She scooted to the edge of her woven sleeping mat and climbed out of the ornate bed constructed from twisted willow and dogwood branches. She moved toward the door. Slowly, she reached for the handle and opened the door slightly. There was an ominous glow coming from above the winding roots that led to the base of the willow. She pulled the door open further and climbed swiftly up the thick, round root steps. A piercing scent filled her mouth and throat the higher she climbed. She was overcome by the odor of scorched wood as she ascended to the broad base of the tree. She slowly circled around the trunk and stepped into what was once the beautiful garden of the great willow. She gasped at the horrible sight before her. Traegonia, as she had known it, was...gone.

Shocked and filled with terror, she began to call out, "Para! Arbalest! Oracle Balstar! Can anyone hear me?" She coughed, and panic began to consume her. All she could see were orange flames engulfing everything around her. There were no other Traegons—no living creatures of any kind, for that matter—anywhere. She cried out again, but she realized that each time she called for the others, she was unable hear her own voice. She reached for her throat; it was becoming more and more difficult to breathe. She fell to her knees and cried out, as best she could, "Mim! Sire Argus! Juna! Can anyone hear me?" But no sound left her mouth, not even a squeak, no matter how hard she tried. She felt the hot earth beneath her hands and could smell the burning forest. She coughed again and collapsed flat to the ground. She lay still, listening to the crackling of the fire as it surrounded her. A tear rolled down her long, smooth muzzle, and she closed her eyes.

Suddenly Karia sat straight up and looked around. She noticed Juna, her brother, in a peaceful slumber on his sleeping mat across from her. Her heart was still pounding; she was unable to release the intense fear and panic that filled her. It was then that she realized she was not at the willow in the main Village of Traegonia after all. She was in her room, at her home deep in the forest, in their huge walnut tree, with Mim, Sire Argus, and Juna. Karia took a deep breath, relieved that the horrible fire was only part of a sleep tale. She wanted so much to reach over and wake Juna, just to hear his voice, to know that she was truly awake and that her brother really was there with her. She listened silently for a moment to his breathing. She stared at his chest rising and falling with each breath as he slumbered comfortably, and she couldn't bring herself to wake him.

She swung her legs off the side of her bed. They felt heavy and tingly. Slowly she stood and walked to the door of her room. Placing her hand flat on the thick wood, she felt to see if it was hot, but it was cool to the touch. She could not tell whether it was day or night. She pulled open the door slightly and peered out. There, she saw Mim standing near the fire hole, preparing the morning meal. Karia stepped out of her room and quietly closed the door behind her. She walked softly across the dirt floor of their tree home to where her mim stood.

Alistia was a simple, yet lovely she-Traegon. A beige apron accented the hand-stitched sage-colored dress that draped to her feet. It had long sleeves with a light brown leather bodice, cinched tightly at her slender waist. Narrow tan and black feathers lay smoothly between her ears and wisped down her back. Her eyes were a beautiful, calming shade of green.

Alistia looked at Karia and noticed immediately that something was upsetting her. "Karia, are you feeling alright? Sit here." She helped Karia over to the table and pulled out a chair. Karia sat down as she was told and held tightly onto her mim's arm for just a few moments more. Alistia looked into Karia's eyes, slid another chair over, and sat beside her. "Karia, tell me what has you so troubled, dear. I can feel you are ill at ease."

"Oh, Mim, I do feel so much fear. You are correct in what you sense." Karia grasped mim's arm tightly again.

"It is alright, my youngling, for you are safe now. Tell me what has frightened you so," Alistia urged in her soft, reassuring voice.

"I had a sleep tale, a very distressing one. It seemed so real, as if I were actually there." Karia proceeded to tell her mim what she had seen in her dream. As Karia told her grim story, she squeezed Mim's arm hard. Alistia placed her other hand on Karia's and gently but firmly pulled her fingers loose. Karia realized then what she had been doing. "Mim, I am sorry. I did not realize I was clutching so tightly."

Alistia looked into Karia's eyes and held her hand firmly. "You are completely safe here. You are in this moment, here with me in this place, your home." Her soft, gentle words poured over Karia like a gentle breeze. "Breathe in and out, slowly and deeply, and just let your body and thoughts relax."

Karia listened and did as mim suggested. Alistia stood and walked to the fire hole. Karia sat still, focusing only on calming herself.

Alistia returned with a bowl of warm walnut mush and a cup of white sage tea. "Sire Argus left at sunrise. It is becoming a bright and beautiful day. The birds are chirping happily, and the forest is showing no signs of fear or impending danger. Listen carefully and be open to my words." Alistia leaned in close, placing Karia's morning meal on the table before her. "Remember your sleep tale, but release the fear, as it will not serve your greatest good. It is not prudent to expend your energies being afraid of something you do not know to be true."

Karia knew her mim was right; her mim was usually right. She knew she had to let go of her fear. She took a deep breath and stretched her arms up into the air, relaxing her back and neck. She looked at her mim. "I do not know what I would do without your wise words to keep me centered." Karia found herself beginning to finally relax.

Alistia filled her own cup with fresh tea and sat back at the table with Karia while she ate her morning meal. After a short silence, Alistia spoke again. "It is probable what you had was just a sleep tale, my dear, but in honoring your training as a young Wayseer, I believe it may be important for you to share your vision with Oracle Balstar."

As Alistia spoke these words, Karia felt the knot returning to her stomach.

Chapter 3
Big Foot

I woke to the sound of the phone ringing on that early Saturday morning in May. I could hear my mother's voice, talking to someone on the other end of the call. I rolled over and buried my head in my soft pillow, hoping for a little more sleep. Later I heard my mother's and father's voices coming from downstairs. I got dressed, brushed my hair and teeth, and went downstairs for breakfast.

"Good morning, Dino!" Mom said, beaming.

"Morning, son," Dad followed, folding the newspaper and laying it on the table next to a plate of eggs, toast, and crispy bacon.

I sat down at the table next to him.

"Would you like some eggs, Dino?" my mom asked.

"No thanks. I'll just have some cereal." She took a bowl from the cabinet and placed it on the table in front of me.

"How would you like to go to California for a week or so?" Mom asked, pushing a couple of boxes of cereal my way.

"What, by myself?" I questioned, somewhat confused, as I poured the cereal into my bowl.

"No, silly, as a family." Mom chuckled. "Your Uncle Joe called this morning and invited us out for a visit. I think it would be a lot of fun. Besides, we haven't seen them in a couple of years." She poured milk over my cereal.

"Isn't it hot there this time of year?" I asked before gobbling a spoonful.

"That's what I said," Dad added.

"Oh, stop it, you two. It's a vacation! Besides, I don't think it is that hot. They live in the mountains, and I'm sure it is cooler up there anyway," Mom said, trying to convince us.

"Of course we'll go, honey. We're just giving you a hard time, right, Dino?" Dad nudged my arm.

"Yeah, right. We're just giving you a hard time." I looked into my cereal bowl and scooped out the last of the floating O's. "I'm gonna go outside for a little while. When are we supposed to leave?"

"I'm going to try and get plane tickets for two weeks from today. I'll let you know for sure when I get them," Mom answered, cleaning up the kitchen.

I pushed my chair away from the table, stood, and walked toward the back door thinking about the trip. Since I had met Karia and Juna, I had been so happy and content that I didn't really miss or even think about vacations. Plus, I didn't want to leave them, even if it was just for a week. We spend so much time together, and they were a part of my life. *What if we can't see each other every day?* I thought as I put on my shoes and stepped out the back door. I walked to the edge of the yard and looked out into the woods. It was quiet—almost too quiet—and I wondered what Karia and Juna were doing.

"Hey, Dino!" a familiar voice startled me from behind.

I turned abruptly. "Hi, Quinn. One of these days, your sneaking up on people is gonna get you in trouble," I warned.

"Oh, you think so?" Quinn replied with a laugh. "Want to go for a walk in the woods? I was thinking we could work on clearing that path we started."

Quinn and I had decided to clear a narrow path to the river. We were planning on surprising my dad with a special fishing spot.

"Sure. I'll go tell my mom. I'll get some work gloves and hats," I said, walking toward the shed.

"Don't worry about me. I came prepared," Quinn said, pulling his hat and an old pair of gloves from his back pockets.

A few minutes later, I met him out back, rakes and yard tools in hand. He was staring off into the woods with a puzzled look on his face.

"What are you looking at?" I asked him.

"Shh! I thought I heard something." He held his hand up to shush me.

I stepped in close behind him. "What was it?" I breathed in a low, deep whisper on the back of his neck, nudging him jokingly.

"I don't know." He looked harder into the woods, squinting.

I leaned in behind him to see if I could see anything.

"Aw, it was probably nothing." He paused. "Or maybe it was BIG FOOT!" he said loudly, turning around and growling in my face.

"Cut it out!" I pushed past him and headed for the woods. "Come on, let's go."

He followed chuckling at his own humor.

We had cleared a path of the plants and grasses about three feet wide and about ten feet into the woods so far. The forest had not been walked through in many years, and we wanted to make sure our path didn't disturb any trees or animal homes. We could have just created the path over time by walking it over and over again, but since it was just the two of us, that would have taken way too long. Besides, we really wanted to get it done quickly to surprise my dad. I handed Quinn one of the rakes, and we got started.

It began to get warmer as the morning turned into afternoon. Suddenly Quinn stopped raking and turned around. "Cut it out, Dino," he grumbled at me, with an annoyed look on his face.

"Cut what out?" I asked, confused. I stopped what I was doing and leaned on my rake, and Quinn turned back and continued what he was doing.

Just then, I saw a small piece of bark fall from the tree above him and slip down the back of his shirt. I glanced up just in time to see a small brown hand disappear into the leaves. I laughed. Quinn reached up and brushed the back of his neck. He turned around and glared at me, and then he threw down his rake and started running straight for me. I dropped my rake, turned, and bolted up the path. I could hear him gaining on me but could hardly keep up my pace because I couldn't stop laughing. I had no idea how long they had been dropping stuff on him, but I knew it was long enough to get him good and irritated. Suddenly I felt him tackle me from behind, and we both hit the ground hard. He started grabbing whatever he could from the ground—grass, leaves, twigs, and dirt—and tried to shove it down my shirt.

"Stop! Stop it! I...I didn't...I didn't do anything." I struggled, trying to hold him back. "What's your problem?" I yelled, trying to catch my breath when I was finally able to roll him off.

"Dude, that wasn't funny." Quinn stood up and un-tucked his shirt. As he pulled it out and stretched it open, I saw a bunch of bark chips fall to the ground behind him. When he lifted his shirt, there were more pieces stuck to his sweaty back.

I snickered.

He turned and glared at me again.

"Quinn, I swear I didn't do it," I said, putting my hands out in front of me.

"Oh no? Then who did? It's just you and me out here." He brushed off his back.

"I don't know. Maybe BIG FOOT!" I growled from a safe distance.

"Really funny, Dino. I guess it's break time. Let's go get something to drink," Quinn suggested.

"Sounds like a plan to me," I agreed.

Quinn offered his hand and helped me to my feet, and we headed back to my house.

⸻◈⸻

Karia and Juna climbed down out of the tree and watched Dino and Quinn walk off toward the house.

"Juna, you should not play such pranks," Karia scolded.

"Oh, come now, Karia. Do not be so serious. Dino himself even found it amusing," Juna chided. "Quinn is fun to play with, like a cat with a mouse, and there is no harm in it. I remember the first time Dino brought him to the woods. He wanted us to include Quinn in our games. He is now our friend, too, you know. Besides, I like him."

"You are right, Juna, and forgive me. I know you are just having fun," Karia conceded. "I guess I am a bit distracted by my thoughts."

"Is it what you and Mim were discussing this morning?" questioned Juna.

"Yes," Karia answered thoughtfully, looking downward and trying not to worry.

"Karia, we are still young ones. We should play and laugh and have fun. You should try not to worry so." Juna smiled and scampered off, chasing a dragonfly. "Come on, Karia."

Karia smiled a crooked smile and ran after him.

————))(())((————

When we walked into the house, my mom was standing at the kitchen sink. "I got the tickets!" she said excitedly "We leave a week from Friday."

"Where are we going?" Quinn asked.

"WE are going to see my brother in California," Mom said, smiling at him.

"I'm not going?" Quinn gave my mom a sad puppy kind of look.

"No, dear, but here's a drink. You look as though you need it." She handed both of us large glasses of ice water.

Quinn took a huge gulp and then smiled and said, "That's good. Okay, I guess I can forgive you for going to California without me."

"A week from Friday? Wow, that seems soon," I mumbled, taking a gulp of the freezing cold water. I could feel it go down my throat and into my stomach. It ached a little, and I didn't know if it was from drinking the water too fast or from the thought of not seeing Karia and Juna for a week. We finished our water and some cookies my mom put on the table, and then I said, "Come on, Quinn. Let's get back to the woods." I stood and pushed in my chair.

"Okay. Bye, Mrs. Dosek. Thanks for the water and the delicious cookies. You know you are the best mom in the world, right? Well... right up there with my mom, I mean." Quinn smiled. He stood, pushed in his chair, and followed me toward the door.

"Quinn, you are too much." My mom laughed. "Bye, boys. Dino, I want to take you shopping for some clothes later. Don't be too long." I could hear her voice trail off as we went out the back door.

We worked on the trail for a while longer and then Quinn announced, "It must be almost lunchtime. I've gotta get home. My mom wants me to help her clean out the garage. Ick. Anyway, I'll call you tomorrow."

"Sounds like fun," I joked as we carried the rakes back to the shed and put them away.

"You're welcome to come with, you know!" Quinn called back, walking to the front yard and picking up his bike.

"No, thanks. I'll take a pass. But have fun." I waved to him as he pedaled down the gravel driveway.

I headed back into the woods. When I came close to where Quinn and I had been working, I began to call out, "Karia! Juna! Are you still here?"

It was only moments before Juna stepped out onto the thick, leafy forest floor. "Ah, Dino you have returned. Where is our friend Quinn? Did we frighten him away?" Juna asked, looking back toward the path into the woods. "I like him, you know!"

"I know you do, Juna...and no, you didn't frighten him away. He just had to go home to do some chores. Where's Karia?"

Karia stepped out of the brush with a dragonfly perched on her small hand. "I am here. I hope my silly brother's prank did not cause you any pain or distress," she said apologetically.

"Nah, don't worry about it. We mess around like that all the time." I assured her. I sensed something was bothering her, and it was more than just Quinn and I roughing each other up. "Kara, is something bothering you?" I asked "You seem...well, quieter than usual."

"Not to worry, my friend, I have just been distracted by thoughts of a sleep tale I had last evening. It has me a bit unnerved," she responded, releasing the dragonfly into the air.

"Oh, I hate it when I have bad dreams. It sometimes takes me a couple days to forget them. Do you want to tell me about it? Sometimes it helps to talk about it," I offered, sitting down at the base of a nearby tree.

"Thank you, Dino. That is very kind of you, but I will be just fine. What do you wish to do today?" Karia patted my knee.

"I don't have much time today. My mom is gonna take me shopping for some new clothes. Oh, that reminds me. I'm going away with my family for a week," I informed them.

"Going away? Where!?" Juna piped in.

"We're going to visit my uncle and aunt in California."

"Cali-what?" Juna questioned, raising one eyebrow.

"California, it's a place, a state. It's far enough away that we'll have to take an airplane."

"An airplane?" Juna asked.

I pulled out my journal, turned to a blank page, and sketched a quick, simple drawing, my best impression of a plane. "It's a really big metal vehicle that takes people from one place to another in the air, like the birds."

Karia and Juna both looked at me and tilted their heads back and forth, showing they didn't quite understand.

"Look here," I said pointing to the picture I drew. "It's like a big bird, except it's not a living thing."

"What makes it fly then? Does it flap its wings?" Juna asked for clarification.

"No. Its wings don't move like that. It has big engines that make it fly."

"Oh," they both said, even though I knew they still didn't fully understand.

"Let's save this for another day. I'll bring some books to show you."

"What is California like?" Karia asked.

"It's kind of like here, but from what I understand, we will be staying in the mountains. Do you know what mountains are?" I asked both of them.

"Oh, yes! Mountains are the highest of hills, and when you are at the top of them, you can see forever," Karia described. "One day I will climb to the very top of a mountain."

"How do you know about mountains?" I asked curiously. "There are none around here."

"Mim and Sire Argus have told us about other Traegonias. Traegonia begins where the sun rises and stretches all the way to where the sun sets and is in all places between," Juna explained. "Someday I will travel to these other Traegonias and see all that Mim and Sire Argus have told us about."

"So there must be a Traegonia in California!" I said excitedly.

"I would imagine so." Karia looked to Juna.

"I believe this to be true," Juna confirmed with a nod.

"I wish I could take you both with me. We would have a great time exploring together—looking for the other Traegonia." I imagined it with a smile.

"That would be a truly amazing experience, but I do not think your mother and father would find it as exciting if we went along," Karia admitted.

"Nor Mim and Sire Argus," Juna added.

We all looked into the trees, imagining just what it might be like.

"Someday we'll travel together. I will figure out a way." I smiled at the two of them. In the distance, I could hear my mother calling me. "I have to go now." I stood and brushed off my pants.

"When will you be making your journey in the big bird?" Karia asked, stepping toward me and sounding a bit sad.

I knelt down on one knee and looked into her eyes. "Not for almost two weeks and I will see you many times before that," I assured her. "Please try not to worry. Everything will be fine.

"I know, Dino, until we meet again." Karia held up her hand.

I placed my palm against hers and smiled, my hand seemed so big against her small delicate hand. Juna walked up and put his hand on her shoulder as I turned and began to walk up the path. When I glanced back, my two small friends were already gone.

Chapter 4
Visit to the Willow

Karia and Juna collected the herbs their mim had requested they bring back. When they returned to their home, Alistia was outside gathering acorns. "Good day, my younglings! I am pleased you are back. There are some perfectly ripe berries on the far side of the sweet grass field. I was hoping you would run over before dark and bring some back."

Karia didn't feel much like berry-picking, but she knew it was more than a suggestion.

Juna grabbed Karia's arm and tugged it playfully. "Race you to the field!" Juna prodded and ran ahead.

Karia took several steps, not feeling in much of a mood to race. Suddenly she caught the scent of something; she raised her muzzle and opened her mouth slightly. It smelled as if there was something burning nearby. *Fire!* she thought, and a feeling of panic came over her. She immediately found herself back in her sleep tale. She could once again hear the crackling sound of burning wood turning to ash. Again she was faced with the image she had seen in her dream. "Juna! Juna!" she called out into the reddish-orange light that blazed before her.

"Karia!" Juna had both hands on Karia's shoulders and was shaking her to bring her back. "Karia! Open your eyes!"

Finally, Karia's eyes popped open. "Where are we?" she asked, looking around franticly.

"We were on our way to the sweet grass field to get berries for Mim, remember? I ran ahead to race you, but when I looked back you were not following. You have not moved more than a few steps from where we began," Juna explained.

Just then, their mim came quickly up the path, hearing the commotion. "What is going on? Is there something wrong?" Juna explained to his mim what had happened, and she looked at Karia with a look of concern upon her face. "Karia? Are you feeling alright?"

"Mim, I believe I should go to see Oracle Balstar soon. May I borrow the wagon at sunrise?" Karia spoke in a faint mumble.

"I do not feel it is safe for you to make the journey alone. We will take you," Alistia insisted, turning Karia to lead her home.

"I should go to see the Oracle alone, Mim. Truly I should."

"We will discuss that later, but for now, do you wish to tell me what just happened?"

"I think I would like to lie down for a while." Karia walked silently back to their tree home. She felt confused by the visions she was having; it made her feel ill. When they arrived at their tree, Karia went to her room for a rest.

"What do you think is wrong with her, Mim?" Juna asked, concerned, as the door to their room closed quietly.

"I cannot be sure, Juna," Alistia stated. "We will talk to Sire Argus when he arrives home for the evening meal. For now, please help me with this heavy kettle."

Juna moved the big black kettle onto the fire hole. He then went on to the sweet grass field to collect the berries for Alistia. When he returned, he helped her finish preparing the evening meal. Time passed, and the door to Karia and Juna's room creaked open. Karia stepped out.

"Karia! You look well. How are you feeling after your nap?" Alistia questioned as she stirred the wild mushroom and carrot soup.

Juna moved the mulberry pie from the fire hole to a worn but sturdy cooking table that Sire Argus had built many years before.

"I slept very peacefully, thank you. Maybe it was just a chance happening. Maybe I just ate something that didn't settle well," Karia observed.

"That is good." said Juna, relieved. "You do look much better."

Just then the door opened, and Sire Argus stepped in. He was slight in height but strong in stature. His ears and muzzle were much shorter than most he-Traegons. His white wavy hair was pulled back into a leather tie at the top of his head. His eyes were dark, appearing deep red in color. This made him even more fearsome looking. He wore a beige woven tunic over a brown shirt. His green pants were tied at the ankle with fabric matching his tunic. He was an excellent hunter and a master wood smith. "Good evening, my family! How has your day been?" Argus smiled.

Karia looked at her mim, silently urging her not to say anything just yet, but Juna hadn't noticed and began. "Sire, Karia is experiencing some strange happenings."

"What do you mean, strange happenings?" Argus questioned, glancing over at Karia in a worried fashion.

"Well, Sire," Karia began, looking annoyed at Juna, "I have been having sleep tales and now waking visions. They seem so very real to me. They unnerve my very being."

"Sleep tales? What about?" Argus questioned curiously as he walked further in and set his hunting bag down by the cooking table.

"I cannot be sure, Sire, but there seems to be some relation to the element of fire and some connection to me. It frightens me a great deal." Karia began to feel the fear well up within her again. "The only thing I know for certain is that I must come to understand what is happening before I begin to unravel within my thoughts."

Argus glanced over at his mate with a puzzled, concerned look upon his face. "What is your thought as to our youngling's fear, Alistia?" he asked her.

"Karia has always had a wonderful way of seeing images within her own thoughts. From the time she was small, she has shared many wonderful and beautiful visions, but none that have set such unease within her." Alistia paused. "She wishes to travel to speak with Oracle Balstar...alone." Alistia looked pleadingly at Argus.

"I am not sure traveling alone is wise. It can be dangerous out in the forest, especially for a lone voyager. It is easy to become turned around and lose your way," Argus pressed.

"Sire, I know I am not fully grown, but I am also not truly a youngling. I am in training to be a Wayseer and must be able to journey to the main village as needed. There shall be many more matters I will have to attend to... alone, and I must become accustom to it. I ask for your trust and understanding to fulfill my calling." Karia spoke in a tone not before heard by Alistia and Argus. She sounded more grown, as if she had suddenly come of age.

Juna had been quietly listening and watching the conversation unfold. "I will take her," he said. "I have spent much time with Sire Argus as of late and have become very familiar with the forest. I know I can take my sister safely to Traegonia and back," he chimed in, puffing his chest out with pride.

Alistia sighed and looked at Argus with a shrug.

He returned her glance and interjected, "There comes a time when elders must trust in the paths of those they love." He turned his gaze to Karia. "Karia, if you agree to allow Juna to be your guide, I will agree to let you journey unaccompanied by us."

Argus, Juna, and Karia looked at their mim. She blinked her eyes slowly and gave a deep sigh. "I must agree with Sire. As much as I wish you were both small again, I know that you are not, and I know your paths hold much exploration and wisdom forthcoming." Alistia turned and carried on the preparation of their evening meal.

"When will you be leaving?" Sire Argus asked.

Juna looked to Karia.

"We will set off before the sun rises," Karia stated flatly.

"Then I suggest you gather your belongings and make ready your journey," Argus directed. "Then you should get some rest before you depart."

Karia walked over to her mim, who had her back to the conversation, and whispered, "Do not worry, Mim. You have taught me well, and though you will not be by my side on this journey, you will be forever in my heart and my thoughts. I am able to do this because you are my guide and mentor—from within." Karia placed her arms around Mim and hugged her gently and then she turned and headed to her room to pack as a single tear rolled down Alistia's cheek.

When morning arrived, Sire Argus hitched the wagon to their turkey and led it around to the entrance of their tree home. Miracle, the squirrel who had lived in the same tree with Karia and Juna's family since he was young, scurried down the tree with several walnuts. He dropped them at Karia and Juna's feet, then turned and disappeared into the full green leaves. After stuffing Miracle's offering into a pouch, Karia and Juna climbed into the wagon. There was a chill in the air, and thick fog blanketed the forest. Alistia approached the wagon and handed Karia a bundle filled with Traegon mix, some dried berries and a pouch of sage tea wrapped tightly in one of the blankets Dino had given them. Karia and Juna said their farewells and set off alone toward the main Village of Traegonia and the old willow.

Juna held the reins, guiding the wild turkey through the forest. Karia stared off into the mist, squinting in an attempt to see anything. They traveled in silence for a long while, with the tin lantern that hung from a pole at the front of the wagon clanking as the wagon made its way over the rough forest floor. A soft, low buzz sounded from within the fog. Juna pulled back on the reins, slowing the wagon to a halt. A large dragonfly with big bright green eyes broke through the dense fog and hung tentatively in front of the wagon. Karia dug into her satchel and felt around. She pulled out a small scroll and held it up into the air. The dragonfly hovered close to Karia's hand and landed on the scroll. Karia opened her hand, and the dragonfly lifted off, carrying the scroll into the fog and on to announce their coming to Oracle Balstar. Juna snapped the reins, and the wagon lurched forward and continued on its way.

The fog hung in the air like a low ceiling above the marketplace as they approached the village. The market was bustling with activity, as the wagon eased through the center of Mazus Grove.

Karia gazed at the wares and goods laid out for trade: homemade herbs and teas, hand-stitched clothing, various food items, and carts laden with assorted found objects from within and outside the boundaries of Traegonia. Suddenly a glint of something caught her eye. "Juna, wait! Pull over! There is something I wish to have a look at," Karia urged, tugging on Juna's arm.

Juna pulled the wagon off to the side of the path, and Karia jumped out. She headed back in the direction they had come from. She walked slowly through the market, scanning each cart for the thing that had caught her eye. She stopped at a rickety old crooked wagon, obscured on either side by two large bushes. She looked carefully over the vast array of items on display. Everything lying on the L-shaped stand that jutted out at the back of the open wagon looked to be very old and somewhat dull. Karia visually examined each piece, hoping that whatever it was that had caught her attention would show itself. She looked over the stand a second time and then wondered if it might have been at a different wagon. As she turned to look at the other wagons, a gravelly voice called her back.

"Is this what you seek, youngling?"

Karia turned slowly back around. Standing before her, shrouded in the shadows, was a Traegon whom she had never seen before, a she-Traegon who looked to be as old as the land itself. When the she-Traegon stepped forward, Karia could see that she was short and bent. She walked with a bit of a limp and had one milky white eye that startled Karia when the old she-Traegon turned her head. On the top of her knurly walking cane was perched a crooked blackbird. He was scrawny, and his feathers were separated, with many missing, as if he were in a constant state of molting. He was unkempt, and his color was dingy, unlike the sleek, shiny black feathers of Oracle Balstar's raven, Sable. His chirp was more of a raspy squawk. Karia's eyes followed down the she-Traegons crooked and outstretched arm to an even more crooked hand with long, wiry, bent fingers that held a shiny, circular object. It was flat but thick, a round silver amulet with crude markings and three curved grooves that came from the edges and met in the center. It was a simple piece, not anything stunning.

Karia knew at once it was what she had spotted, even though she had no idea what it was. Little did she know the power it held. "Yes, that is it! That is what I was searching for," Karia replied in a puzzled tone. "Was that sitting on this cart moments ago?"

"No, my dear. It has been in a box inside my wagon since I first came to possess it. This, youngling, is not for just any Traegon." The old she-Traegon coughed a bit. "I believe everything has one to which it belongs, and I believe this belongs to you." Her crooked arm reached further out of the shadow of the shaded cart and placed the item into Karia's hand.

"How do you know this?" Karia asked.

"It is not for me to know, Karia. It just is," mumbled the old she-Traegon in her frightfully croaky voice.

"Who are you, and how do you know my name?" Karia demanded. "What is your na—?"

Karia was interrupted as Juna stepped up behind and startled her when he tapped her on the shoulder. "I almost lost you. Why did you jump from the wagon and hurry off like that?"

Karia turned to answer him. "I needed to get back here to find what had drawn my attention," Karia told Juna, turning back to the old she-Traegon. But when she turned back, the crooked old she-Traegon, her crooked bird, and her crooked wagon were gone. Karia looked around, completely perplexed. She looked down and slowly opened her hand. Nestled inside it was the round object. It was no longer shiny but was just a time-worn, battered piece—pretty, but not bright or eye catching. Karia took a deep breath and looked around again.

Dino C. Crisanti

Out of the Shadows

"Why are you standing here?" Juna pressed. "Can you not find what you were seeking?"

Karia looked directly into Juna's eyes. "I found exactly what I was meant to find. We can go on to the willow now." Karia's tone had changed, for it was now soft and mellow. She opened a pouch that hung at her waist and placed the object inside. She walked with Juna back to their wagon and climbed in. Even though her encounter was strange and unexplained, she felt a deep calm come over her.

At the willow, they were greeted by Nintar, the squire who was assigned to Karia's keeping when she had first visited the village the year before. "Welcome, once again, young Karia and young Juna. Oracle Balstar will meet with you in the willow garden, once the sun has fully shown itself."

Karia and Juna looked back at the eastern sky. "It will be some time yet," Juna observed.

"Yes, Juna, you are right. Let us go and see if we can find Para. I do miss seeing her." Karia smiled remembering the kind and joyful she-squire that was appointed to Karia's keeping after Nintar.

"Lead the way," Juna stated.

Karia looked to Nintar for direction. "Follow the winding roots of the willow, back beyond the lighted entryways. The servants' quarters are back there." He handed Karia a lit candle in a handled holder. "Fourth root to the round," he said as he stepped back into the gnarled knot in the side of the large trunk.

Karia and Juna turned, following the roots around to where Nintar had directed. The light of the candle flickered off the heavy bark and the rolling root steps. The shimmering glow of the candlelight bounced off the roots, giving the appearance of slithering snakes intertwining within the ground.

"Para? Para?" Karia whispered loudly.

A distant glimmer of light shone from behind a large arched root, where a knotty door stood open.

"Ahh, my dear Karia! What a pleasant surprise. Have you eaten yet?" Para said excitedly.

"Do you recall my brother Juna?" Karia introduced.

"Oh my, yes. Such a strong face! Come in. How are you? Do you have some time? Would you like a little something to fill your bellies? I just laid out my morning meal, and I would be pleased if you both would share it with me," Para invited.

Juna glanced at the food with a lustful look on his face. "It would only be polite, you know," he said, as his mouth began to water.

Karia nodded in silent agreement that a meal would be perfect while they waited. They followed Para into her quarters, where they chatted and ate and enjoyed their time together. When the sun began to rise higher in the eastern sky, they bade farewell to Para and headed back up to the willow garden.

Chapter 5
Understanding

Oracle Balstar was the oldest known Traegon living in the village. He was also the leader and standing Wayseer for this Traegonia. He lumbered slowly toward them from the south end of the garden, leaning on his carved, twisted staff for support. His deep green robe draped his frail figure, tied at his waist with a smooth woven belt. Hanging from his belt was a glass bottle that held a glittering potion and a single old and tarnished key, the key to their village. The many crystals sewn into the robe caught the morning light as it streamed through the long, leafy whips that hung from the sturdy, broad branches of the great willow. A slight breeze stirred the leaves sounding the harmonious chimes that hung high in the branches throughout the garden. Though he was quite old, Oracle Balstar had a strong presence and deep wisdom that was his pure essence. It was unmistakable.

"My dear Karia, I understand you have found yourself in need of some guidance," Oracle Balstar said in a very calm, quiet voice. "Juna, it is good of you to accompany Karia. She relies on your strength. You are a perfect balance for her."

Juna looked at Oracle Balstar and bowed his head in honor. "I would do anything for the good of my sister, Oracle."

Karia looked kindly at Juna.

"Please sit and find comfort. Tell me, Karia, what guidance do you seek?"

Karia explained her strange experiences, the sleep tales and waking visions. She shared the fear that had been haunting her inner being and outer life.

Oracle Balstar listened intently, just as he always did, and then he sat for a time in deep thought. At times he closed his eyes, which made Karia and Juna wonder if he hadn't fallen asleep. Finally, he spoke. "Fire, young one, has many aspects. In its physical form it can serve us well by illuminating our dark nights and early mornings. It serves to warm our physical bodies and heat our meals. Fire can also be destructive, though, as it can devastate our homes, land, and our lives, leaving much suffering in its smoldering path. Fire, in its ethereal sense, can also be illuminating. It can bring light and clarity to our thoughts and quandaries. Fire can be a message of transformation and change. It is the energy that fuels our desires and passions.

"As to the destructive element that has haunted your dreams, I am not aware of any great fires that have threatened Traegonia in our recent past, nor of any danger set before us. Traegons are most cautious and respectful of fire. We understand the treasure and power that it is." Oracle Balstar paused, looking intently at Karia. "Karia, I believe this fear feels very real to you. It is possible that you are tapping into an awareness within, that which is slowly uncovering your undiscovered potential. You must allow yourself to be open and unafraid of this awareness. If you choose to dismiss it, it will continue to return. You may not gain awareness or realize the connection until a much later time. Now is the time you should meditate on the message being set before you. These are all lessons, lessons that will become a part of who you are and who you will one day become."

Karia looked at Oracle Balstar. She remained silent, allowing all of his words to seep deep into her consciousness.

"I will discuss your concerns of the physical fire with Master Zoal and the members of the Village Council. If we become aware of or have any further information, we will call upon you. I invite you to stay a few days, or as long as you need. Use the willow as your place of peace and the crystals to help you to decipher your thoughts. This may reveal some insight to you. But remember, you must try to find your calm center. If you become too overwhelmed, your thoughts will become tangled and twisted and will not serve you in their intended way. Use the tools you have learned, for they are always with you." Oracle Balstar used his cane to stand, and Karia stood and stepped before him. He placed his hand upon her shoulder, and she understood. And with that, he turned and departed from the garden.

"Do you feel any better?" Juna asked hopefully.

"It is not a feeling as much as an understanding. I must be open to the thought that this may not have anything to do with physical fire. That alone is a huge relief. The truth that the understanding may truly lie in the ethereal is something I can much more easily accept and work through," Karia replied.

Juna wrinkled his brow. "I am not quite sure what all of that means, Karia, but I hope you do. I'll tend to the wagon and navigate the physical. It is you who will have to navigate the unseen."

"That sounds like a well-laid plan, and I am truly grateful for your companionship. What Oracle Balstar is telling me is that I must not allow the sleep tales overtake me."

"We traveled all this way for that? Mim and I already told you that." Juna raised his eyebrows.

"I know Juna, you and Mim are both quite wise. Let us go and see Dino. He'll be going on his journey soon to the mountains." Karia took a deep breath and seemed to feel a bit better.

They retrieved their wagon and headed off in the direction of Dino's home.

"I want to see the mountains, Karia," Juna confided on their ride.

"I, too, would like to see the mountains, but that journey is one that this little wagon will not make. We would have to fly on a goose or some other way, and even then it would be a very long, possibly treacherous journey," Karia explained.

"Why do we not go with Dino? He will be able to get us there. He said one day we could journey together, so let us do it now!" Juna had an excitement in his tone that Karia had not heard from him before.

"Juna, did you leave your good sense back at the willow?" Karia teased.

"No. I am serious. We can tell Mim and Sire Argus we will be staying at the willow for a time. It is a bit of a fib, yes, but it will enable us to go on a great adventure with Dino." Juna sounded as if he had it all planned out. "Let us at least share the idea with Dino, alright?"

"Alright, Juna, but I am sure Dino will think us nuttier than a walnut tree," Karia conceded.

"I already think that about you, my sister," Juna said with smirk.

"And you likewise, my nutty brother," Karia giggled.

Chapter 6
Suggesting a Journey

It wouldn't be too long before we would be leaving for California. I could tell my mom was excited. She was busy organizing clothes for all of us and making lists so we wouldn't forget anything; my mother, the Queen of Organization. I only had one day of school left, and I had been looking forward to the time I would spend with Karia and Juna, but now it would have to wait another couple of weeks. I had no homework, so I decided to go out into the woods behind our house to see if Karia and Juna were around.

I walked down the path, listening to the warm summer breeze gently blowing and whistling through the fresh new leaves. The sun peeked through the trees, casting light and shadows across the ground, the fallen logs, and me. A few more weeks, and the trees would be completely full, giving all the animals and creatures lots of hiding places, but right now I could look up and still see the birds caring for their young. I watched the squirrels chasing frantically through the trees, jumping from branch to branch and chattering away. The woods were alive, and I loved it. I glanced down at the path ahead of me and noticed a tail disappear behind an old fallen log. I slowed and then stopped, waiting to see what it was. I could hear the rustling in the old leaves that were left over from the prior fall. Suddenly I saw a small raccoon struggling to make his way on top of a log. One, two, three of them walked carefully but quickly toward the far end of the hollow log. Following behind were Karia and Juna. I watched for a few more minutes as they played. I really had never seen Karia and Juna in this way before, watching over the little ones until they finally brought them safely back to the tree where their mother waited watchfully.

Once the little raccoons were safely in their hole, I called out to my friends. "Karia! Juna! Over here!" They had become comfortable in this area behind my house; they knew it was safe for them.

"Dino!" I heard Juna first.

They jumped over the log and bounded in my direction.

"We were hoping we would see you here today." Karia smiled.

"What are you two up to, other than playing with the raccoons?" I teased.

"They are so sweet, are they not? I just love this time of year, seeing all of the new ones exploring the forest for the first time," Karia mused.

"I do, too, though I don't get to see them that much. I can see they trust Traegons, way more than humans," I said, sitting on the ground and leaning against a nearby tree.

"Dino, we want to come on your journey with you!" Juna blurted out.

"Juna!" Karia snapped, shaking her head at him for being so blunt and unable to hold his tongue.

"What? Do you mean to California?" I questioned.

"Yes! We wish to see the mountains. Please take us with you," Juna pressed.

My mind spun with thoughts of them joining me for vacation. *How can we do this?* I visualized them walking through the airport carrying little suitcases, and I laughed a little at the thought.

"What is it that makes you smile so, Dino?" Karia asked.

"Oh, nothing. I'm just thinking about how we could possibly make this happen. Are your mim and Sire Argus Okay with you coming?" I asked.

"They will be fine with it," Karia said without looking at me.

"They believe we will be staying at the willow in the village. No one keeps very close track of us there, so when they observe that we are gone, they will determine we have returned home. We should be back home before it is found that we are not in either place," Juna explained

"Sounds like you have it all figured out," I observed.

"Is this something you believe we will be able to do?" Karia asked excitedly.

"I don't know. I'll have to think about it a little. We have to be able to get you from here to the airport, onto the plane, and to my uncle's house, all without anyone knowing, and then back to the airport, onto the plane, and home. Hmm...that's a lot of figuring," I shared with them, as I worked on the plan in my head.

"You can simply hide us in your backpack," Juna suggested. "We are small."

"You do remember the last time you were both in my backpack, don't you?" I reminded them.

"Oh, yes, I certainly do." Karia said, remembering. "I think something a little larger would be necessary."

I began to get excited at the thought of them coming with. I could take care of them in my world, and we could explore together the Traegonia in California. *This could be an awesome adventure.*

"What do you think, Dino? Can we come?" Juna said in apparent anticipation.

"Let me think about this overnight and try to figure it all out. Don't get your hopes up though." I could see in their eyes that they were counting on me to make it all work, and I didn't want to let them down.

We let that subject go for a while and went about our business of playing and having fun. Hours went by, and I heard my mother ringing the triangle bell that hung outside the back door of our house. Her faint call followed.

"I've gotta go. I will meet you here tomorrow after school. I will let you know then what I've figured out."

"I am feeling hungry as well. We should get back to the village." Juna rubbed his stomach.

"We will see you soon. Think well on these things." Karia winked at me before she and Juna turned and disappeared from the path.

Chapter 7
Drawing a Plan

I walked back to my house, distracted and deep in thought. *How am I going to get Karia and Juna all the way to California? What an adventure it will be if we can work it out.* I smiled as I again thought of Karia and Juna walking through the airport pulling along their wheeled luggage. *Many people would walk by, too busy to even notice, but others would gawk, unable to look away. It would cause a people and luggage pileup in the terminal. Some people might even scream and run for the doors, and then I would have to explain to Karia and Juna that they shouldn't feel bad. "Just ignore them," I'd say. Then security might stop us at the gate and hold us in a little office until police and scientists come, and then they might take Karia and Juna away, and...*

I shook my head, trying to get those thoughts out of my mind. *I will have to come up with a better plan than that. They can't be seen. I will have to hide them.* It seemed like they really want to go, and I wanted them to go too. I just couldn't imagine how we were going to do it. I had to get working on a real plan. My mind was elsewhere as I walked into my house.

"Dino, take off your shoes! Where is your head?" my mom snapped as I walked through the kitchen and toward the stairs.

"Oh, sorry, Mom." I tiptoed back through the kitchen. Kicking off my shoes, I scanned the floor for traces of dirt or mud that I might have tracked in. Luckily, there was nothing. I started up the stairs when my mom stopped me.

"How close are you to being packed, Dino?" she asked, passing me on her way to the laundry room. She had some kind of checklist in her hand.

"I'm getting there, Mom. Don't worry. I'll be ready in time. We still have a week to go, right?" I replied, skipping a step or two on my way up the stairs.

"Just don't wait until the last minute or you are bound to forget something." I heard her say as I turned the corner into my room and quietly closed the door.

I pulled my journal out from beneath my mattress. I drew an open suitcase and stared at it. I knew they would fit into my backpack, it was a little cramped but they fit. *A suitcase would be like a real room for them,* I imagined. I drew them tucked into my suitcase with my clothes snuggled in around them. *But how will they make it past the X-ray machine?* I knew they would have to go to the baggage area and hopped it wouldn't be too dangerous for them. I drew and thought and planned and imagined and did that over and over again until I drifted off to sleep.

"Dino! Come down for dinner!" I heard my mother call.

I pulled myself to the side of my bed and leaned down to put away my journal. I caught a glimpse of the box under my bed that held the White Acorn and the Sunbow Crystal. I picked it up and opened the box. I peered into the box, remembering all of the seemingly impossible things that had happened that first year we met. In that moment, it was clear: we really could make just about anything happen. We just needed to want it bad enough. And that we did.

"Dino, what are you doing up there? Dinner is getting cold!" my mom called from downstairs.

I dropped the lid on the box and pushed it under my bed. I knew then what my answer would be to Karia and Juna the next day, and I couldn't wait to tell them.

Chapter 8
Vision of Change

Karia and Juna returned to the village and found their room beneath the winding roots of the willow. Juna was hungry, as always, and decided to fill his belly with the meal that was waiting on the table in their room when they arrived.

Karia told Juna she was going up to the garden for a while to think on things. The sun was moving into the western sky and began to dip into the horizon. Karia always loved being in the garden at sunset. The light sparkled and danced in the leaves, and the chimes played their haunting evening songs. She walked to the north end of the garden and sat in front of the crystal that protruded up through the ground seeming to reach toward the openness of the domed leaves within this magnificent willow tree.

She closed her eyes, breathing in and out, listening only to the rhythm of her breath and the beating of her heart. She relaxed and noticed the sound and the feeling of her own heartbeat—*bah-bum, bah-bum, bah-bum.* A curtain of light appeared before her and opened, calling her in. She stepped forward through the curtain and found herself standing in the middle of the forest. She knew it was not the forest where she had grown and her family still lived, not the forest where she, Juna, and Dino would play, but a very different forest.

Karia walked forward into the massive, beautiful trees. She became very aware that they seemed strangely large, much larger than the trees in the forest at home. Her eyes were drawn up the tall, rough trunks of the trees into the leaves that towered even further into the sky, seemingly never to end. It was beautiful and peaceful there. As she walked, she noticed the sounds of the birds and other forest creatures moving about in the warm glow of the evening sunset. The animals were busy in the forest: the raccoons scurried down trees, looking for their evening meal; and birds chirped and flitted through the leaves. So many of the sounds were the same as she had heard back home, but then she heard it—a new and foreign sound, some kind of deep, low, menacing growl. She stood very still, listening. She could not determine the direction it was coming from. Fear welled up within her, and she frantically looked quickly from side to side. She backed up slowly toward a large tree she had spotted out of the corner of her eye. Pressing her back into the tree, she swallowed hard. "This is a vision. Nothing can harm me. I am...I am safe," she whispered to herself.

A dark shadow rushed past her, followed by another threatening growl. She felt as if she were being stalked by a predator she could not see. Suddenly she heard a crackling sound that drew her attention away from the growling shadow—the same sound she had heard in her sleep tales. She leaned out, looking around the large tree she had her back against. There she saw a reddish-orange glow through the trees in the distance. She would have thought it to be the sunset, except for the crackling, sizzling sound that accompanied it and that the sunset was now behind her. The strange light with its brilliant colors was stunning and beautiful, but with its beauty came a danger that Karia could feel—one that would cause change and lots of it.

She heard a sudden hurried movement in the brush behind her. She turned to see birds, deer, raccoons, and many other animals hurrying away from the crackling sound. When she turned back to the light, she could see flames reaching through the trees toward her like a demon with a savage, horrible smile taunting her. It seemed sickeningly satisfied with its wild devouring of all that lay in its path. The sense of danger overwhelmed her. She turned to run, but she took a step and felt herself drop hard back into her body. "Change," she heard herself whisper without even feeling herself speak.

It had become very dark in the garden, and the only remaining light was from the glowing lanterns scattered about. She sighed deeply, knowing she was back at the willow. There was a sound near the pond at the willow entrance, she stood and moved slowly toward it. She squinted and blinked, trying to focus, and then she recognized the shadowy figure.

"Ahh, young Karia. I was not aware there was anyone in the garden." Nintar spoke softly as he stepped out of the shadows, holding his lantern up to reveal his face. "I was just coming to put out the lanterns, but I can return at a later time."

"No, Nintar, that will not be necessary. I was...I was just returning to my room." Karia nodded as she walked past him. "Good evening."

Back in her room, she watched Juna sleeping and debated in her mind as to whether she should wake him and tell him what she had seen in her vision. She sat quietly looking at him. It was at that moment she noticed for the first time how he somehow looked older, stronger. She stepped over to a mirror that sat in the corner of the room. She looked into the mirror at her own reflection. She noticed subtle differences in her appearance as well. "Change," she whispered again. She gazed at her face in the dimly lit mirror and then turned and walked to her sleeping mat. She lay down and pulled the woolen cover over her.

Chapter 9
Emergency Blanket

I woke up early. The last day of school is always exciting, but this one was especially so. I looked at the clock and realized it was early, so early that no one else would be up yet. I dressed, pulled out my journal, and stared again on the picture of Karia and Juna snuggled into a suitcase, using my socks for a pillow. Thinking again about getting them through security, I remembered a visit we had taken to our local fire station. *Maybe I could use one of those metal-looking blankets. I wonder if that would obstruct the X-ray view of Karia and Juna inside my suitcase. Hmm. Where can I get one of those?*

My drawing became more detailed. I added a straw or some sort of tube that they would use to breathe out of, just in case. They would be in the suitcase for probably around six hours, quite possibly longer. I wondered if that would make them rethink their wish to go see the mountains. I drew what they might look like in the suitcase, and then I drew what it would look like with the blanket and clothes packed in around them. *I will need to pack food for them. Trail mix would be good.* That reminded me of breakfast, and I felt hungry. I quietly crept downstairs and looked through the cabinets for something to eat. As I was getting myself a bowl of cereal, my dad walked into the kitchen.

"You're up early," he said.

"Yup. Last day of school. I guess I couldn't sleep," I said, sitting down at the table.

"Not much longer before we go on vacation. Are you looking forward to seeing your aunt and uncle and California?" he asked, pouring a cup of coffee.

"Yeah, it should be fun," I replied.

A few minutes later, my mom came into the kitchen. "All ready for your last day of school?" she asked.

"Yeah. Actually, I was just getting ready to leave," I said as I put my bowl into the sink.

"When you get home, I would like you to help me clean up the car before our trip," she told me.

"Sure. I'll take care of it, no problem," I assured her. "See you later!" I said goodbye to my mom and dad, grabbed my backpack, and headed out on my bike to meet up with Quinn.

After school, Quinn came home with me and helped me wash and clean out my mom's car, which was really nice of him since I'd skipped out on helping him clean out his garage. I was pulling some junk out of the trunk when I found a big first aid kit. I peered around the open trunk to see where Quinn was; he was vacuuming the inside of the car. I opened the kit like I was opening a treasure chest. It was a medium-sized red bag with a white cross on the front and the words "First Aid" in bold white letters. I unzipped it and flipped up the lid. I looked at the stuff in the bag, all neatly packaged and labeled. There were bandages, antiseptic, scissors, cotton swabs, and some other things. I pushed aside some of it and saw the words "Emergency Blanket." I read the package" "Made of durable insulating Mylar material, designed by NASA for space exploration. Retains and reflects back 90 percent of body heat." *This just might work*, I thought to myself. I looked around the open trunk again and saw Quinn, still vacuuming. I slipped the blanket into my shirt, zipped closed the first aid kit, and pushed it into the darkness of the trunk. "I'll be right back!" I called to Quinn as I ran toward the house.

"Where are you going?" Quinn called back.

"Bathroom! I'll bring us back something to drink," I said as the door closed behind me.

I bounded up the stairs and into my room, closing the door behind me. I pulled the blanket out from under my shirt, looked at it again and smiled. *Everything is coming together perfectly,* I thought to myself tossing the blanket under my bed. I went back downstairs and stopped in the kitchen for drinks before returning to finish the car with Quinn.

Chapter 10
Packing the Kids

The morning we were to leave, Karia and Juna came to my window just before sunrise. They had gotten quite good at scaling the rainspout to get to my second-floor room. They sat on the floor by my suitcase and ate some of the food I brought up from the kitchen. Being inside my house was very different and a little strange for them. They watched me intently and excitedly as I went over the plan again.

"You will be in the suitcase for a long time," I explained. "First we will travel in the car, and then we will be separated for a while—a long while. No matter what, you cannot allow anyone to see you. Do you understand?" When they nodded excitedly, I continued. "You will be going in the cargo hold of the airplane. You will have to remain quiet and under the blanket until you are safely loaded onto the plane. It's important that you follow the plan. There's no way for me to check on you once you're loaded." I paused and looked at them.

Juna was eating a half of a banana. He had slit the peel around the center with his single long, curved tooth that poked out from his lower jaw. He flipped one half back onto the plate and was trying to eat the inside of the other half without pulling back the remaining peel.

"Here, let me show you something," I said. I took the banana and peeled it down and handed it back to him.

He took it and smiled sheepishly at me.

"The next time we will see each other is at the luggage pickup, and even then we won't actually be able to see each other." I paused and looked at them while they continued to listen and eat. I was concerned about how the whole plan would play out, but they didn't seem to have any idea of the danger involved. "Are you sure you still want to do this?" I questioned them.

"This will be the greatest adventure yet!" Juna mumbled excitedly, his mouth full of banana.

"Dino, bring your bag down now! I want to put it in the car." My dad called from the bottom of the stairs.

"Be right down!" I replied.

"Okay, guys, this is it. You're absolutely sure you want to do this?" I asked, giving them one last chance to back out.

They looked at each other and then back at me. "Absolutely!" they replied in unison. "We can do this, Dino. We can do anything we are determined to do," Karia insisted. "You know that."

"I know." I smiled and held open the lid of the suitcase. They climbed into the emergency blanket I had folded several times and had laying open in half. I handed them each a straw. "You will use these to breathe out of, through the zipper." I folded the blanket over them and waited for them to situate themselves. I laid a couple of lightweight shirts on top of the blanket and gently zipped the suitcase closed. "Okay, you two. Try your straws." I waited and then I saw the zipper at one side of the case slide open a bit and a straw push through a moment later another at the other end. "How does it work?" I asked, leaning in by the straw.

"Just fine," a muffled voice assured me.

"See you in California," another muffled voice stated.

This was my queue. I gently picked up the suitcase and took it downstairs.

"What took you so long? We are almost completely packed," my dad said. I could tell he was a bit annoyed.

"Why are you acting so funny, Dino? Don't you want to go?" my mom asked.

"Sure I do. Can I put my suitcase in the back seat with me?" I asked.

"I suppose you will have to now that you have waited till the very last minute and the trunk is practically full," my mom replied.

Perfect! I thought.

I carefully pushed the suitcase in and unzipped the two zippers on either side about three inches. I thought it would be good to let them get some extra air before they were stuffed in the cargo hold. It was a long and quiet ride to the airport. I sat with my hand resting on the side of my suitcase. At one point, I thought I felt a small hand on the other side. It wasn't until I could see the airport that I really began to get excited and a little nervous. *We are really doing this!* The plan was actually starting to take shape, but I was still a little worried about getting through the airport. I was really hoping my luggage would not draw any attention. We parked in the long-term parking lot and took the shuttle to the airport. I left the zippers open a little so that Karia and Juna could see out if they wanted to.

Of course, from inside the suitcase, it was a different story. It was pretty comfortable as long as the suitcase was lying down flat or standing with the side handle at the top, but when my dad saw me struggle with the weight of the suitcase, his bright idea turned things topsy-turvy.

"Here, son. Let me help you with that," he said as he set his own suitcase down. He walked over and flipped mine up on its side, and then he pulled the slide handle out. "Now you can just pull it behind you on its wheels. It will be much easier that way."

I know he was trying to help, but when he flipped the suitcase, I could almost hear Karia and Juna go flying to one side. I walked slowly, following my parents. I could feel the bag jerking gently from side to side. As I stepped onto the moving walkway, I had the chance to look back. My suitcase was soft sided, so I could see them moving around inside the bag. I glanced up at the people behind me. A boy about my age with a baseball cap on backwards was staring at me and my bag with a really strange look on his face. I just smiled sheepishly and shrugged my shoulders.

"Pay attention, Dino!" My mom's voice startled me.

I turned around just as the moving walkway was about to end, glad her warning had kept me from stumbling off of it like an idiot.

———— ((◦)) ————

"Umph! Oh! Juna, get off me!"

The two of them clamored to reposition themselves and the emergency blanket that twisted around them as they scooted and turned.

"Be still!" Juna piped in, wanting to remain silent but needing to stop the commotion inside the suitcase.

Karia stopped immediately and waited, breathing heavily. "What is it, Juna?"

Juna stretched out his arms, straightening the blanket. Karia was then able to turn herself more freely and get untangled. As she and Juna were settling themselves, Karia's foot slipped through the open part of the zipper. She grabbed for Juna, trying to keep from sliding further out.

"What is it?" Juna grunted, grabbing Karia by the arm.

"My foot! It has slipped through the hole that Dino created for us to breathe out of." Karia struggled to feel which direction her foot was turned.

"Can you pull it in?" he urged.

"No! It is stuck. What if someone sees?" Karia mumbled, struggling to get her foot back inside.

"Lean over my back, and I will see if I can free your foot." Juna leaned forward so Karia was able to rest on his back. She could feel his hand at her ankle; she felt a little tugging and then heard the zipper move. Fearing they might both fall out the bottom, she reached for something to hold on to. Finally she felt her foot slip back into the bag and again heard the zipper. Juna straightened himself, as did Karia, and they were once again face to face.

"Your cloth tie around your leg was caught in the slide hole. That is a strange mechanism, that zipper thing," Juna shared. "I closed it all the way now so we don't have to worry about slipping out again."

"Thank you," Karia said, finding a comfortable way to sit.

"Well, I couldn't very well leave you hanging out the bottom of this thing, now could I?" Juna grinned.

I saw my parents heading toward a man who would check in our luggage. As we waited in line, I squatted down to secure the zippers on my bag. I whispered into the side of the bag, "This is it, you two. This is where we separate. Be good and be safe, and I will see you soon." I brushed my hand down the side of my suitcase, and I could feel them. I hoped they would be okay. *Just a few hours. What could happen in that short time?* I thought, trying to calm my nerves.

The man grabbed my parents' bags first and then mine. He wasn't gentle, that's for sure.

"Come on, Dino. We have to finish checking in. There are others waiting behind you," my dad pressed.

I looked at him and then at the people behind me. It was the same boy in the backwards baseball cap that I had seen on the walkway. The man at the baggage check-in took our bags and tossed them haphazardly onto a conveyer behind him. My dad put his arm around my shoulder to guide me away from the counter. I turned back and saw my bag as it disappeared through a plastic curtain on the baggage conveyor.

"I hope our luggage doesn't get lost," my mom joked to my dad.

Now I will be worried the entire flight, I thought to myself. I hadn't thought of that very real possibility.

Chapter 11
Load 'Em In

Karia and Juna could feel the bag riding on the conveyor for a long time. They were bumped and jostled around time and time again. There was a quick jerk, and they could feel the bag take a turn and slow to a stop. A few moments later, it moved again and stopped. This happened several times.

"What is happening, Juna?" Karia asked.

"I cannot be sure," Juna responded. He scooted to the side near the zipper and tried to peek out, but all he could see was darkness.

The bag continued to move slowly and stop. Finally Juna's curiosity got the best of him, and he pulled back the blanket so he could get a better look.

At that very moment, the suitcase was sliding through the X-ray machine. The security screener was carefully looking at the contents of each bag as it passed. The airport worker caught a glimpse of the skeletal profile of Juna's head as the bag exited the screen. Quickly she stopped the conveyor and put it in reverse. Dino's suitcase slowly came back into full view. The screener looked again. What she saw or thought she saw was no longer there, and the bag looked perfectly normal.

"Is something wrong, Agnes?" another screener asked her, noticing the puzzled look on her face as she now glared at the screen.

Dino C. Crisanti

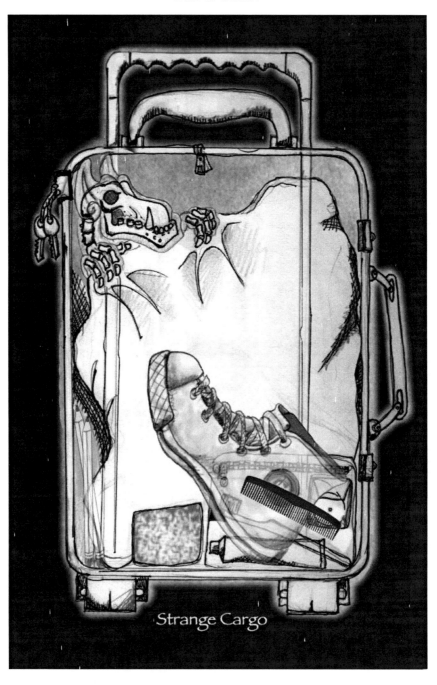

Agnes shook her head and said, "No...uh, nothing, I think I am due for a break. My eyes are starting to play tricks on me. I'll be back in fifteen, after a good strong cup a Joe," she said, hitting the conveyor button sending the bag on its way.

Karia and Juna were back on the move again. The conveyor seemed to pick up speed. They felt the bag bumping and jerking some more. They were pushed and squished, and finally they felt themselves falling. The suitcase landed with a *thud* in a pile of others, causing Karia and Juna to crash into each other. Again they felt themselves moving, only this time it didn't feel like they were on the conveyor. All of this was so new and strange to them.

Juna moved to the inside corner of the suitcase. When he had closed the zipper earlier he had tucked the pull inside. Now he carefully unzipped it, revealing piles of other luggage. He could see part of the blue sky and knew they were outside. He pulled the zipper back far enough to be able to pop his head through.

"Juna! Where are you going?" Karia blurted, grabbing onto one of his legs.

"Don't be alarmed. I am not leaving. I just want to see where we are," Juna explained. He proceeded to pull himself further out of the case. Finally, he could see. He was amazed, excited, and anxious all at the same time. He looked back from where they had come and saw the airport getting further and further away. He saw other carts pulling baskets like the one they were in. He stared with wonder at the flying machines—the big metal birds—in the distance. Suddenly a dark shadow fell over them. He turned and looked up. There, before him, was an enormous orange and blue flying machine. Until he was under its wing, he could not have ever realized its immense size.

The vehicle came to a stop, and Juna heard one voice holler to another, "Let's load 'em in, Al. This is the last load."

"I'll back it in!" Al bellowed back.

Juna pulled his head in and re-secured the zipper. "Karia, you will never believe the size of this airplane contraption. It is unlike anything

I have ever seen. It is like a giant metal eagle. Bayalthazar would be amazed!" Juna proclaimed. His eyes became wider, and his excitement filled their small luggage home.

Karia's eyes also grew wide with anticipation as she listened to Juna describe what he had seen.

The vehicle started moving again and was coming to another stop.

"Shh! I think we are going to be moved again."

Dino's suitcase was lifted again onto another conveyor. They could feel themselves being pulled along, but this one didn't last long. They were then lifted and swung onto another pile. They could hear the other luggage being loaded onto the plane as well. They sat quietly and waited until they could no longer hear the men talking, and then they heard the hatch close and lock.

"I believe we will be here for a while," Karia whispered.

"I believe you are right," Juna agreed.

Chapter 12
Strange Cargo

I was sitting in the terminal with my mom and dad, waiting for our flight to be called. Occasionally I would go to the window and watch the small trucks pulling the luggage bins to the planes. I squinted hard trying to see if I could spot my suitcase. All of the luggage looked the same, though, and I couldn't tell which plane we would be getting on. I began to get more and more worried about where Karia and Juna were and if they were alright.

"They should be calling our flight soon," my mom's soft voice predicted. "Are you getting excited?"

"Yeah, sure," I answered, turning away from the window. I walked slowly back to the chairs in the waiting area and plopped down. I watched people come and go until they finally called our flight.

My mom nudged me and said, "That's us!"

We picked up our carryon bags, walked to the line, and waited to board.

My mom put her arm around me. "You seem really quiet this morning, Dino. Is something bothering you?"

The line shifted forward.

"No, nothing's bothering me," I answered flatly. "Just a little tired I guess."

We handed our boarding passed to the lady at the gate. "Enjoy your flight!" she smiled.

As we walked down the long corridor to the plane, I wondered what Karia and Juna were doing, and I hoped they had made it on the plane.

———◄(●)►———

Karia and Juna were on the plane and were finally settling in.

"I have not heard any movement for a while now," Juna observed slowly unzipping the luggage to get a better look. "It sure is dark in here."

Karia remembered something Dino had put in the suitcase. She pushed aside the emergency blanket and felt for the inside pockets. She patted the pockets until she felt it. She reached inside a narrow pocket and pulled out a small flashlight. She pressed the button like he had shown her, and suddenly light flooded the inside of the suitcase.

Juna pulled himself back in through the zipper. He shielded his eyes from the unexpected bright light. "That is just what we need!" Juna exclaimed excitedly, reaching for the flashlight. "I wish to see where we are."

Karia handed Juna the light. She heard the zipper open more and watched as his head, shoulders, and arms disappeared through the opening. "Wait for me!" Karia squeezed out behind him.

What they saw was a sea of luggage. They stood atop the suitcase mountain, and Juna shined the light slowly across the cavernous room.

"Shine the light over here!" Karia requested.

Juna did as she asked and pointed the light back at Dino's suitcase. The bag was situated between several others, like books on a shelf.

"Let us pull it out. We can lay it flat and create more comfortable travel quarters," Karia suggested.

Juna set the flashlight on another piece of luggage, and they each got a grip on the bag. Together they pulled. As the bag began to move, they felt and heard the loud roar of the jet engines. It was louder than anything they had ever heard before. They both released their grip on the luggage and covered their ears. They stood for a few moments, staring at each other, as they felt the plane taxi to the runway. Once their ears became adjusted to the sound, they again began pulling at the luggage. It was difficult at first, but the suitcase finally slid free. They had it almost completely out when they felt the plane jerk and lurch forward hard. Karia and Juna, still holding onto suitcase, tumbled backwards. The roaring noise became louder and then turned into a high-pitched whine.

"Hold on!" Juna hollered, in mid fall.

The flashlight rolled off of the other suitcase and fell to the floor out of sight.

Karia, still holding on, found herself under the very suitcase she was looking to for protection. She lay there as she felt the plane leave the ground. The noise was deafening, and she struggled to free her hands to cover her ears. She felt herself being pulled to the floor and decided to just wait. The plane began to level out, and the noise began to subside. "Juna!" Karia called. She struggled to move the suitcase that was on top of her. "Juna, can you hear me? Are you alright? Juna!" When he didn't answer, she feared that something happened to him. She tried harder to free herself. She twisted and turned and pulled her legs up. She worked to get her feet in position to push the bag off. Just as she went to shove the bag, it lifted off of her, and standing behind it was her brother. "Juna, you're alright!" she exclaimed.

Juna reached out his hand, took Karia's, and pulled her to her feet. "Are you alright?" he asked her.

"I am now, but I was beginning to worry about you. These airplane things are so, so, so very loud. I do not know how humans can stand it." She brushed off her dress. "Where is the light?" She remembered seeing it roll away.

Juna pulled the flashlight out of his belt and turned it on. "I saw it roll off and went after it so it would not get lost."

"Very good, Juna. Now let us get back to setting up our quarters."

Karia reached down and pulled on the handle of the suitcase. Juna grabbed the other end and pushed it up. They found a nice flat spot to rest it on. Karia walked to the zipper pull and opened it all the way. They each took a side and flipped the lid of the suitcase up. Juna pointed the flashlight in. The suitcase was a complete mess. Karia climbed in and began to straighten the clothes to make a place for them to sit comfortably. As Juna held the flashlight, occasionally the light wandered.

"Please, Juna, I cannot see what I am doing," Karia scolded.

"Oh, I am sorry," He mumbled.

"There. This should be quite comfortable for the journey," Karia said, admiring her work.

Juna climbed into the suitcase, and they both sat down. Karia pulled some Traegon mix from her pouch and found a container of nuts and trail mix that Dino had put in the suitcase for them.

Juna lay back shining the flashlight all around. He carefully looked at the luggage, the walls of the plane compartment, the ceiling, and just about all he could see from where they sat. "Let us go for a walk!" Juna blurted hopping to his feet.

Karia stared at him in complete disbelief. "Did you bump your head when you fell? Sit back down. It should not be too long," she said.

"Aw, come now! You are always the adventurous one. Let us just see what else is down here." Juna pressed her to join him. "I am going. You can come or you can stay, but I would rather you come."

She looked at his pleading eyes. "I have a feeling this is not a very good idea," then she stood and climbed out of the suitcase. "Where exactly are we going?" she questioned Juna.

"Over this way." Juna motioned to Karia as he started climbing onto stacks of luggage.

She followed closely, and Juna climbed as if he knew exactly where he was going. "Are you sure you know what you are doing?" Karia quizzed.

"You should not worry so much. Did you have something else to do?" Juna glanced back teasingly, as if she might. "What happened to your adventurous spirit, oh great Oracle Karia?"

"Please do not tease, Juna. This path, these dreams, they feel like a big responsibility, and leaving home the way we did doesn't feel terribly responsible," Karia continued on behind Juna.

"I understand what you are feeling, Karia, but we are becoming older and must grow in our experiences. It will make us better and stronger Traegons. Think of all we will be able to tell the community," Juna persuaded.

"Like what the inside of an airplane luggage area looks like?" Karia joked.

"You never know what may be important in our life plan," Juna said wisely.

"Oh, brother," Karia huffed.

Suddenly there was a noise from ahead, but all they could see was a wall. Juna stopped and crouched on one knee. They listened carefully while Juna shined the light around.

"What does that sound like to you, Karia?" Juna asked, bringing the light to the two of them so they could see each other.

"Animals? I would say wolves in distress if we were in the woods. Where is it coming from?" she asked.

"It sounds like it is just behind this wall." Juna flashed the light back in the direction of the wall. "I am not sure how to get over there.

Karia noticed a small grid at the top of the wall. "What is that?" she asked as she began crawling in that direction, passing Juna.

Juna grinned as Karia took the lead. *That is the sister I remember.* "The bags are not high enough over there," he observed.

"A small obstacle, not to worry. Come over here and help me pile these bags higher," Karia instructed as she began pushing and pulling bags.

Juna came to help. "Ah, the adventurous Karia has returned!" He smiled.

Some of the bags were just too heavy for them to move, even both of them together. They gathered several that were smaller and lighter and began making their way to the grid in the wall. The stack swayed and wobbled, but Juna steadied it while Karia climbed to the top so she could peek through.

"What is it? What do you see?" Juna asked impatiently.

"Boxes or crates. The fronts are like cages. I can see things moving inside," Karia described.

"Come down. I wish to see," Juna requested.

Karia carefully climbed down the bags. She then held them steady while Juna climbed up for his turn.

"I can see them!" he said. "I think that they are dogs. They must be going on a trip with their humans," said Juna.

"Why do you think they whine as they do?" Karia asked, listening to the yips, yaps, and howls.

"I cannot be sure," Juna answered as he slid his fingers into the holes of the grid and gently pulled. It did not move.

"It is held in by pins of some sort, in the corners," Karia shared. "I noticed it when I was up there."

Juna pulled out his crude knife with the curvy blade and began working at the corners. Moments later, Karia heard something fall. "One complete!" he stated. A few moments more, and she heard the sound of another falling, and then another and another. He put his knife back into his sheath and again pulled on the grid. Finally, it slipped free of the wall.

"Excellent work, Juna," Karia complimented. "Now hold tight. I am coming up." Karia released her hold on the tower of bags just to see if they were stable. She tilted her head back and forth as she watched the bags sway a little. "Try and steady it as I climb."

Juna held tight to the hole in the wall. Using this leverage, he balanced the tower of bags with his body, holding it steady as his sister ascended it. When she was within reach, Juna leaned toward her and extended his hand. The tower of bags moved slightly, startling both of them. Karia grabbed Juna's hand, and he pulled her up. Together they teetered on the small bag at the very top.

"You first," Juna directed as he helped Karia to go through the small hole in the wall.

Her legs went through first, and when she was about halfway through, she realized there was nothing on the other side to step onto. She looked around and saw a piece of luggage that looked kind of soft, so she aimed and let go of Juna's hand. Flinging herself out, she landed directly on top of it. A high-pitched yelp came from inside the bag when she landed. Startled, Karia gasped. She looked up at Juna and then leaned over and looked into the bag. Inside, cowering in the back, was a small white dog.

"Oh, there, there, little one. I did not mean to scare you." Karia spoke in a calm and quiet tone and placed her hand on the screened side of the bag. A low and vicious growl came from the dark end of the cage, and then it burst forth. Karia fell off, startled. She heard a chuckle from above.

"Aw, sweet ornery thing. How about you help me? At least I like you," Juna teased.

Karia stood and looked around for something soft and not living for Juna to climb down on. She noticed several brightly colored ladders strapped together. She moved over to them and struggled to sand them up. "A little short," she informed Juna. Then she found a plastic box. She checked to see if there was anything living in it, and then she moved it over to the wall. She placed the ladders on top and leaned them into the wall. "Go ahead. I'll hold it," she told Juna.

He backed himself through the hole and hung down, feeling with his foot for the ladder. Finally he felt it and released his grip on the hole. His foot touched the top rung, and then he slipped. Karia saw him coming and tried to quickly get out of the way, but she didn't move fast enough before he fell right on top of her. He rolled off of her almost as soon as he landed. "Are you alright?" he asked, rolling up onto one knee checking to see if she had been harmed.

"Watch out!" Karia warned.

Juna looked back just in time. He reached out and grabbed the rungs of the ladder and used the momentum to toss the ladders over their heads and into a stack of pet supplies.

"Are you alright?" Karia asked, bringing herself to a stand.

"Better than that bag." He pointed to where he had thrown the ladder. It had hit a bag of dog food and tore it wide open, spilling the brown kibble out onto the floor.

"Oops," Karia said, squinting. Then they heard a door open. "Somebody is coming!" she whispered, looking for a quick hiding place.

Juna disappeared behind a large animal crate, and Karia slid between two smaller ones. She could hear the footsteps and thought the crate would be a good place to hide, but she remembered the little white dog and thought again. She peered into the crate next to her and saw a fat gray tabby cat. He purred and seemed harmless enough, so she thought it would be safe. Quickly she went around to the front of the crate. *Oh, good! A zipper contraption,* she thought as she unzipped the front and slipped into the cage just as a human came around the corner. Karia looked at the cat and placed her finger to her mouth. "Shhh," she whispered. The cat lifted his big furry body and moved toward Karia, so she sat very still, not wanting to be mistaken for a juicy mouse. The cat stepped forward, coming nose to nose with her. Karia felt his cold wet nose touch the end of her long smooth muzzle, and then he pushed his face hard into hers, purring. She put her hands out to steady herself. "I guess you like me, huh?" Karia whispered. She squeezed past him to the back of the cage and sat down. The cat turned also and laid his large fury body right in her small lap.

"Look what happened over here!" an angry man's voice boomed from right in front of her. "I asked you to make sure to secure these ladders. Now you can come over here and clean up this mess."

"But I did. I did secure the ladders. Or at least I thought I did," a younger man said as he noticed the dog food all over the floor.

"You've gotta take this job seriously, Jimmy, or they won't keep you on. Understand?" the older man stated. "Now clean this mess up and then go through and check the animals."

"Okay, Boss," Jimmy replied.

A few moments later, the door opened and closed.

Karia squeezed from the back of the carrier to the front, nudging by the chubby tabby cat. Karia peered through the screening as the cat purred loudly in her ear. She searched for any sight of Juna but could only see the younger man cleaning up the torn bag of pet food. She watched him a moment and found herself feeling bad that he had gotten in trouble for the mess they made. Then she heard a "Pssst." she glanced around again and saw Juna, directly across from her in a large dog crate. She had missed him earlier because he was sitting between the legs of a really big, floppy-eared dog. She giggled a little as the dog with long droopy jowls rested its chin on Juna's head, sniffing and nudging him like he wanted to play.

Juna shot her an annoyed look. "Do you have a plan?" Juna whispered loudly.

"No. I was hoping you did," Karia whispered back as the cat pushed hard on the side of her face, purring even louder.

Jimmy continued his cleaning, all the while mumbling under his breath.

Suddenly the door once again clicked open. The older man had returned with a roll of clear heavy tape. "Here, Jimmy!" he said, tossing the tape at him. "Make sure it is closed and the name of the owner is still visible. Then get yourself back up top. We'll need you up there for the landing."

"Yeah, I'll be right up," Jimmy said, wrapping the bag with tape.

Juna shot Karia a look of concern and whispered, "Landing! We must get back to Dino's bag."

Karia was staring at Juna when Jimmy walked past quickly. Moments later, the door closed. Karia slowly unzipped the door of the carrier she was in and backed out. "It was very nice to meet you, Sir Kitty," she said as she re-zipped the carrier. The cat bade her farewell with a sound like a cross between a yawn and a meow. Turning around, Karia saw Juna latching the carrier that he had just exited himself. The big dog was nosing the cage door and whining.

Dino C. Crisanti

"Good to meet you, Fanblade," Juna said.

"Fanblade? Why do you call him that?" Karia had a very puzzled look on her face.

"It is the name on his collar," Juna replied, walking back toward the hole at the top of the wall.

Karia followed Juna, walking past Fanblade's large crate. She looked at him, and he watched as she passed by. He jumped, slapping his front paws on the bottom of his crate and yowling loudly. Then he shook his head wildly, and his large floppy ears made a tremendous noise on the inside of the crate. "Fanblade, huh?" she mumbled.

"I am not sure how we are going to get back through that hole," Juna observed, staring upward.

Karia began looking around. She walked over to the ladders they had used earlier and found that Jimmy had definitely secured them better this time. "We will not be using these again," she informed Juna.

Juna was looking around for anything that he might be able to stack high. The only things he could think to use were the animal crates. He eyed them and tested several to see if he would be able to move them.

"We cannot do that," Karia stated, guessing what Juna was thinking. "It would not be right. If those crates fall when the airplane lands, the animals could get hurt."

"I agree. I wouldn't want anything to happen to Fanblade." Juna looked at Fanblade's crate, and the dog flapped his ears wildly and scratched at the cage door. "I think I might like a dog. I like this one."

They could feel the direction of the plane changing, and they looked at each other.

"We had better figure something out, and quickly," Karia announced.

Chapter 13
Not So Great Surprise

"Please return your seats to their upright position and secure your trays. The flight attendants will be coming around to pick up any remaining cups or garbage you may have. It is a beautiful eighty-two degrees in sunny Sacramento, California, and we will be landing shortly. We hope you have enjoyed your flight with us. If you are here on a visit, we hope you enjoy your stay and choose to fly with us on your return trip. If you are here to stay, we thank you for flying with us and hope you will choose us again. Sit back, relax, and enjoy the remainder of your flight. As your pilot and flight crew, it has been our privilege to serve you."

"We are almost there!" my mom said, leaning over me to look out the window. "I am really getting excited. How about you?"

"Yeah, me too. How long do you think before we land?" I asked.

"Oh, I don't know. Maybe fifteen or twenty minutes. Then we have to go get our luggage, you know," she answered, sitting back in her seat as we felt the plane gradually reduce altitude.

I sat back too, relieved that the flight was almost over and soon Karia, Juna, and I would be together again. The plane came in for the landing. We felt it touch down, rumbling and bumping and jerking. I knew Karia and Juna had to be glad it was almost over as well. The plane turned and taxied toward the gate. Finally, it came to a stop, and all of the people began gathering their things. We waited patiently as the flight attendants directed us off of the plane. We made our way down the long corridor to the terminal.

"This way," my dad directed us.

My mom followed my dad, and I followed my mom as we headed toward the baggage pickup area. It seemed like the longest wait of all. We passed the area where people were waiting to pick up their pets. The baggage carousels had not even started. Mom leaned against dad, and they talked quietly to pass the time. I paced back and forth, waiting anxiously. Finally, the first bags descended carousel. As I watched intently for my bag, my dad walked up behind me.

"Do you see it yet?" he asked, startling me a little.

"No, not yet. Do you see yours?" I asked him back.

"Nope. Come on. Let's stand over there." My dad pointed to a empty spot off to the side. "We will be able to see the bags as soon as they come onto the conveyor."

Mom picked up her carryon and followed. She was looking through some brochures of California. "There's yours, Jack," my mom pointed out. She shoved the brochures in her bag. Dad came back and set his bag down by my mom. "There's another one." She and my dad were like a tag team; she saw them, and he gathered them.

"Do you see yours yet, son?" my dad asked as he started for the other one.

"Not ye—" I started and then saw it come down the conveyor. As it made its way around so, did my dad and I.

"Go grab it, and I'll meet you by your mom," my dad directed me.

My anticipation quickly turned to horror and disbelief as I noticed that the zipper on my bag was open and not just a little like I had left it for Karia and Juna. It was open, really open. I watched the bag intently as it made its way around the carousel. When the bag came close, I grabbed for the handle and pulled it off. Immediately, I could feel a difference in the weight. My stomach sank and my heart raced as I opened my bag. They were gone!

"What's the matter, Dino?" my mom asked, coming up from behind me.

"My bag! It was opened," I said, looking helplessly up at the carousel and wondering what happened to Karia and Juna.

"Well, sometimes they do random checks. Is anything missing?" she asked, sensing my concern.

I couldn't answer. I couldn't even think. I started looking around desperately. *Where could they have gone? Where could they be?* I wondered, my mind racing.

"Come on, son. Grab your bag. We'll check it better over where your dad is," she said, trying to get us out of the crowd of people who seemed to surround us. The whole place seemed suddenly extra crowded.

What am I going to do now? How am I supposed to find two creatures no more than sixteen inches tall that no one has ever seen before, in an airport with more people than I've ever seen in one place? I felt myself begin to panic. I could hear my parents speaking to me, but it all sounded muffled. I just felt...sick.

"Dino, are you alright?" My mom put her hand on my shoulder and her face in front of mine, forcing me to look into her eyes. "Honey, you look really pale."

"I have to use the bathroom," I blurted out.

"Well, let's get out of this luggage area and find a place to sit," she suggested.

"No, I have to go right now." I pulled from her grip and headed in a direction as if I knew where I was going. "I'll be right back"

———— ⟫⟪⟫⟪ ————

All of the animal carriers came out in their own designated area. They were stacked, awaiting the arrival of their owners. Karia and Juna peered through the crate door and marveled at the sheer number of humans in one place.

"We must release ourselves from this cage before Fanblade's humans come to get him, or we will be going home with them," Karia said.

Juna reached through and slowly unlatched the crate door. He watched carefully so they would not be seen. "Are you prepared, Karia? We will need to move quickly once we are free. I am not sure where to go from here, as I cannot see well what is around us."

"I am prepared." Karia took a deep breath, but before they could slip out of the cage Fanblade playfully pushed them free—and himself as well.

A woman working behind the counter turned when she heard the commotion. The shocked look on her face was a good indication that she had seen more than just the dog. Fanblade stopped and shook his head vigorously, and his large, floppy ears made a thunderous sound as his shaking worked its way through his entire body all the way to the tip of his long tail. Karia and Juna scurried under him as he shook and slid behind a stack of carriers. Fanblade decided that everyone in the baggage area was going to play with him. A woman from the airline reached for him, but he was too fast. He nosed each person as he ran by. He hopped and slid on the shiny tile. Kids were laughing and pulling to go and pet him. The other dogs were barking, and cats were hissing. People were guarding the entrance so the dog wouldn't get out. This chaos was the perfect cover for Karia and Juna to find their way back to Dino. They hid behind the legs of people watching the crazed dog. They ran from suitcase to suitcase, trying not to be seen.

Juna spotted a large pile of luggage on a cart. "There! That will be our way out." He pointed. "Follow me and stay close." Juna moved quickly, with Karia following close behind. Once they reached the cart, they jumped on and hid themselves among the bags. People kept piling on more and more bags, and then the cart began to move. Karia and Juna had a unique view now.

They heard a man call out, "Blade! Blade, come here!"

Fanblade was so excited to hear his human that he darted across the room and jumped right into the man's arms, almost knocking him to the ground. The attendant was near him, apologizing over and over again. As the cart moved toward the terminal, Karia saw Dino walking in the opposite direction.

"Juna! It is Dino! I see him over there," Karia said excitedly.

In the terminal, Juna noticed a large, elevated cluster of plants and small trees. It looked like an island in a sea of humans.

"Prepare to jump, Karia!" Juna called. He watched a large group of humans standing near the place where they were heading. "Wait... wait...NOW!" Juna grabbed Karia by the arm, and they jumped from the cart. Among the crowd there were bags, suitcases, and an assortment of hiding places. "Meet me at the island." He pointed before he spun away from her in another direction. They quickly made their way through the crowds, pausing under a cluster of chairs or behind a pile of bags.

At one point, Karia had caught the eye of a man walking quickly through the crowd. He stopped suddenly and turned to look again. His eyes scanned the area, he shook his head in confusion and continued on. Karia found a child's backpack and slid in next to it. She stood very still, hoping to be mistaken for a toy. The child sat on the floor next to her mother's feet, playing with a small book. When she saw Karia, she smiled and leaned to reach for her. She held out her hand. Karia looked into the innocent eyes of this lovely human child and felt compelled to reach out as well. Their hands touched, and a smile was shared once again by a young human and a young Traegon. Then Karia spun back and continued on her way toward the island. Reaching the island, she leapt onto a seat nearby and jumped to the island, rolling into the shrubbery and into her hiding place. Karia brought herself to her knees and pulled back a branch, trying to locate Dino or Juna.

"What kind of trees are these?" Juna whispered into Karia's ear, startling her.

"Do not do that!" Karia snapped. "Have you seen Dino? He should be coming from that direction."

"He hasn't emerged yet. I have been watching. Did you look at these trees and plants? I think there is something wrong with them." Juna put Karia's hand to the firm plastic leaves.

Her eyes left the crowd, and she glanced at the plants that were hiding them. "What are these?" She pulled a leaf from a nearby plant and bit into it. "These cannot be real. I cannot even bite through it, and it tastes awful. I have never before seen such strange plants and trees."

Juna struggled to pull some of the leaves off and stuffed them in his pouch for later. "There! There he is!" Juna announced, looking up at the very moment Dino was passing by their island hiding spot.

———————◆———————

I was distraught. I returned to my parents after my short bathroom search turned up nothing. *Where could they be?* I knew I couldn't leave the airport without them. Somehow, I needed to keep my parents from leaving until I find them. If I couldn't come up with something, I knew I would have to tell them everything. I felt really sick, and the crowd only made it worse.

My mom stopped and turned to talk to me. Since I wasn't watching where I was going I bumped right into her. "Dino!"

"Oh, I'm sorry, Mom. I didn't mean—"

She cut me off. "What is going on with you? You are acting very strangely," she persisted. "You have been since we left the house this morning."

I looked into her eyes. "I am not feeling very well. I think I need to eat something," I answered weakly.

"Jack, let's get our lunch here before we leave. Dino is not feeling well," Mom said, grabbing the back of my dad's jacket.

"Do you know how much lunch here at the airport is going to cost?" my dad objected.

"Please, Jack. Look how pale he is. I think he needs to eat," she pleaded.

"Alright!" He looked around for a sign to indicate where the nearest restaurant would be. "Come on. Follow me."

We made our way through the airport toward the food court. I felt relieved, but I also knew we didn't have much time.

Chapter 14
Recovery

Karia and Juna remained undercover as they crept to the opposite end of the concrete island with the odd trees. They waited until the coast was clear and climbed down. They watched as Dino and his family turned the corner.

"Come on! Stay under here." Juna directed Karia to follow him under a cluster of chairs.

Karia followed along, watching to ensure they were not spotted. At the end of the long stretch of chairs, they paused. The terminal was strangely quiet. Karia looked one direction and Juna the other.

"Head for that!" Juna said, pointing at a rolling cleaning cart near the restrooms. They ran and ducked behind it. Concealed by the cart, Karia was able to look down the corridor where Dino had gone. She could see that there was an opening at the end of the hallway. *They must have gone in there!* she thought. The cleaning cart began to move, and Karia pulled Juna around the corner. They ran as fast as they could with nothing to hide them. They could hear footsteps. "Someone is coming!" whispered Karia.

Juna grabbed Karia, pulling her backwards into a doorway with him. "Close your eyes and be very still!" he demanded.

"It won't work here, Juna," she objected.

"Just do what I tell you," he urged.

They remained very still, until they no longer heard footsteps.

Juna and Karia slowly opened their eyes. "It worked!" he announced. "Now let's go."

They reached the end of the hall and peeked around the corner. They saw many tables and could smell many different scents.

"I am hungry," Juna declared.

"As am I, but we have no time for eating. We must find Dino before he leaves this place," Karia said. "Over there!" Karia pointed at another smaller concrete island. "There are more of those strange plants. We can hide there until we see him. Hurry! Under here." Karia grabbed Juna's arm and ran to a nearby empty table, then on to another table with a man and a woman eating lunch. Juna was very distracted by the aroma of all the new kinds of food that he wasn't used to. Karia pulled him again, and this time they were under two tables pulled together, where a man, woman, and four children were seated. As Karia planned their next move, Juna was busy gathering the crumbs that the small humans dropped. He placed a few French fries in his pouch and then felt a tap on the top of his head. He slowly looked up.

There was a very small human child leaning over on her chair. She had two very short ponytails on the top of her head. "Hi!" she whispered with a big, kind smile on her young face.

Juna gave her a nervous grin as she handed him another French fry. Karia grabbed his arm, and they were off and running again.

"Doggy!" the little girl cried out after him.

When they reached the concrete island with the strange plants, Karia said, "Climb up and then pull me up."

Juna looked at Karia and then at the wall. She was holding her hands so Juna could climb on her first. "It is too high, Karia. We will need something to climb on." Juna looked around and saw a table and chairs with nobody sitting there. "Wait here."

Karia waited nervously, feeling completely exposed and vulnerable. She saw Juna pushing a chair toward her. She glanced around to see if anyone was watching, and when she turned back the chair was in front of her, but Juna was nowhere in sight. "Uh, Juna?" Karia gasped. "Juna, where are you?" Karia climbed up on the chair and into the plants. There she felt safer.

———⊰⦿⊱———

I waited while my mom and dad went to the counter to order our food. I was looking around when I noticed an unattended chair moving across the floor. I stood and walked around a display of artificial plants, and there was Juna! I snatched him up from behind, startled he began struggling. I quickly walked to the other side where we couldn't be seen and set him down. "Where have you been?" I demanded. "And where is Karia?"

Juna turned around and immediately took a fighting stance. "Dino! We found you!" Juna cried. "Do you have Karia as well?"

"No. Isn't she with you?" Dino questioned.

"I am right here!" Karia popped out from the plastic plants.

"Oh, thank goodness. You two had me scared half to death. Where did you go?" I began questioning them and then remembered my parents, who were now back at the table with our food, scouring the room for me. "I have to get back to our table. We are just on the other side of these plants. Stay here and DO NOT go anywhere. I am going to go to the table and eat. I will unzip my suitcase and stand it next to me. Whatever you have to do, get in that suitcase before we are finished eating. Do you hear me?"

Karia and Juna nodded and backed into the plants just as my mom came around the corner.

"There you are! What are you doing? We go to get lunch and when we come back you're gone." My mom sounded annoyed.

"Um, I felt a little dizzy. I thought I would go to the washroom, but when I got this far, I felt better. Funny, huh?" I said.

"No, not really," she responded clearly not amused. "Dino, you have been acting very strange. I don't know what's gotten into you, but you need to pull yourself together."

"I'm sorry, Mom. I will." We walked back to the table where my dad was standing, still scanning the room for me.

"What is going on?" He sounded just as annoyed as my mom.

"Dino is going to sit down, eat, and stop acting so strangely. Is that right, Dino?" My mom shot me a disapproving look.

"Yeah, I am," I responded to both of them with an awkward smile, feeling much more myself. I leaned over and quietly unzipped my bag.

"Now what are you doing?" my mom barked.

"Nothing!" I sat up and ate my lunch.

Chapter 15
Uncle Joe's and Aunt Carol's Place

I watched the forest grow thicker as we ascended the mountain. My dad pulled the rental car into the long mountain driveway of my uncle's home. *We're almost there*, I thought to myself. I noticed birds and squirrels moving through the trees and wondered if there were really any Traegons there. I squinted, trying to focus, but the car was moving too fast. I laid my hand on the side of my bag and wished Karia and Juna could be looking out the window with me. "Will we be there soon?" I asked loud enough for Karia and Juna to hear.

"Very soon," my mom answered back.

I patted the side of my bag.

A few moments later, there was a fork in the driveway, and my dad pulled the car to the left. Up ahead, I could see a log home. Uncle Joe and Aunt Carol were standing on the porch waving as we pulled in. My mom hopped out of the car just as it rolled to a stop. She hurried to her brother, my Uncle Joe, and his wife Carol. They were hugging when my dad and I brought the first few bags up.

"Good to see ya, Jack! How was the trip?" Uncle Joe greeted my dad. He walked over to me and messed my hair. "How are ya, Dino? It's been a long time, and boy have you grown. Do you even remember me?" he asked.

"Sure I do…a little." I tried to be honest.

"That's alright, son. Come on in. Let me take that for you," he said, reaching for my bag.

"Thanks, but I've got it," I responded, pulling it away.

"Yeah, he's been weird about that bag all day. I've got a couple more, though, if you want to help me with those," my dad suggested to my uncle.

I continued on toward the house. I looked intently at the tree line as I made my way up the steps to the front door. I walked into the living room and was amazed at how big and open it was inside. Huge timbers stretched the full length of the house. There was a large stone fireplace, and the walls were roughhewn logs just like the outside. The view out the back windows was spectacular. It looked out over a deep ravine, and the sun was shining on the rocks.

"Your room is right over here, Dino," Aunt Carol told me.

I followed her into a small room off the back of the house. It felt quiet and secluded, and I liked that.

"I hope this is alright. It isn't very big, but I like the view in here," she said, pulling back the curtains and revealing an awesome view of the forest. "There is a bathroom just out your door to the left. You'll have it mostly to yourself."

"No, actually it's perfect. Thanks, Aunt Carol," I said.

"Come on, Anna. I will show you where you and Jack will be staying." They turned and left my room.

I closed the door quietly behind them and laid my bag down on the floor beside the bed. Carefully, I unzipped it and opened the top. It looked like a normal suitcase, a bit messy but otherwise normal. Then I spotted a little foot sticking out from under the emergency blanket. I reached in and very lightly ran my finger over the foot. It immediately pulled away.

Karia carefully peeked out from under the clothing. "Is it safe? Can we come out now?" Karia whispered.

"Yes. The coast is clear," I said as I helped to uncover them.

They climbed out of the suitcase and stretched.

"This is lovely," Karia observed. "It feels a bit like home."

Juna climbed up on the bed and strained to see out the window.

I walked around the bed, picking up Karia on the way. I set her on the desk by the window and brought Juna over too. They both gazed out the window in silence. I opened the window to let some of the mountain air in. Just as I did that, Karia and Juna both took in long, deep breaths. I couldn't help myself either. The air was so clean and smelled so fresh. It was different from home somehow.

"It is beautiful here," Karia proclaimed.

"Where are the mountains?" Juna quizzed.

"We are on them. They are out there." I pointed outside.

"I want to see them out there," Juna insisted.

"Okay. Stay here. I'll go and see if it's alright if we go outside. I will be right back. Stay out of trouble," I told them.

When I left my room, my mom and Aunt Carol were sitting on the couch in front of the big fireplace talking. I could see my dad and Uncle Joe sitting on the front porch. "Can I go outside for a little walk?" I asked my mom.

She looked at my aunt.

Carol said, "I suppose, but don't go far. We have some friends dropping by in a little bit who we want you to meet. It is also more dangerous here than by your house. There have been sightings of a rogue cougar roaming the mountains, so please stay close to the house and pay attention to your surroundings."

"I will, I promise. I'll be really careful. Holler for me when your friends get here," I said, turning and heading back toward my room. I grabbed my backpack and set it on the desk so Karia and Juna could climb in. "Just until we get outside," I promised them.

They reluctantly climbed in. Once we were outside, I walked toward the side of the house with the least windows and then about ten feet down a forest path. I came upon an outcropping of rock with an incredible view of the mountains around us. I found a safe, flat spot to open my backpack. When Karia and Juna climbed out and looked around, they were mesmerized. From where we stood, we could see into the valley and up to the adjoining mountain. Juna immediately moved to the edge of the rock, seemingly without any fear.

"Wait, Juna! Don't get too close. I don't want you to fall," I ordered.

"Do not forget the land is our home. I can move through the forest with much more ease than you. Fear not for me," Juna said confidently.

Karia moved in behind Juna for a look. "This is most amazing," she said. "It is so very different from our home, yet so similar."

I scooted on my butt to a safe distance from the edge. "Well, then you two will be on your own if you go any closer to the edge, 'cause I'm not coming along."

I heard my mom call for me. "Dino, come on back!"

"Come on, let's go. We have to get back," I said, backing further from the edge until I could comfortably stand and walk back.

"I think we will stay here for now," Juna stated.

"What?" I gasped.

"Yes, Dino, we will be fine out here. We will not go far. This is where we belong—with the land," Karia insisted.

"At least follow me back up to the house so you know where to find me. You have to be extra careful here," I begged. "Besides, my aunt said there is a rogue cougar running around out here somewhere, and I don't want you guys to get eaten."

"We will follow you back, but I think we will be safe enough until you return," Karia said. "When you are finished, come back. We will be waiting."

They followed me back and peered through the bushes at the house. "Which window is yours?" Juna questioned.

I pointed to the lone window on the side of the house.

"We will go and have a look at the trees over that way as well. There is much to explore. Don't worry. We will remain close," Juna assured me.

"We will be safe, Dino. There is no need to worry for us," Karia agreed.

"Alright. I'll be back in a little while," I said reluctantly.

I walked to the back porch. When I looked back, I couldn't see them, but I knew they were there. I walked in the back door and heard voices coming from the living room.

"Dino, come in here!" my aunt called.

There in the living room were my Aunt Carol, my Uncle Joe, my mom, my dad, a man, a woman, and two girls. One of the girls looked about my age with long, straight blonde hair. The other one looked to be a little younger with short brown hair pulled up in a ponytail.

My uncle stood and walked over to me. He placed his hand on my shoulder and introduced me. "Dino, this is Mike and Miriam Linder and their daughters Autumn and Jade. They are old family friends. We've known Mike and Miriam since before these lovely ladies were even born. Everyone, this is my nephew Dino."

"Hi," I said and waved my hand shyly.

"It is nice to finally meet you all. Joe and Carol have always spoken so fondly of you," Mrs. Linder shared. "We live just up the hill and thought you might enjoy spending some time with the girls while you're in town. We have a few horses, so you kids can go out on the trails with them. The girls are pretty familiar with the trails and the terrain around here. Maybe they can show you around a bit," Mrs. Linder explained.

I was feeling a little uncomfortable as she spoke, and when I looked at Autumn and Jade, it seemed they might be feeling the same way.

"Why don't you kids go out back and get to know each other a bit?" Mrs. Linder instructed.

"That sounds like a nice idea," my mom agreed.

There was an awkward silence in the room. Mrs. Linder put her hand on Autumn's back and gently pushed her in my direction.

Autumn gave her mom an annoyed look and then proceeded toward me with Jade following close behind. "Nice to meet you, Mrs. and Mr. Dosek. See you later." Autumn smiled and walked past me with Jade on her heels, and I fell in behind.

We stepped out onto the back deck; we all stood for a moment just staring at one another.

"Sorry if that was awkward. My mom can be a little pushy," Autumn admitted.

"It's okay. I understand," I replied. "Want to go for a walk?" I suggested.

"Sure!" Autumn agreed.

"You don't say much, do you, Jade?" I questioned as I led the way down the steps into the yard. She reminded me of Juna when I'd first met him and Karia. Speaking of which, I looked around and wondered where they were. I hoped they would know enough to remain hidden.

Jade smirked and cocked her head at me. "I do when I have something to say," she retorted.

"Let's walk down by the outcrop. Have you seen it yet?" Jade suggested, taking the lead.

"Um, yeah I walked down there a little earlier," I said, still looking for Karia and Juna.

"These trails are a lot of fun but can be dangerous too. Would you like to go out on the horses tomorrow? We can cover a lot more ground that way," Autumn proposed.

"Yeah, that would be good. Where should we meet?" I asked, wondering what I would do with Karia and Juna for the day.

"We'll bring the horses down here and get you in the morning," Jade called back from the front of the line. "Watch your step!" she warned, stepping over a thick branch that was lying on the path.

We climbed down to the outcrop. I stopped back a bit and waited while Autumn and Jade walked right up near the edge. "Don't you think you should stay back some?" I cautioned.

"We're not really that close," Autumn said, slightly rolling her eyes at me. "You should come down here. The view is awesome," she prodded.

"No, thanks. I am good right here, I can see just fine," I said, watching from the safety of the mountainside.

"You're not chicken, are you?" Jade teased.

"No. Just smart and safe," I defended.

I heard a rustle in the brush nearby, and I looked over my shoulder and could see Karia and Juna. It seemed they were trying to get my attention.

———⊙———

"Let me go, Juna! I need to have a talk with that girl. I cannot let her tease Dino like that." Karia struggled with Juna in the brush.

"Now settle yourself, Karia. She is just a child. Besides, what are you going to do about it? Just walk right up to her and tell her you do not like the way she speaks to Dino?" Juna chided.

"That is what I was considering," Karia replied.

"Karia, you are brave but are not thinking sensibly. Calm yourself. It seems Dino is able to defend himself just fine," Juna reasoned.

"Yes, I suppose you are right, Juna." Karia relaxed a bit.

———⊙———

"I'm just teasing you, Dino. Come on over here. Really, it's safe. I promise. We wouldn't put you in danger," Jade insisted.

"It really is okay, Dino," Autumn encouraged me.

Not wanting to be outdone by a couple of girls, I stood and walked reluctantly toward the outcrop where Jade and Autumn were standing.

"Just walk out, slowly. Feel the ground under your feet. That's really the biggest thing. Just pay attention to what you're walking on. The ground can change at any moment, so you just need to pay attention," Autumn guided.

I looked at the ground. I thought about scooting down on my butt the way I had earlier, but I didn't want to look like a chicken. I made my way slowly down the hill and onto the outcropping. I held onto small trees with a tight grip as I took notice of the vast distance down. Then I felt a hand grab my arm.

"You're okay. Look, you made it!" I looked into Autumn's cool pale blue eyes and noticed she was smiling as she pointed out across the valley.

I looked out at the valley surrounded by the mountains with all of the clusters of trees. Out past all of this was the horizon and an incredible sunset. The oranges, reds, and pinks blended and swirled, creating a sunset like none I'd ever seen before, almost like a painting. We all stood staring into the warm orange and pink brilliance.

I looked back for Karia and Juna. I wanted them to see the amazing view, but they were nowhere in sight. Then I heard a rustle in the trees and looked up and saw Karia and Juna standing on a limb, camouflaged behind a canopy of leaves. I was happy to know they were sharing the view with me.

"Jade! Autumn! It's time to come back now," their father called for them.

"Cool, huh?!" Jade smiled as she worked her way back up the hill.

"Yeah, really cool," I agreed. "Thanks for showing me that."

"Next time, just trust us. Really, we're not gonna get you hurt. Our mom would kill us." Jade laughed.

By the time we got back to the house, the sun was sinking fast into the horizon. It was getting dark, and the adults were all standing on the back deck.

"We had better get going. You must all be tired from your trip," Mrs. Linder said.

"We're going to take Dino out on the trails in the morning. We'll see you around nine if that is not too early," Autumn confirmed.

"Nine is good. I'll be ready," I replied.

They all walked through the house, and Mr. and Mrs. Linder and the girls left.

"I'm tired. I'm going to go on to my room to rest," I told them.

"There are sandwiches on the counter in the kitchen. Why don't you take one with you?" Aunt Carol suggested.

"That would be great, thanks. I'll see you in the morning. Goodnight," I told them.

"Goodnight, Dino, and sleep well." My mom walked over and kissed me on the forehead.

I grabbed a sandwich and on my way back to my room, but ducked out the back door instead.

Karia and Juna appeared at the bottom steps off the deck.

"Oh, good! I'm glad you came back. Follow me." I turned and slipped back into the house with Karia and Juna following behind.

"Those girls seem nice," Juna began.

Karia shot him a look. "You should not let the short one speak to you in such a way," Karia told me.

"She was just kidding around, Karia. They really seem nice once you get to know them," I said. "Just give her another chance," I suggested.

"Alright, but if she is not nice, I might bite her," Karia teased.

We shared my sandwich and talked about the plane trip before finally falling asleep.

Chapter 16
Good Morning

The sun peeked in between the part in the curtain and woke me before the others. I lay in bed and breathed in the clean, cool morning air that came in through the open window. A slight breeze moved the curtains.

"When will it be time to go?" Karia's soft voice questioned.

I propped myself up on my elbows and looked at the desk that was set below the window.

She was sitting on an upside-down pencil cup, leaning on the letter opener as if it were a walking stick, and staring out the window. "It is so quiet here and so beautiful. The sunset we saw last evening was unlike anything I have ever seen before. It was almost as if we could reach out and touch the colors." She took a deep breath and continued to gaze out the window. "I am grateful you brought us with you."

"I would love to take you both with me everywhere I go. I dream about it, but the world isn't ready if you know what I mean." I sat up and swung my legs off the side of the bed. "I am going to go get washed up and dressed. I'll bring back some food. Is there anything else I can get for you?"

"Not at the moment. I will dress as well and rouse Juna." Karia stood, turned the cup back over, and returned the letter opener to its home.

When I came back into the room, Karia and Juna were nowhere in sight. Then I saw Juna's face peeking out from behind the corner of the bed. "Dino, would you do something for me?" he asked timidly.

"Sure, anything. What is it?" I answered.

"Could you lower me out the window?" he asked, climbing onto the chair and making his way to the desktop.

"Oh, well, sure. Um, do you want me to show you to the washroom here?" I asked guessing by the look on his face what he was hinting at.

He looked at Karia and back at me. "What is a washroom?" he asked tilting his head slightly.

"Come on. Follow me, and I'll show you. No one is up yet, and if you don't think it will work, then I will let you out the back door, okay?" I suggested.

They looked at each other and then followed me into the hall and to the bathroom. "Good morning, Dino!" my Aunt Carol said, exiting the bathroom as we approached.

"Oh, good morning, Aunt Carol. You scared me!" My heart was pounding, and I could feel Karia and Juna trying to hide behind my legs.

"You startled me too. I was just making sure you have everything you need in here," she said.

I felt Karia and Juna slip into the bathroom behind me. "Oh, I have everything I need, thanks," I replied taking a step back into the doorway.

"Well then, in that case, I'll get out of your way. Come into the kitchen when you're finished, and I'll get you something to eat." She turned and walked back down the hall toward the kitchen.

"Okay, thanks," I said, closing the door. "That was close." I turned around and saw Juna sitting on the side of the toilet dipping his feet in the water.

"You are right about that," Juna said, looking around at the tiny bathroom. "Why do you have this little pond in here?" he questioned.

"It's a toilet," I answered, looking at him strangely.

Karia and Juna looked at each other and then back at me.

"Well, I guess we haven't talked about these things. Here, I'll show you. I mean...well, just watch." I explained to them about how a toilet works and then showed them how to flush it.

Juna looked at me with a strange, yet inquisitive look on his face.

"What's wrong?" I asked him.

He swallowed hard but didn't say anything. He pulled his feet slowly out of the toilet.

Karia giggled and shared, "While you were speaking with your aunt, Juna was quenching his thirst in the small pond."

"Oh! Well, whenever someone flushes it, the water is replaced with clean water." I hoped that would make him feel better, even though it was still kind of gross.

I turned to the sink and explained what it was for and told Juna he could drink out of that anytime. They seemed to understand, so I turned around to offer some privacy.

"What is this?" Karia asked me while she had her back to Juna. She began to pull back on the shower curtain and peek in.

"That is a shower. You take off your clothes, and the water comes from that showerhead up there. This is where you wash up," I explained.

"Mission accomplished!" we heard Juna say, and we turned around just in time to see him standing on the back of the tank, his knife held high in the air, flushing with his foot. "Yet another interesting human contraption." He stepped on the top of the toilet seat and rode it as it slammed closed, and then he jumped to the floor.

"Would you like to try, Karia?" I questioned her.

"Thank you, but I think I shall wait until we are outside," she answered.

We watched Juna climb over to the sink. "What is this?" he asked, looking at the soap dispenser.

"Put your hand under this part."

Juna put his hand under the pump, and I pushed. A squirt of soap plopped into his hand, and I turned on the faucet.

Dino C. Crisanti

"Go on and put your hands under the water and rub them together," I said as Juna sniffed at the soap. It made bubbles between his hands, and he touched them with his tongue. He made a face that made it clear he did not like the taste. He reached to place his hands under the faucet and lost his balance. Luckily, I was close enough and was able to catch him. "I'll hold you, and then next time we'll have to figure out something else."

Once we finished the exploration of the bathroom, I carefully opened the door and made sure there was no one around. Then I escorted them back to my room and went on to the kitchen. I ate with the family and excused myself with some extra food for Karia and Juna.

Chapter 17
First Exploration

After breakfast I went outside, I brought along my backpack with Karia and Juna in it. I unzipped it as soon as I was out of sight of the windows and let them out. Karia and Juna hurried toward the densest part of the woods. I walked around the house, looking at the logs that were stacked one on top of the next, which created the walls. It was a beautiful house. It felt very rustic but was also very cozy and inviting.

I was killing time waiting for Autumn and Jade to get there and Karia and Juna to return. I walked on and began looking at the tall trees. They seemed to stretch unending into the forest. When I came to the end of the driveway, I saw the girls coming up the road. Jade was in the lead on a brown and white spotted horse, and Autumn was behind her on a white horse with a gray braided mane. She was holding the reins of a tan horse with a black mane and black legs from his hooves to his knees.

I slipped back behind the bushes. I didn't think they had seen me, and I rushed back to the side of the house where I'd left my backpack. "Karia? Juna? Are you here? The girls are coming, and I need you to get in the pack," I whispered loudly, as the windows were open and I didn't want anyone to hear.

A moment later, there was a rustle in the brush, and Karia and Juna hurried over to the bag.

I heard the hooves of the horses turning onto the gravel drive and looked back over my shoulder. "Hurry! Get in! They're almost here!" I blurted.

Karia and Juna quickly climbed into the backpack and settled in.

I carefully lifted my pack and gently swung it onto my back.

"Hey, you! Are you ready to go?" a girls voice chimed from behind me.

I turned around and saw Autumn and Jade pulling the horses to a stop. "Yeah, I'm all set."

Autumn jumped down from her horse and began showing me how to get up into the saddle. "Put your left foot in the stirrup, grab onto the saddle horn, and pull yourself up. I'm right behind you, whenever you're ready."

I heard the front door open, and my mom and aunt stepped out on the porch. "You kids be careful out there. Do you girls have your mace?" asked Aunt Carol.

"Sure do, Mrs. Baker," Jade responded.

"Mace?" my mother and I interjected in unison.

"Don't worry." Autumn laughed as I lost my concentration and leaned back a little. I could feel her push me back into position. "It's just in case."

"In case of what?" I swung my leg over the horse and pulled myself onto the saddle.

"In case that cougar shows up. We haven't had to use it yet," Jade spoke up, "but it's better to be prepared. We've heard it's been coming closer to people, probably looking for food. There are a lot of other animals out in these mountains, too, it's good to be ready for anything. You know?"

My mom looked pleadingly at my aunt.

"Anna," Carol said, "it's just better to be safe than sorry. The girls have lived here all their lives, and they know what they are doing. Believe me, their parents wouldn't let them go if they thought it was too dangerous."

I looked down at Autumn as I situated myself in the saddle.

Autumn adjusted my stirrups. "Your aunt's right. We'll be perfectly safe," she said, looking up at me with a smile. "Think of it as an adventure. You like adventures, don't you?"

Autumn climbed onto her horse, Wind and pulled on his reins, turning him around. We headed on down the gravel driveway. Jade followed her lead, and I fell in behind her. I waved to my mom, who was still standing on the porch with my Aunt Carol. She waved back with a slight smile that didn't do much to hide her obvious look of concern. "Don't be too late!" my mom called after us.

"We won't, Mom, and don't worry!" I hollered back.

On my trusty steed, who I'd met all of ten minutes early, I followed the girls up the winding paved mountain road. Luckily, the horse that Autumn and Jade brought for me had a really good temperament. Her name was Rory, and she was very patient with me. I think at times it wouldn't have mattered what I did with the reins, she would have just followed the girls anyway.

Just as I began to feel more comfortable on Rory, Autumn pulled her reins to the left, leading us on to a narrow dirt trail and up a steep incline. Jade looked back to make sure I was still following. "How, are ya doing, Dino?" she called, leaning back on her horse's rump. They were so comfortable on their horses that the animals almost seemed like an extension of the girls themselves. Now that she was looking at me, I wondered if the horse was on auto pilot.

"I'm good. This is a really nice horse. She doesn't seem to mind that I am new at this," I replied.

"Haven't you ever ridden before?" Jade asked.

"Only a couple of times at the local stables back home." I adjusted myself in the saddle to get more comfortable.

"Well, I think you're doing fine, Dino. Rory is a good trail horse and is really tolerant of new riders," Autumn called back from her front position. "Just remember to lean forward on the uphill and lean back on the downhill, and she'll do the rest."

"Okay, I got it. Thanks for the tip." I caught her smile as she turned around.

We rode on for a long time. The woods were beautiful. The trees were tall, and the trails were seemingly untouched by anything other than horse hooves and other animal paws. It was quiet except for the sound of twigs cracking under the weight of the horses, and the dull, soft *clomp-clomp* of their hooves in the dirt. Birds chirped their songs, frogs could be heard croaking in the distance, and other creatures moved about silently in the dense forest. *This is what I love—to be in the forest away from people and traffic.* Then I heard my backpack slowly unzip.

"Psst, Dino, may we have a look?" I heard Karia request.

I whispered out of the side of my mouth. "Yeah, it should be okay. Just stay low, alright?"

I could hear the zipper open more and could feel them moving around in my backpack. "Where are we headed?" I inquired, loud enough for Autumn to hear.

"There are some old caves up in these hills," Autumn announced, this time without turning back. "I thought we would show them to you."

"There are lots of really cool places out here," Jade added.

We rode quietly on the trail for a long time. I could hear Karia and Juna occasionally whisper to each other and felt them move a few times. As we rode, I looked deep into the forest and far up into the trees. At one point, Jade whistled and Autumn slowed to a stop. They both looked silently into the woods.

"What is it?" I whispered loudly. I could feel the weight in my backpack shift to the side we were staring toward.

"Shh!" Jade hushed me. Then she raised her arm and pointed very specifically out into the woods. "There! Watch right over there."

I looked at Jade and Autumn. They were both turned and staring intensely into the forest. I squinted and leaned in the direction she was pointing. I waited and watched and waited some more. Then, there it was, moving just out of the cover of the thick brush, a huge buck with the biggest antlers I had ever seen.

"Holy cow!" I mumbled.

"Wait! That's not it. Keep watching," Autumn instructed.

A doe moved slowly through the trees and into the clearing. She began to eat the plants while the buck stood by protectively. Just then a fawn could be seen only slightly through the trees eating alongside its mother.

"It isn't often we see them all together. We usually only see the does and fawns together. I just love that," Autumn admitted. "Come on. Be quiet so we don't scare them." She lightly snapped her reins and gave her horse a soft kick, and the horses slowly began on their way again.

"How much farther to the caves?" I asked, still enjoying the ride.

"Not too much farther—maybe another mile or so," Autumn replied.

It was cool in the forest, for the canopy of tree branches kept the heat down. After a while, the horses stepped from the shelter of the forest into a clearing near a large rock formation. The temperature changed about ten degrees just from leaving the cover of the trees.

"This is really cool," I said as the girls climbed down from their horses.

"It is, isn't it? This is one of my favorite places to come to," Autumn answered, tying her horse to an old dead tree. She walked over to where I was still sitting on Rory. "Are you coming down?" she said, looking up at me with her cool blue eyes.

"Oh, yeah," I responded, trying to remember how to get down from a horse without falling.

"Here. Throw me your reins, and I will hold her steady for you," Autumn offered.

Jade walked up and stood next to the stirrups. "Come on. You'll be a pro at this by the time you go home. We won't let ya fall."

Jade was tough, but I could tell she had a soft side to her as well. One moment, it seemed like she might trip me just for the fun of it, but in the next she'd be saving someone's life.

I climbed down and shifted my backpack to one shoulder. Karia and Juna were tucked down inside; I could see a glint from their eyes through the unzipped slit.

"Come on over here," Jade directed as she started walking toward the rock formation.

"You want to leave your pack with the horses?" Autumn suggested.

"No. I think I'll take it along," I answered, putting it squarely on both shoulders again.

"Suit yourself." Autumn smiled and skipped along behind Jade.

"Where to now?" I asked, trying to catch up.

"Right over here."

They stopped in front of a large pile of rocks. Jade climbed up on the rocks and disappeared behind. Autumn winked and walked around. On the other side of the rock pile was a dark opening to a cave. It wasn't small, but it wasn't large either.

"How do you know something doesn't live in there?" I questioned cautiously.

"Well, a bear probably sleeps here in the winter, but we haven't seen anything when we've been out here. I have this just in case." Jade flashed her mace. "We'll tell you if you need to run." She smiled mischievously and winked at her sister, who smiled back at her, shaking her head.

We walked into the cave and immediately felt the temperature drop again. It was dark inside, so Jade clicked on her flashlight and shining it up into her face for dramatic effect, then turned slowly and whispered, "Move very slowly and be very quiet. We don't want to scare them." Jade crouched down and moved very slowly to the side of the narrow cave. "Shh. Follow me."

"Here." Autumn clicked on her flashlight and handed me another. "That's better, huh? Just keep it pointed to the ground."

"What's in here?" I asked nervously.

"You'll see. Don't worry. You can trust us." Autumn grinned.

We followed closely to one another as Jade flashed her light carefully at the cave floor and occasionally at the ceiling. "There! Look up there!" she exclaimed in a loud whisper. She placed her hand over the flashlight to soften the light. "Do you know what those are?" she asked, removing her hand and flashing her light at me.

I squinted as the light passed my eyes. I pointed my flashlight at the ceiling of the cave for a better look.

Jade gently pushed my hand. "Don't shine it directly on them."

I could feel Karia and Juna moving around as well, so I was guessing they wanted to see too. "BATS!" I whispered quietly. "What kind are they?" I asked, hoping to hear they wouldn't be flying down to suck my blood or get caught in my hair.

"They are Townsend's big-eared bats. If you look closely, they have long ears and look somewhat like tiny bunnies'. They are rare and threatened in this area. These are mostly female bats. It is what is known as a *maternity colony roost*. We must be very quiet and respectful of their home. They have been here for a long time. That is why we like this cave. It is almost completely hidden, so not a lot of people come here. They have become used to us. I think they know they are safe here. They eat mostly moths, flies, and dung beetles, so they won't bother us. They are actually quite gentle. They are very sensitive to disturbances at their roost sites. If someone messes with the site, they might leave and never come back. It is really important that we keep this place a secret, or they may lose their home."

"I'll never tell," I said as I gazed at their small group, feeling a little sad about their struggle.

"You know, it is really unfair how people think of bats. They fear them because they don't bother to learn about them and about how important they are. Or they see bad things about them in scary movies, so they get the wrong impression." Jade paused and stared through the darkness. It was clear that she really cared about them. "They will come out at dusk. That's when they go for food. There are probably only forty or fifty of them in here. It is such an awesome thing to see them fly. We just lie on the ground and wait for them. They fly right over us and into the forest. Maybe we can come back and show you before you leave." Jade was more than happy to share her wealth of knowledge and love of these creatures.

I stared at the ceiling of the cave and could actually feel Karia and Juna up by my neck. I felt kind of silly for being afraid before I knew the truth. I really should have known better. I squinted to try to see them a little better. "How do you know so much about these bats?" I asked Jade.

"She did a project on them in school last year, and now they have become her personal cause," Autumn shared.

"Well, someone has to look out for them. They are too awesome to let them disappear forever," Jade defended.

"I think that's great. Last year in our town, we found a frog species that was thought to be extinct," I told them.

"Wow, really? That's so cool," Autumn said, sounding surprised.

"See? So you can understand what I am talking about." Jade smiled.

Just then my stomach growled.

"Are you getting hungry, Dino?" Jade asked.

"Yeah, but I didn't bring anything."

"Then what are you carrying around in that backpack of yours?" Jade snickered.

"Don't worry. We brought food," Autumn said. "Come on. We can eat outside the cave so we don't disturb the bats."

We quietly left the cave and walked back toward the horses. Autumn went to her saddlebag and opened it, pulling out a small cooler bag. Jade went to her saddlebag and pulled out a blanket. She walked back toward the rock formation and laid the blanket out in the shade of a small tree growing out from the rocks.

"Thanks, you guys," I said as I took my backpack off and set it behind me, hidden by some rocks.

The girls pulled out three sandwiches, three water bottles, and a handful of granola bars. They handed me a sandwich, a bottle of water, and a napkin. "Here you go. I hope you like ham and cheese," Jade said.

"I sure do. Thanks again," I said sincerely. "This is really nice of you to bring this for me."

"Don't worry about it. Your Aunt Carol said you really like the outdoors, and so do we, so why not enjoy it together?" Autumn smiled.

We finished eating and started to pack up the food and blanket. I looked over my shoulder and noticed Karia and Juna were not in the pack. "Where to now?" I said loudly.

Jade and Autumn looked at each other and smirked. "We are going to head out along the far side of the mountain. There is a path along the cliffs. It is really pretty over there," Autumn replied, walking toward the horses.

"That sounds like a lot of fun," I blurted more loudly than normal, hoping Karia and Juna would hear me and get back in the pack. I pretended to forget it as we walked over to the horses. I figured that would give them more time to get back in. I had one foot in the stirrup when I said. "Oh, I almost forgot my backpack," again more loudly than my usual tone. By this time, the girls were beginning to think there was something wrong with me. I could tell by the way they were looking at me and each other. I slipped my foot out of the stirrup and walked back to the picnic site, reached down, and peered into my pack. I was relieved to see four little eyes looking back up at me.

"All set?" Jade said loudly, mocking me. They both laughed.

"Yup, I'm good to go." I smiled at them and climbed up on Rory with ease. I snapped the reins and followed the girls toward the path.

Chapter 18
Over the Edge

I felt more confident on the horse this time and had not put my backpack fully on my back. It was swung over my left shoulder. I was just thinking it might be more comfortable for Karia and Juna than if I put it on fully.

I wasn't paying attention when I heard Jade say. "Hold on and pay attention! This part can be a little scary."

Just then I looked up and saw Rory following the other horses onto a cliffside path that didn't look near wide enough. I felt Rory stumble over some rocks in the path. It startled me, and I quickly reached for the reins with one hand and the horn with the other and in the same moment felt my backpack slip from my shoulder and leave my arm. "NO!" I cried, reaching for it, but I was too late. My stomach dropped as I leaned over and saw it fall. It all happened so fast that there was nowhere for me to safely dismount the horse, and I couldn't see where it went. I looked up and saw Jade stopped and staring at me.

"Dino, are you okay?" she asked.

"No! I...I lost it! My backpack!" I could hardly speak, could barely even breathe.

"Dino, you look like you are going to pass out. You are completely white," Jade observed.

"I see it!" Autumn called from the front of the line. "It is hooked on a branch sticking out of the cliff."

"I have to get it. How far till we can get off the horses?" I pleaded.

Jade and Autumn looked at each other. "It is a ways ahead, Dino. We are almost better off going back," Autumn stated.

I looked behind me and realized we had just started on the path. "How do we get back?" I asked, looking desperately at them.

They looked at each other and back at me. "We will have to walk the horses backwards on the path," Jade stated. "Dino, what is in your backpack anyway? Is it really that important? Can't you just get another one? This is really dangerous."

I looked at them, and they were staring at me intently, waiting for my answer. "I can't, I'm sorry, what's inside it is irreplaceable. Just tell me how to back Rory up, and then you two can go on ahead. I will meet you at the end of the trail. I don't want you to get hurt because of me."

"How do you intend to get it once you are off the horse? You cannot even see it from here on foot. It's in a really bad spot," said Autumn.

"Is it open or closed?" I asked her.

She leaned over and looked down. "It's closed. Whatever was in it should still be there."

"I have to get it," I insisted.

They looked at each other one last time. "Let's back it up!" Autumn called.

Jade turned around and looked me in the eyes. "You will have to listen to me very carefully. These horses will follow each other all day long, but YOU have to back them up. You will need to very gently pull back on the reins. If you pull too hard, her feet will come up off the ground. You DO NOT want that to happen. As you gently pull back on the reins, Rory will begin to take steps backwards. Since we just started on the path, it is still pretty straight. Keep her head straight. If you turn her head, she could accidentally step off the path. Slow and steady and straight back. Got it?"

I swallowed hard. "I can do this. You guys go on ahead, and I will meet up with you."

"We are not leaving you, Dino. We've backed these horses up before. It is dangerous but not impossible. At least we are not any further on the path. We can do this together," Autumn insisted. "Whenever you're ready, back her up slowly."

I took a deep breath and began pulling back gently on the reins until I could feel Rory's head begin to tilt back. She resisted, probably just as scared as I was. "Please, Rory, really slow." She took one step back and another. I was looking back and saw that she only needed to go a few more steps and she would be safe. I pulled again on the reins.

"Dino, look at me!" I heard Jade call. "You are pulling her head to the left. She has to go *straight* back. Look at me, and I will guide you."

I looked at her.

"Pull back slowly," she said as she watched Rory's feet.

I felt the horse take another step and another.

"Almost there, Dino. Keep going!" Jade said.

I got excited and pulled back hard. Rory's front feet came up off the path.

"Keep her up! Pull her back hard Dino. Harder! If she comes down now, she will fall off the edge. You have to get her off the trail. You're almost there...almost there."

I could hear both Autumn and Jade hollering at the same time. Their voices blended together. I just kept pulling hard. I felt Rory moving backwards on her hind legs, and all I could think was *Don't let her down.* For me, that statement meant so much in so many ways.

"Okay, Dino. You're there. You can let her down now. Let her down slow." Autumn's voice broke into my thoughts.

I released the tension on the reins, and Rory came down hard and whinnied. I rubbed the side of her large neck; I could feel the sweat on her short fur. She snorted and whinnied, breathing heavily. "It's alright, Rory. Calm down. You did great." I spoke to her in a soft voice, trying to calm her as I shook all over.

When she calmed down enough to stand still, I looked up and saw Jade taking Junebug backwards down the narrow path on the edge of the cliff. She was calm and quiet. Junebug was taking halting but confident steps. A few more steps and she was on safe ground with me.

Now it was just Autumn and Wind. I heard Autumn make a clicking sound with her mouth. Wind's feet stayed close together, as he backed down the path in what looked like a dance. We could hear Wind breathing heavy and snorting. Autumn continued to click at him and call his name. She was strong and commanding, and Wind could sense her confidence. She had the longest way to go. My heart was pounding. Jade was sitting on Junebug with her hand over her mouth. The clicking, the snorting, and the dancing hooves that moved this awesome white animal along the narrowest path I had ever seen were amazing. After what seemed like forever, she, too, was safe on the flat ground with Jade and me. Autumn immediately jumped off of Wind, stepped in front of him and hugged him. We were all safe, but it was just the beginning.

"What's in the backpack, Dino?" Autumn was standing over me as I knelt at the edge of the mountainside surveying the backpack, perched precariously on the side of the cliff.

"You owe it to us to tell us. If you can't trust us now, what was all this for?" Jade exhorted.

I crawled backwards from the edge of the cliff and brushed off the front of my shirt and pants. "I know I can trust you both. You didn't have to help me or risk your own safety for me, but you did, and I thank you both for that. What I am going to share with you is something I promised never to share with anyone and never have, so you have to promise me you'll never tell a living soul," I pleaded before I opened up.

They looked at each other and then back at me. "We promise," they said in unison.

"Okay. Then I'll show you. Come here." I knelt back on the ground, laid on my stomach, and scooted all the way to the edge where I could see the backpack again.

Autumn and Jade did the same.

"Karia! Juna! Can you hear me? Are you alright? Karia, open the zipper slowly. Not too far or you'll fall out!" I called from the edge.

Autumn and Jade were lying on either side of me as I yelled down to Karia and Juna. They looked at me with a puzzled look and then stared at the backpack. Finally the zipper began to move. Slowly it opened across the top, and we could see movement. Karia was the first to poke her head out of the backpack, and I was relieved to see her.

"Karia! Are you alright? I am so sorry. I'm coming to get you!" I reassured her. "As soon as I figure out how," I said under my breath. "Don't worry."

"We are alright, and we are not worried. I knew you would come for us. But please be careful, Dino!" Karia called back and then disappeared into the bag.

Juna popped his head out next and looked down and around and then up at me. "When we told you we wished to see the mountains, this was not quite what we had planned." Juna looked down, squirming a little as Karia pinched his leg inside the bag. "Hey!" he said to her.

Jade giggled.

"Dino, do you have a rope? Something long enough to drop down to us?" Juna asked.

"I'll see what I can find. Don't move around too much. I'm not sure how strong that branch is. I'll be right back." I eased back from the edge of the cliff and sat up.

Autumn and Jade were sitting there, just staring at me. "We would have done the same thing," Autumn said simply after an awkward silence. They didn't even ask what the creatures were.

I was confused by their calmness. "Don't you even want to know what they are?"

Jade stood and walked to the edge of the forest. She cupped her hands around her mouth and gave a high-pitched bird call or something like one of the calls we made when we played Track 20 back home, and then she hollered. "Fletcher! Fletcher, we need your help!" Then came the bird call again. She waited a moment then turned back to us and said, "He may not be close. Let's get started and see if he shows up."

Suddenly something burst out of the forest at lightning speed. It flew past the horses so fast we could see their manes and tails move as if blown by wind. Then there was nothing. I looked around and then back at Autumn and Jade, who were looking at each other.

"Come on, Fletch. This is serious, and we need your help. Besides, I think you are going to want to help with this one." Autumn spoke to the air.

Wind let out a loud bray, and we all looked in that direction. To my surprise, standing on Wind's back was a male Traegon! He was similar to the he-Traegons back home but also very different. He had jet-black hair, a stark contrast to Juna's, which was white and wavy. He appeared to be young like Karia and Juna. He was a little thinner than Juna and looked a bit awkward. His clothing was a patchwork of color, which seemed to be reflective of his interesting, bold, and highly energetic personality. He had an assortment of pouches hanging from a wide belt around his waist. He had a bow and quiver slung over one shoulder and was heavily laden with ropes, hooks, and other gear. He looked ready for anything. "What excitement have you for me on this fine day?" he asked.

"Fletcher, we would like to introduce you to a friend of ours. This is Dino," Jade began.

Fletcher looked curiously at Autumn and Jade and asked, "Why do you make my existence known to another?"

"You have always trusted us, Fletch. You have to trust us this time too." Autumn walked toward Wind and watched as Fletcher jumped down.

I stared at him, stunned and amazed. "There are others!" I whispered under my breath.

"Come with us. We need to show you something," Jade urged Fletch.

We walked to the edge of the cliff and once again got on our bellies, scooting to the edge in order to see the backpack. When we looked over, we saw Juna still working on a way out.

Fletch walked boldly right up to the edge and saw him too. "Who is that?" he asked.

"It is Dino's friend from a faraway place called Illinois. They came here with him on a visit, and now this has happened. We need to save them," Jade explained.

"Them? I only see one." He leaned over further.

"That is Juna. His sister Karia is in the pack too. Please, will you help us?" I pleaded.

"Of course he will. Right, Fletch?" Jade nudged him.

He turned back and smiled. "There is never a need to ask when another Traegon, is in danger!"

Chapter 19
The Save

Jade walked over to Junebug and opened her saddlebag. She pulled out a rope, some gloves, and some clips called *carabineers*. I took the gloves and rope and carefully moved out onto the narrow cliffside path. I found a young but strong tree and secured one end of the rope. Autumn and Jade stood at the start of the path, nervously watching and waiting. I squatted and got on my knees then leaned forward and looked over the edge. I could just see the backpack. I lay on my stomach and called to Karia and Juna. Juna was looking around for me, trying to follow the sound of my voice. "I'm up here! Above you!" I called. "We're coming for you. Hold on."

I let the rope out slowly, so as not to risk dropping it directly on them. It fell straight down but was still almost five feet from where they were hanging. Juna watched the rope and looked up at me. "I know! Just hold on!" I called to Juna.

Fletch moved out onto the path now and was coming toward me. He looked much more comfortable than I felt. "I'll take it from here," he declared confidently. He grabbed the rope and began lowering himself down.

I could see that Juna could now see Fletch, and the look on his face was priceless. He was surprised, confused, in disbelief.

"What is your name?" Juna questioned as Fletch descended closer.

"I am Fletcher P. Webenaki, but you can call me Fletch," he

proclaimed. "We will be on our way to the top quicker than you can say...uh...Fletcher P. Webenaki!"

Juna looked bewildered as he watched Fletch slide down the rope kicking off the side of the cliff, as if he did it every day. Then Juna disappeared into the backpack. Moments later, Karia poked her head out. She watched Fletch working his way down the rope. He kicked off the cliff wall and glanced back to see how much farther he had to go. That was when he saw Karia, and suddenly he looked even more cool and determined. Their eyes met, and then, for an instant, he forgot what he was doing. That was all it took. He hit the side of the cliff hard and began sliding uncontrollably down the rope.

"Fletch!" I heard Jade scream, but there was nothing I could do.

As he came to his senses, Fletch managed to find a crevice in the rock and catch his foot. He stopped hard and fast and hung limp on the rope upside down like a fly caught in a spider web.

"Fletch! Fletch? Are you okay?" Autumn cried.

Embarrassed by his mistake, Fletch slowly pulled on the rope and righted himself. He twisted the rope around one of his legs and then around his body. He looked down at Karia and then up at Autumn and Jade. He was very close now. "I am alright. My hands have seen better days, but they will be alright as well." Then he looked back at Karia. "Ah, young maiden, it is I, Fletcher P. Webenaki, your hero to the rescue."

Karia raised her eyebrows. "My brother and I are grateful for your assistance."

"Anything for a similar. I am looking forward to making your acquaintance in proper fashion," Fletch responded.

Juna, peering from behind Karia, let out a deep sigh as he rolled his eyes.

Seeming not to notice, Fletch shot her a wink. He pulled a piece of cloth from his belt and tore it in half with his sharp little teeth. He wrapped each of his hands securely in the pieces of cloth. He untwisted his body and once again began to slowly descend the remainder of the

Dino C. Crisanti

Fletch to the Rescue

way. When he was directly parallel to the backpack, he again twisted himself in the rope and found handholds in the rock. He scaled the cliff away from where the backpack hung to create a pendulum effect. Once he was far enough away, he kicked off of the rock face, released, and swung away from the cliff toward Karia and Juna. He didn't stay out far for long. He once again hit the side hard and scraped back toward where he had begun.

"Oh, Fletch," Autumn sighed.

"Wait! I have an idea!" Jade ran into woods and returned with a long, strong branch. "Here!" she proclaimed.

"What are we going to do with that?" I asked.

She carefully made her way out onto the cliff, carrying the branch. The branch had a Y shape at the end, and she slid the rope into it. Then she wedged it under a log on the opposite side of the path.

"That's not going to hold," I speculated.

"Autumn, come here!" Jade called her sister and then turned to me. "We are going to sit on it. You swing Fletch over to Karia and Juna."

"This seems really dangerous," I commented.

"You got a better idea?" she asked, obviously tired of my questioning her ideas. "We need to get them off the side of the cliff now!"

Autumn made her way out to us, and they both sat on the far end of the branch. There was nothing but dense woods on the far side of the path, so they were basically sitting in the brush.

"Let's make this quick, before the bugs start crawling all over us," Autumn stated.

I lay down with one leg over the branch and saw Fletch hanging freely away from the cliff. "You okay, Fletch?"

"Sure enough. Swing me over," he responded anxiously.

I pulled and pushed and pulled and pushed again until he started swinging back and forth. Each time, he came closer and closer to Karia and Juna. Juna pulled himself fully out of the pack, grabbing the branch with one hand and Karia's hand with his other. Karia held on tight and leaned in the direction of Fletcher. Karia and Fletch reached out for each other as he came close but only touched fingers. The next time, they were nearly able to grab each other's hands but slipped free. The third time, Fletch was able to get a good grip on Karia's. The momentum of the rope pulled Fletcher back; he held on but in turn pulled on Karia, who then pulled Juna. Juna held tight, but the backpack slipped sideways a bit, putting them all in a very precarious position.

"I'm losing my grip, Karia!" Juna stammered.

"Don't let go, Juna! Just hold on!" Karia urged.

She pulled hard on Fletcher's hand, and he continued to move closer to them. Finally he was close enough to grab the side of the cliff and steady himself. They released their hands, and Juna was able to pull the backpack and Karia back securely onto the branch.

Fletcher tied himself into the rope, reeled in the remainder, and handed it to Karia. "Tie this around yourself then give the rest to your brother," he instructed.

Karia did as she was told and then handed the rope to Juna. He, in turn, tied himself in. They all felt slightly safer but knew they were not out of danger yet.

I looked back at Jade and Autumn. "Get ready! We are going to pull you up." The girls waited for me to pull some slack into the rope and then grabbed on. I looked down over the cliff and called to Karia, Juna, and Fletcher. "Are you ready? We're going to pull you up now."

Fletcher looked to Karia and Juna and they all checked their knots and nodded tentatively.

"Wait, I have a thought!" Juna interjected. "Once we swing free of this branch, if Dino removes that branch, we will then be able to assist in our ascent by climbing on the rock wall. If not, we will be dead weight."

"Oh, Juna, please do not use the term *dead* until we are safely on solid ground," Karia requested.

"You have an effective plan. Go on and share it with your friend," Fletcher stated.

Juna called up to me and explained the idea. I agreed and held tight to the rope, and one by one, they released their hold. The rope swung back and forth like a pendulum as I tried to steady it and finally, it came to a stop.

"The backpack!" Karia yelled. "It is still on the branch."

"Don't worry about it. Just hold on," I told them. Then I had Jade and Autumn, one at a time, get up off of the branch they were sitting on. They both still held it with their hands. It slipped without their weight, and the three Traegons felt the rope move suddenly. I held the rope steady while Autumn and Jade pulled the branch back. Fletch, Karia, and Juna drew closer to the cliff wall. They found footholds and handholds in the cliffside where they could hold on and ultimately climb. Jade, Autumn, and I brought the rope in as they climbed. Before we knew it, they were at the top and climbing onto the path. Karia grabbed onto me and I to her. "Let's get off this path," I suggested.

Once we were safely on solid ground, we all were able to relax.

"I am so sorry," I said, looking at Karia and Juna. "Thank you for your help," I continued, turning to Jade and Autumn.

"Dino," Karia began, "you and these two brave girls risked your lives to save us. We know what happened was not intentional, so there is no need to apologize, and Sir Fletcher P. Webenaki, your bravery and skill are praiseworthy." Karia gave a slight curtsey.

Fletcher stood, puffed out his chest, and walked toward Karia. He dropped to one knee and took her hand like a true gentleman. "My Traegonian maiden, it has been my pleasure to serve you."

Karia blushed noticeably.

Juna stood next to Karia, staring at Fletcher and glancing at Karia. He was dumbfounded at what he was witnessing, as he had never seen any Traegon act in such a way.

Jade grabbed Fletcher by the arm and pulled him back. "Alright, Fletch, we get it. Now come and sit. Don't crowd our guests."

Autumn giggled, Karia batted her eyes, and Juna shook his head as Jade pulled the clearly smitten Fletcher away from his sister.

"I think we should probably be getting back," I said, breaking the awkward silence.

Autumn looked at her watch. "Oh, Dino, you're right! I didn't realize how late it is. Everyone will worry if we don't get back soon," she said, standing and brushing the dust off of her jeans.

Jade stood and climbed onto Junebug. "Come on, Fletch. You can ride with me."

I climbed onto Rory without help this time and looked at Karia and Juna. "You will have to ride on the horse with me," I said.

They looked at each other. "I have never ridden on a horse before, at least not outside of a backpack," Karia stated.

"Karia, why don't you ride with Dino, and Juna, if you would like, you can ride with me," Autumn suggested.

"Yip, yip!" Fletcher hollered and took a running leap, grabbing onto Junebug's tail. The horse flipped him into the air. Fletch did a midair somersault and landed on the back of Junebug's neck, right in front of Jade.

"Show off," Jade remarked.

Karia and Juna stood staring at the horses and then at each other. Autumn walked over to them and held out her hand. Karia took it. Autumn lifted her and passed her off to me. Then she went back for Juna. She took his hand and pulled him up in to her arms. "How about you hold on to my back till I get up?" She carefully swung him around by one hand, and he grabbed onto her shoulders. Autumn mounted Wind, and we headed off down the trail toward home.

Chapter 20
Kamara

That evening, Karia seemed quiet, sitting on the desk and looking out the window. "I wish to go off into the forest for a while, if you both do not mind." She looked across the room where Juna and I, were sitting on the bed.

"Do you not wish to watch Dino draw images of our day's adventurers?" Juna questioned her.

"Are you feeling alright, Karia?" I asked.

She turned back toward the window. "I am quite fine. I just need to wander through my thoughts, I suppose. I do wish to see your drawings, but may I look at them when I return?" Gesturing to the window, she continued, "I would just like to be out there for a bit."

I looked at her and finally realized that I had become so comfortable with them being around that I kind of forgot they belonged outside in the forest. It is sort of like animals, they need to be where they are most comfortable. The forest was that place for Karia.

"Sure, Karia. I get it." I stood and grabbed a blanket from the foot of the bed. "Here. If you hang on to this, I'll lower you out the window."

She looked at me and smiled. "Thank you, my friend. That would be just fine."

"Do you wish for me to accompany you, Karia?" Juna asked her.

"No. I will not be gone long, and besides, you two are enjoying yourselves. I will be fine," Karia responded. She stood and stepped aside.

I looked out the window to be sure no one was around. I popped the screen off and helped Karia out the window. "Just use your bird call when you come back. We'll wait up for you, okay?" I said, lowering her gently to the ground.

"Thank you!" Her tone and her demeanor had lightened and become less melancholy. She reached the ground, tugged twice on the blanket, and scurried out into the darkness.

***

Karia walked leisurely through the forest. The moon was full and offered her plenty of natural light to see by. She walked for a long time. She listened to an owl hooting in the distance and all of the other night creatures moving about. For many, night is a time for rest and sleep, but for some it is their most active hours. After a while, she stumbled across a small stream running through the forest. The sound caught her attention, and she stopped, closed her eyes, and listened. The water rippled over the stones and made a serene bubbling sound. She opened her eyes slowly and looked over the area. Noticing a large rock resting next to the stream, she decided to sit for a while and enjoy the moment. The moonlight streaked through the branches, creating sparkles on the water. Karia breathed in deeply, becoming full with the clean, cool night air.

Across the stream she noticed jewels of blue light jumping and dancing in the brush. She watched for a few moments and then whispered excitedly, "Fairies!" Watching them made her smile and also made her think of her mim. "I see you, my fairy friends. My name is Karia. I am a Traegon," she said and then silently awaited a response. As she waited, she gazed thoughtfully at the trees. Her eyes followed the light cast by the moon, up the trees, and through the scattering of leaf-covered branches to a small opening at the top. Through the gap she could see the inky black sky, peppered with glittering stars—more stars than she could ever remember seeing in all her life. "How beautiful!" she whispered.

When she brought her gaze back to the forest and the stream, there before her in the shadows stood the old crooked she-Traegon she had seen at the market! "Lovely, isn't it, my young one?" the gravelly voice beckoned.

"Oh! You startled me," Karia shared. "Where did you come from? How did you know where to find me?"

"Youngling, we have been brought together for a purpose. I will always know where to find you. I will always be with you. I will always see you," she said very directly. "Now let me get a better look at you." The old Traegon leaned on her cane and knelt with one knee on the ground. She held out her hand, brought her thumb and finger together to create a circle, and then dipped her hand into the clear flowing water. When she pulled her hand out of the water, within the circle of her fingers was a thin membrane of water. Using her crooked cane, she pulled herself up and moved slowly toward Karia.

"What is your name?" Karia asked, squinting through the darkness to get a better look.

The old one took another hobbled step forward and the moonlight poured over her. Standing at an angle, she reminded Karia of a matriarch, an elder whose place was much like a grandmother or great-grandmother to humans. Her hair was as feathery as Karia's only somewhat fuzzier and pure white, taking on a glow in the moonlight.

"My name is Kamara." She turned, revealing her one milky eye, which startled Karia once again. She deliberately brought her water monocle to her good eye, using it to look Karia up and down. After a few moments, she switched her hand over to her other eye. The water seeing glass that she had created made that eye look large and distorted. Once again, she carefully looked over Karia.

"What happened to your eye?" Karia inquired.

"It is as it should be, my youngling. It is still a good eye, you know, for with it I am able to see far better than many with two ordinary eyes. Can you understand that?" She glared eerily at Karia, awaiting her answer.

"Yes, I suppose so," Karia answered.

Dino C. Crisanti

Not your Grandma's Fairy Godmother

Kamara blew at her hand, and the water eyeglass popped into tiny droplets.

"Yes is not a sufficient reply," the croaking voice snapped. "When I question your understanding, you must answer in a way that shows me that you fully understand."

Karia was silent as she thought about the strange old she-Traegon's request. Finally it came to her. "What you see with your poor eye is beyond what is before us. It is from within. Is that correct?"

"Very good, youngling. Yes, it is from within, but it is also pure wisdom and truth.

These, my dear, are the lessons we learn, the truths we consume, and the wisdom of the ages. These will be my gift to you, in time." Kamara took a deep, rattling breath.

Karia also took a deep breath, just trying to soak in what Kamara was saying to her.

"Today's events are a new course on the path that you, your brother, and the human child are destined for. Pay close attention. Do you have the amulet you received from me?" Kamara looked deep into her eyes.

"Yes. I carry it with me always, though I do not know what it is or what it is used for," Karia responded.

"You will know in time, young one." As Kamara spoke, the blue light of the fairies began to flutter around her. More and more came, and a crooked smile spread across her face. They surrounded her until all Karia could see were the dancing lights of the fairies. The lights swirled and skipped through the air, ascending into the trees, and then, just as mysteriously as she had come, she was gone.

———◦《◉》◦———

Juna and I had been talking about the day and coming up with many ideas to draw. The time went by very quickly, and when we realized we were getting tired, we also realized that Karia had been gone for a very long time. "Should we be worried?" I asked Juna, getting up to look out the window.

"I have been trying not to for some time now," Juna responded. "I should have gone with her. I am supposed to protect her."

"I'm sure she is fine. She probably just lost track of the time. We'll give it a little while, and if she doesn't come back soon, we can go and look for her, alright?" I tried to assure him.

There was a knock on my door. "Dino? Are you awake?" my mom whispered through the closed door.

Juna rolled off the bed and quickly crawled under.

The doorknob turned slowly and the door creaked open. My mom poked her head in. "Hi, honey. We're back from the show," she informed me.

"Hi, Mom. How was it?" I asked.

"It was nice. I hope you weren't too lonely," she said, pushing open the door and stepping into the room.

"No. I took a walk, drew in my journal, and watched TV. I think I'm going to go to sleep now," I said.

"Alright. See you in the morning." She kissed me on the head and pulled the door closed behind her.

Juna crawled out from under the bed and climbed up the side. "I think I should go look for Karia," he said.

"I know," I replied.

I stood and walked over to the window. I pulled off the screen and unrolled the blanket I had used to lower Karia out.

Juna put on his pack and stood at the window. "I will return as soon as I am able," he said with a nod before he climbed down the blanket.

I held tight to the blanket, waiting for the tug to let me know he was down, but it never came.

Suddenly, Juna appeared back in the window.

"What are you doing? Why are you back?" I asked him.

"Mission complete!" he stated, climbing in the window with Karia right behind him.

"Karia, where have you been? We were getting worried!" I unintentionally scolded her.

"I am sorry to you both. I was sitting by a beautiful stream and must have dozed off. Before I knew it, it seemed terribly late. I did not mean to make you worry. But I am quite sleepy from my walk." She yawned.

"Us too," I answered for both myself and Juna. "Let's get some sleep."

Chapter 21
Request from an Old Friend

"Anna, please listen." Dino's mom rolled over in her bed and opened her eyes. She sleepily looked around but didn't see anything, so she closed them and went back to sleep.

"Anna, I need your help." A soft, kind voice entered her dream, and the image of a face began to appear before her.

"Alistia, is that you?" Anna spoke in her dream. "It has been so long since I have seen you. You are as beautiful as I remember, although a bit older, as am I."

"I need your help. You must listen to me closely," the voice continued with a slight smile.

"I would do anything for you Alistia. I think you know that," Anna responded.

"I know your son Dino," Alistia spoke slowly. "He and my younglings know each other as well. I have reason to believe my younglings are with your son right now." Her image faded in and out as she spoke, making it difficult to be sure of what she was saying.

"We are not at our home, Alistia. We are away on vacation. I do not think your young ones are with Dino. Have they been missing long?" Anna, being a mom herself, felt that sense of maternal fear in her chest for Alistia.

"I need you to find out, and if they are, please keep them safe and bring them home to me..." Her voice trailed off.

"Wait!" Anna called, but Alistia's image faded and then was gone.

The next morning when Anna woke up, she didn't immediately remember her dream from the night before. She was in the kitchen helping Carol prepare breakfast when it began to come back to her. First, Alistia's face popped into her thoughts, and then she began to remember what she had told her. "I'll be right back," she told Carol and abruptly left the room. "Dino? Dino, are you awake in there?" she whispered through the door. She heard some movement from inside and reached for the doorknob.

Just then I opened the door, but only a crack. "Morning, Mom." I smiled.

"What are you doing in there?" she asked, trying to look past me.

"Nothing. I was just going to get dressed and come out for breakfast. I'll be there in a few minutes," I told her, trying to close the door.

With one hand on the door and the other in the middle of my chest, she gently but firmly pushed her way into the room. I turned around quickly and scanned the room for Karia and Juna. She, too, was looking for something, it seemed. "What is it, Mom?" I questioned her. I think she could hear the irritation in my voice because she looked at me in that certain way as if to say, "Close your mouth."

"I thought I heard voices. Is there someone in here with you?" she quizzed.

"Who? Who would be in here with me?" I looked at her, puzzled.

"Dino." The tone in her voice meant business. I didn't know what she knew, but she had something on her mind, and she was serious about it. She walked further into the room, and I could see her eyes darting back and forth from wall to wall, hunting for something.

"Mom, what are you looking for?" I prodded.

Then she saw something and quickly walked over to the desk. My heart sank when she picked up a small maroon pouch that was lying there. "Whose is this?" she said, turning around and confronting me. "And don't even think about telling me it is yours."

I just stared at her. She knew; somehow she knew. But I wasn't going to confirm it. I couldn't. I would be breaking a promise. *Do I lie or do I break a promise?* I chose to say nothing.

"What are their names? How did you get them here? You have to tell me, Dino. Their mim is scared to death." The concern in her voice hit all of us, along with the fact that she said "Mim".

I noticed out of the corner of my eye the bed skirt move. I looked down, and my mom's eyes followed mine. Her mouth dropped open as she watched Karia and Juna crawl out from under the bed. They walked over and stood at my feet.

"Mom, this is Karia and Juna."

Chapter 22
Past Revealed

The madams and male council members, including Sir Antar, stood in the garden among Alistia, Sire Argus, and Arbalest Bendbow. A hum of concern spread through their conversations. A door appeared in the knotty trunk of the willow, and Master Zoal stepped into the garden, followed by Oracle Balstar. Oracle Balstar and Master Zoal moved slowly across the garden to where the group had already gathered. Oracle Balstar seated himself in an ornate wooden chair made from the stump of a long departed tree. The group fell silent and patiently waited for Oracle Balstar to settle himself. Master Zoal stepped to the back and found a small bench next to a stone wall, where he was able to create a desk to work from.

Sir Antar stepped forward, pacing before the group. "Who will go and bring them home?" He posed the question everyone was contemplating.

Arbalest Bendbow immediately stood. "I should be the one to retrieve them."

All eyes fell upon him.

"I will be best able to find and bring them safely home."

"How will you get to them? They are quite far away," Alistia reminded him.

"Although getting to them will be a most daunting task, it is not impossible. I will require a more rapid method of transport to bring me to them, and then we will need to devise a method for our return," he pondered aloud.

Sir Antar cleared his throat. "I will speak with Bayalthazar, leader of the Unpuzzliers. He should be able to assist us in this matter."

"Alistia," Oracle Balstar spoke in a strained whisper.

She stood, stepped forward, and knelt on one knee before him. "Yes, my Oracle?"

"You have been in contact with Dino's mother. This is how you knew. Your intuition is strong. That is what brought you to the willow in your quest to find them. I knew it was imaginable that you would come to find out who Dino is."

The council members stood silently and listened.

"My Oracle, I knew as soon as I saw his eyes. I knew he was hers. You do not forget those moments in your life. Even though she was not the prophesied one, we formed a bond, one that tore at my very core when I was to never see her again. I was not sure I would even be able to get through to her, but I am a mim, and I had to attempt to reach out to her."

Oracle Balstar looked upon her as he did when she was young. He knew her heart was good and pure. He placed his hand on her bowed head and whispered, "We will bring them home alive and well. I assure you."

The group had a look of shock on their faces. Oracle Balstar raised his hand and motioned to Master Zoal. He stood, unfolded a scroll, and began. "Many moons erstwhile, a youngling by the name of Alistia brought to the community a human child. It was a female named Anna. It was thought the Sunbow Prophecy was coming to fruition. Following the course taken to determine her worthiness, it was found that the Sunbow Prophecy was not, at that time, to come to pass." Master Zoal rolled the scroll and slipped it into a bag that hung from his shoulder.

"It was a most sad and difficult time for me. I have never forgotten that pain. I was as astounded as all of you to come to know that it was my own youngling and Anna's child as well that would bring the prophecy to life," Alistia shared.

There was silence in the garden.

Finally Sire Argus spoke, "As Oracle Balstar has stated, your heart is pure, and your intentions are honorable. I do not judge you, your past or your life's journey, nor should your community. Together we endured the Prophecy of the Sunbow, and together we will bring our younglings home. It is our strength and courage that will guide us to assist our own in their life journeys." He stepped forward and took Alistia's hand.

She looked into Argus' dark eyes. "From the moment fate brought us together, you have been my companion, my familiar, my shield. To you and for you I am grateful."

A sigh could be heard from the direction of the madams.

"We all have secrets. It is what we learn from those moments in our existence that shapes the Traegons we become. You are a strong and honorable she-Traegon, Alistia, and just as we feel with your younglings, we do with you. This is part of your path and part of all of our paths as well. We will stand together as a community, as confidants, just as we always have," Madam Calthia spoke wisely.

"Well spoken, Calthia," Sir Gortho commended.

Alistia looked around the beautiful, serene garden at the alliance of her peers. "Then let us work together to find a way to bring them home safely."

There was silence, and all were in deep thought.

Finally, Sir Antar spoke. "What if we summon Dino here and speak with him directly?"

"Could that work?" Alistia asked. "Can we bring them all here? Is this a way to bring them home?"

"This is an intriguing assumption, but is it possible?" Sir Pexor inquired.

"I am afraid it is not a feasible solution," Oracle Balstar stated. "The White Acorn is a very powerful tool, but it can only be used to move them back and forth temporarily. Prolonged stays through summoning can eventually cause harm. Humans and Traegons must move through the current time for it to be permanent. But if Dino has the White Acorn with him, we could summon him to gain information and devise a plan," Oracle Balstar explained.

"Would it then be necessary for Arbalest to go?" questioned Madam Shoran.

"They still need to be protected, guided and brought home. This can be considered with some debate," Master Zoal added.

Oracle Balstar cleared his throat and spoke. "Alistia, communicate with Anna again tonight. Question her about Dino having possession of the acorn. If it is with him, tell her to have him place it under his pillow. Make sure she understands, as many moons have passed, and she may not remember the process."

"I will do as requested, my Oracle," Alistia agreed.

"We shall meet again upon our next nightfall. Are there any further questions?" Oracle Balstar paused, but no one stirred. "Then we are finished for now."

Chapter 23
Rain Shadow

The thunder clapped loudly above the house, startling all of us. The rain began to pound at the roof and windows.

My mom reached down and gently picked up Karia and Juna one by one and set them on the bed. She looked closely at Karia. "You look just like her," she whispered in a soft, kind voice. Then she reached out and stroked her head. "You are lovely, Karia." She turned to Juna. "My, aren't you a handsome Traegon. I knew your mim a long time ago." She paused. "We were friends." The wonder in her eyes fell away, and sadness came over her. She sat back on her knees on the floor at the edge of the bed.

Karia stepped forward. "She remembers you. She always has. She used to tell us stories. We thought they were just that, stories, but now I know it was her way of keeping you close."

"Your mim is so worried about you both. This was not a very smart thing you chose to do." My mom stood and turned to me. "What would make you think this was a good idea? What if they were caught on the airplane? I don't even want to imagine it." She noticed me looking at Karia and Juna as she spoke about the plane. "So that is why you were acting so strangely! Something went wrong with your plan, didn't it?" She paused, but before I could answer she said, "No, wait. I don't want to know."

"I don't know, Mom. It seemed like a good idea when we came up with it. They just wanted to see the mountains," I tried to explain.

"Dino's mom," Karia addressed, "I do believe this is all part of some plan, something bigger than any of us."

We all looked at her, puzzled by her words.

"What are you speaking of?" Juna questioned her. "We came to see the mountains and to help you forget your dream. That was all, was it not?"

"Do you remember at the market the morning we went to see Oracle Balstar?" Karia began. "I met a very old she-Traegon that day, and she has followed me here. Her name is Kamara. That is why I was gone so long last eve'."

"What does she want?" Juna asked.

"I am not sure, but I sense we have work to do together, and I think it is here." Karia continued, "I think it involves the two of you as well, for Kamara mentioned you both." Karia paused and looked at Juna and me.

We looked back at her in a strange and confused way.

"Oh no. Not again!" I heard Juna mumble under his breath.

"Us?" I asked, just to be sure I heard right.

"Yes, all of us," Karia confirmed.

"What is she like?" Juna asked.

"She is an odd sort, but very wise. When she speaks to me, she does so as though she is always imparting teachings upon me. I think we were meant to come here—all of us together."

"Oh, my," my mom injected. "This is a lot to take in," she said, sitting on the bed. "I just ask that when you are away from me and out doing whatever you are here to do that you keep yourselves and each other safe. Please!"

Karia walked over to my mom and took her hand. "We have been together for a while now and always look out for each other. Do not worry."

"I think I need a cup of coffee. I will let you three alone. Be good." Mom stood and let herself out of the room.

It rained lightly on and off for most of the day, so Autumn called to make a plan for the next day. She gave me her phone number in case we wanted to go out later, and then I could call them. We watched TV in my room most of the day. Juna seemed intrigued, though Karia not so much. She preferred to try her hand at drawing and practicing writing in my journal.

After dinner, the rain stopped, and Karia suggested we go out for a while before the sun set. I called Autumn and Jade, and they agreed to meet us by the road with the horses.

"So where are we off to?" Jade asked.

"I'm not sure. Karia, it was your idea to go out. Anywhere special you want to go?" I asked her.

She pulled a piece of paper out of her pouch and unfolded it. "What is a *Rain Shadow*?" she asked spontaneously.

We all looked at her, puzzled, and Autumn finally spoke. "How do you know that word if you don't even know what it is?"

"It came to me while I was practicing writing this afternoon. Do you know what it is?" prodded Karia.

Autumn hesitated and then answered, "It is the place on the side of a mountain where it doesn't rain, ever." Autumn gently kicked her horse to get moving, and the rest of the horses followed her lead.

"Can you take us to that place?" Karia asked, climbing in front of me to get nearer to Autumn's horse.

"No. I don't know where it is or if it really even exists. I only know of it because I've heard Fletch mention it. I thought he was just telling me a story, so I didn't ask."

"Well let's find Fletch and ask him then. I'm up for an adventure," Jade piped in.

"No more cliffs, okay?" I emphasized.

We all laughed as we made our way up the path.

Out in the woods, Jade cupped her hands around her mouth and let out her strange call, and then she followed up playfully, "Fletch! Fletch, come out, come out wherever you are."

We all sat motionless atop the horses waiting. Suddenly there was a rustle in the brush off to our left. We all turned to look, expecting Fletch to pop out of the trees, but instead a fawn stepped tentatively from the woods.

"Oh, shhh. Look!" Autumn whispered.

We all stared at the baby deer, not moving a muscle so we wouldn't frighten it away. Its ears perked up and turned in opposite directions.

"Here he is, mother deer. Not to worry. I knew we would find him," Fletch said, slowly stepping out of the woods with a large female deer behind him.

The fawn immediately turned and ran toward his mother, and the two bounced off into the woods.

"Fletcher P. Webenaki preforms, yet, another good deed." Fletch announced proudly. "What are all of you doing out here?" he asked, pretending to just notice us.

"You're so silly, Fletch." Jade giggled and held her hand low at the side of Junebug.

Fletch took a running leap, grabbed Jade's hand, and hoisted himself into her lap. "Silly, huh?" He opened his hand, revealing a tiny purple butterfly. He blew gently, and the butterfly hopped onto Jade's nose. "Silly is good!" he proclaimed.

We all laughed. "Okay, charmer, we need your help," Jade said as the butterfly lifted into the air.

"Ahh, my help is what you need, eh? My pleasure. Fletcher P. Webenaki at your service, as always. What can I do you for?"

Jade smiled and shook her head. "We need to know where the Rain Shadow is. Will you take us there?"

His look turned from silly to surprise, and he glanced at Autumn. "You were not supposed to tell anyone of the Rain Shadow."

"I didn't, Fletch, I swear," Autumn pleaded.

"Do not cast doubt on her," Karia protested. "It was my request."

"How did you come to know of the Rain Shadow?" Fletch questioned.

"It came to me, into my thoughts. I do not know of it really," Karia responded.

As we lingered in the clearing with dusk approaching, Fletcher shared with all of us the secret of the Rain Shadow.

"It is a magical place, like a fairy circle where the fairies are found dancing and playing, or the land within the jungles where the Abatwa gather," Fletcher began. "I cannot tell you how to get there, as I myself have not been there, but I can tell you what I know."

"How is it that you know it truly exists if you have never been there yourself?" Karia asked curiously.

Fletcher and Karia looked at each other as if they knew something no else did. "The knowing comes to us when we are ready to accept it and act upon it. It is always there. You know this, don't you?"

Karia paused for a moment and answered, "I do. Please continue."

"A she-Traegon named Zuri shared with me the story of the Rain Shadow. Her Matron Traegon was a Wayseer within their community," Fletcher stated.

"Will she tell us how to reach the Rain Shadow?" Karia asked.

"I can only take you to see Zuri. She will have to make the determination as to whether we are to know anything more. We can go when the sun rises. Meet me just beyond the ridge by the cave of the bats. We must go alone—only Traegons and no humans," Fletch said, glancing at Autumn, Jade, and me.

I looked at Karia, and she must have sensed the concern I was feeling because she immediately said, "Juna will accompany us. This is something we must do. I feel it deep within my being."

"It's getting dark. I think we should be heading back," Jade said, glancing up at the sky.

"Yeah, I agree. Our parents are going to worry if we don't get back soon. Thanks for sharing your story, Fletch. Maybe we'll see you tomorrow," Autumn said.

"Until we meet again, sleep well all." Fletch jumped to the ground and began to walk toward the tree line of the forest. "Do not be late, Karia!" he said, turning back toward us.

"I shall be here when the sun rises, I assure you," Karia responded.

We watched as Fletch disappeared into the forest. We headed back down the path toward home. The sun fell quickly into the horizon. Suddenly the horses became increasingly uneasy. They started to snort and stomp, moving and jerking in a nervous way. It wasn't like them at all, as they were usually very gentle and obedient.

"There's something out there," Jade remarked. "The horses sense it, and it's spooking them." She grabbed her mace and held it tight in her hand.

Autumn gently kicked Wind to get him to pick up speed. "Stay close. It could be the cougar," she said.

Karia and Juna were especially alert, watching as we rode quickly through the forest. Jade held back, letting me pass so she could stay in the back. She was watching carefully but couldn't see what was following us. "Don't bolt, Autumn. You don't want to challenge it to a chase," Jade reminded her sister. "I can't see anything. It's too dark."

"I don't see anything either," I piped in, scanning the darkness.

We could hear movement in the brush. Controlling the horses became more difficult, as they wanted to get out of the forest as quickly as possible. A deep, loud growl came from the darkness of the woods. We all panicked, and the horses bolted up the path. Karia, Juna, and I grabbed the reins in an attempt to keep from falling off. Suddenly the path spit us out on the mountain road just as the headlights from a truck came around a curve. The truck horn sounded a warning.

Wind reared up as Autumn pulled him to the side of the road. "Pull back! STOP!" Autumn screamed.

I pulled back hard, and Rory reared up. I pulled the reins to the right and gave some slack. Rory came down hard before stepping into the road. Karia and Juna were hanging on to the reins and Rory's mane for dear life. I could hear Junebug slide in the dirt behind me and just hoped she and Jade would be able to stop in time.

"That was close!" Jade said.

Our hearts were pounding. We sat for a minute by the side of the road and tried to regain our composure before continuing on. Karia and Juna climbed up on Rory's back and into the saddle in front of me. The horses seemed to calm down, and we no longer heard any sounds coming from the path or the surrounding woods.

"I think the truck scared it off," Autumn said, still shaking from almost getting mowed down by the truck.

"Good. Now can we go home," I said, not caring how scared I sounded.

"I'm with you there, Dino," Jade agreed. "That was a little too close for me."

Autumn nudged Wind to continue on, and we headed toward home.

Chapter 24
Separate Ways

"Anna! Hear me now! I must speak to you."

Anna rolled over in her bed and became aware of Alistia's voice.

"Anna, now!" the whispered voice half awakened her.

"I am here. I hear you," Anna spoke in her dream as she watched Alistia's image fade in and out.

"Listen carefully to my instructions. It is imperative that you understand." Alistia paused, giving Anna time to focus. "Ask your son if he has the White Acorn with him. If he does, direct him to place it beneath his pillow on this next eve. He will be summoned by Oracle Balstar. He must come, for the council requires answers. Do you understand?" Alistia paused again.

"I understand. I remember, and I will give him the message. Will Karia and Juna be going with?" Anna questioned.

"It will be decided." Alistia's image faded, and Anna drifted back to sleep.

———— ✧ ————

I woke to Karia's hand pushing firmly on my cheek and an urgent tone in her voice. "Wake up, Dino. You must let us out now. We have to go to meet Fletcher."

I opened one eye and saw that it was still very dark. Karia and Juna were standing over me. The curtains were drawn back, and I could see a distant hint of the coming light. I sat up quickly, remembering Karia's important meeting with Fletch. "Okay, I'm up. Let's get you two on your way." I hopped out of bed and headed for the window. I popped off the screen unrolled the blanket and folded it in half. Before Karia climbed on, I looked at her. "Be very careful out there. Remember that cougar, and come back as soon as you can. Do you remember the way?"

"We do, and I assure you we will be fine." She looked at me, and I could see calmness in her eyes; I knew she was doing exactly what she knew she had to do. "Until later." She smiled, climbed into the curve of the blanket, and waited as I lowered her out the window. Once she was down, I dropped one end and watched as Juna grabbed on and climbed down on his own. They headed toward the woods, turning back once, they each held up one hand, palm toward me, in an expression of goodbye and I returned the gesture.

I climbed back into my bed. I've always felt protective of Karia. I know she is strong, and I know she can totally handle herself, but I still feel like I have to look after her. I began to think about the conversation Karia, Juna, and I had after we returned home the previous night. We had lain awake and talked for a long time about our mothers. They shared what they knew about their mim and confirmed my suspicions about my mom. *No wonder she loves the forest so much.* I felt bad for her not being able to see Alistia again. I can't even imagine not being able to see Karia and Juna ever again. I felt lucky, and it gave me a new understanding of who my mom truly is.

The next thing I knew, there was a knock on my door. Before I even got up, I heard the doorknob turn and the door creek open. "Dino, are you awake?" My mom stepped in the room and closed the door quietly behind her.

I sat up slowly.

"Where are they?" she asked.

"They had to go out early this morning," I responded.

"Go out? Where?" she asked surprised.

"There are more of them, Mom," I shared.

"Here?" she asked.

"Everywhere!" I responded. "Karia and Juna went to meet another young Traegon named Fletch. He is going to take them to meet others," I told her.

"Amazing!" she whispered. "I knew it. How incredible! How wonderful!" She paused, and suddenly I saw in her a sense of wonder and excitement, a side of her I couldn't ever remember seeing before. We had finally shared the secret, the truth we had both kept protectively hidden, her for much longer than me. Suddenly she remembered what she had come in the room to tell me. "Do you have the White Acorn?" she asked.

I was surprised because I didn't realize she knew about it. "Yes, I brought it. Why?"

"Tonight, place it under your pillow. You will be summoned to Traegonia," she said.

"How do you know?" I asked her.

"Alistia, Karia and Juna's mim, came to me in a dream last night. They wish to speak to you," she continued.

"What do you think they want?" I asked, feeling like I was facing a punishment. "Are Karia and Juna supposed to come with me?"

"All I know is that you are supposed to place the acorn under your pillow. That is all I was told." I think she could sense my worry and placed her hand on my shoulder. "It will be alright. You know them. No harm will ever come from them." She smiled that knowing smile of hers.

Our conversation returned to our vacation, and we talked for a while about how much we liked it there. Then we went to see the others and have some breakfast.

Chapter 25
Into the Mountain

Karia and Juna climbed the rocks of the bat cave. Karia breathed in deeply. "I suppose we are early," she said, looking around at the forest.

"He will be here," Juna said calmly. "He is too self-proud to be late."

They looked back toward the horizon. The sun glowed behind the morning clouds before it fully emerged. Just then there was a rustling in the woods nearby.

Juna pulled his knife from its sheath and took a protective stance, fearing the cougar was on the prowl, looking for a morning snack.

"It is I, Fletcher P. Webenaki, on time and prepared for adventure," Fletch said as he burst dramatically out of the woods.

"Do you always announce yourself?" Juna asked, in a slightly disgusted tone, slipping his knife back into its sheath.

"A grand entrance is befitting a skilled archer, hunter, and protector," he responded.

"Oh!" Karia breathed. "And are you all of those things?" she asked.

"One day I will be if I am not already. I am in a state of perpetual preparation, you see," he proclaimed.

Juna stood in the background and watched. *He should meet Arbalest Bendbow. Now he is all of those things, less the boastfulness,* Juna thought.

Karia asked, "What must we do now?"

"Follow me," Fletch announced.

He turned, heading back into the woods from where he had come.

Karia and Juna looked at one another and obediently followed. They walked for a long time, through some of the largest trees Karia and Juna had ever seen. They crossed a fallen log lying over a rapidly flowing creek that seemed more like a river to them. They walked into the darkness of a grove of sugar pine trees. The soft needles created a thick padding on the ground. The forest floor beneath was bare of brush or any other growth, only a scattering of giant pine cones that were as large as a Traegon. Karia looked up into the dense towering trees as they passed beneath them. "Home to many, I am sure," she contemplated.

Finally Fletch came to a stop. Karia looked around and could no longer see any other type of tree. A ceiling of wide, far-reaching branches covered with soft short needles, jutted out from the broad trunk. It was comforting there in that shadowy expanse.

Karia asked quietly, "Are we here?"

"Yes," responded Fletch in a low whisper. He stood and carefully scanned the quiet and motionless area. Then Fletch drew his hands to his mouth and let out a series of clicking sounds. He stopped and waited. Once again he announced their presence with these clicking sounds. A few moments passed, and they heard a sound to their right.

They turned to see an opened door in the side of one of the pine trees with light streaming out. Standing in the door way was a she-Traegon with a very kind smile on her face. She motioned them in. Her home was warm and inviting. Karia and Juna both thought of their Mim when first they met Zuri. She was tall as she-Traegons go, and with child, dressed in fabrics of deep purple, grays and leafy green. A bodice laced tight accentuated her round belly. A fragrance of wild flowers and freshly baked sugar cakes surrounded her. She was younger than Alistia but older than Karia. She had long, dark feathers that fell softly upon her shoulders, and she walked with a slight waddle. Both Karia and Juna had a sudden twinge of home sickness and wondered if Mim and Sire Argus were very worried.

Fletch proceeded to introduce them. "Karia, Juna, this is Zuri

Shima." Fletch motioned from one to the other.

Zuri blinked her eyes slowly and bowed forward. "It is with great pleasure that I welcome you into my home."

Karia bowed in response and pulled on Juna's arm to follow. "We are grateful that you have agreed to meet with us."

"My dearest friend Fletch is a trustworthy and insightful judge of character. If you are here, you are supposed to be here." Zuri smiled.

The sounds of a scuffle emanated from another room. All eyes turned to the approaching commotion. Suddenly a youngling of only a few winters noisily tumbled into the room. With bright sky blue eyes and ears too big for his head, the fine smooth skin of his face blushed red. Ige looked at Karia and Juna, bashful in front of the newcomers. Zuri shook her head as the little one jumped to his feet and ducked behind his mim. Suddenly the youngling noticed a familiar face.

"Fetch!" the small Traegon hollered excitedly.

"Ige!" Fletch responded, dropping to one knee as the little one ran into his arms.

"You bring me sumting?" Ige questioned Fletch, looking closely into his face.

"Ahh, yes, little one, I did." Fletch opened a pouch tied to the belt on his waist. He dug into it with all eyes upon him and pulled out a small object. It was a golden, transparent, crystal like stone— flat, smooth and round. It shimmered as it lay in the palm of his hand.

Ige gazed at it and then looked up at Fletch.

"Hold it," Fletch directed.

Ige took the item from Fletch's hand and looked at it closely.

"Take much care of this. It is a rare treasure," Fletch instructed.

"Where did you get it?" Ige asked innocently.

"It was on my last expedition. I was guiding a small, weak fawn away from the grips of a large Grimalkin when I stumbled upon the carcass of a sizable unidentifiable beast. The fawn safely disappeared into the forest, and I was left to fend off a large angry mountain cat. I turned to face the Grimalkin and found myself between her and the

Dino C. Crisanti

The Gift Fletch and Ige

carcass. The dirty, matted Grimalkin slowly approached, crouching, crawling, and growling lowly and fiercely. I pulled an arrow from my quiver and readied my bow. I knew I was no match for this incredible hunter. Suddenly, an enormous shadow descended upon us. I did not dare look away from the ravenous beast."

Ige had his fingers in his mouth by this time, and his eyes were as wide as they could possibly get. The rest of the group was also staring in anticipation of what was to come.

Fletch continued, "From behind me, I heard a deep grunt, almost a growl, followed by a hiss. I was concerned at this time that I might be eaten at any moment. I then heard a loud, strong, unfurling sound and saw the shadow of wings from above—wings larger than any I had ever seen before. Then again came the guttural grunting. The Grimalkin cowered as her eyes drew up from me to directly above me, and then she began to back away. Moments later, she turned and ran. I cautiously turned to see a towering blackbird at least fifty times my size standing over me. He closed his wings and shifting his head back and forth looked at me out of one eye and then the other. His head was bare of feathers and a bright red color, and a collar of fluffy, white feathers encircled his neck. His body was massive. It was then that I heard him speak to me."

"What did he say?" Juna asked, completely engrossed in the story.

"He said, 'You are safe now. This is my meal. Be on your way.' I answered him and told him I was grateful for his assistance. 'You are a mighty bird,' I said, 'one of which I have not seen many,' and then I asked him his name."

"And did he tell you?" inquired Karia.

"He said, 'We are but very few. You may never see another like me again. I am Condor. I must eat and gather food for my mate and young.' I asked why I might never see another like him, and he said, "My kind has been hunted, and we have lost many of our homes. It is a struggle just to survive. We find ourselves tangled within the world of humans. It has become difficult for us to live among their intrusive machinery.' When he told me that, a tear dropped from his dark black eye, and then he told me again to be on my way as he began to tear away at the carcass. I looked down, and as I turned I saw a glint in the dirt below. I reached down and picked it up," Fletch said, looking at the object he'd given to Ige. "This, which I give to you, is the tear of Condor."

Karia and Juna stood in silence, staring at Fletch.

Ige gently placed his arms around Fletcher's neck and whispered, "Tank you. I will take good care of it." He turned and ran off, disappearing into the other room.

"That was quite a story!" Juna chimed in.

"It was more than a story," said Fletch, looking more serious than usual. "It is the truth—a magnificent tale befitting a magnificent creature."

"Let us sit for a while," Zuri suggested, leading the way to a cozy area near the fire hole.

As she turned to motion the three to sit, Karia noticed the large bump at her belly beneath her dress. "Are you preparing for another youngling?" Karia asked, taking a seat.

"Yes. We expect the new one near the time of the changing leaves. We are very excited, as is Ige." She smiled, patting her baby bump. "Now, you have come to me for a purpose. What is it that I can assist you with on this day?"

Karia scooted to the edge of her seat and leaned in, as if preparing to release a long held secret. "Can you tell us how to get to the Rain Shadow?" she asked.

Zuri glanced at Fletch and then back at Karia. "Is it my understanding that this be your sole request?"

"Yes. It came to me in a vision. I feel it is important and that I seek out its purpose. I would be sincerely grateful if you would assist us," Karia explained.

Zuri sat quietly. She closed her eyes and rubbed her belly in a circular motion. She breathed in deeply, held it, and then released her breath. She did this several times and then looked as though she had stopped breathing altogether. Her eyes opened slowly. She gazed at each of them one by one and then spoke, "It is by way of the Rain Shadow that you will find the passageway to our Traegonia. It is the center of our community. It is the home to Oracle Qendrim and the Ternion. It is our safe haven..."

To Karia, Zuri's voice trailed off. Karia found herself once again in the forest. She could hear Kamara's voice. "You are meant to be there. The truth you seek, the power you will gain will be given to you there. You will be expected." Then Karia returned to the present and heard Zuri speaking again.

"Do you understand what I am telling you?" Zuri said.

"I understand, I am expected," Karia stated. Karia's and Zuri's eyes met, and there was an understanding.

"Go to the cave of the large-eared bat. Climb down to the outcrop on the farthest side of the rock face. You will not be able to find it alone, but Fletch can lead you. Wait there for further direction." She paused. "Be wary of the demon shadow that stalks the forest. She has snatched Traegons from the forest floor before they ever knew she was near. She has taken unprovoked and not just for food. Her hunger is for destruction, fed by fury. Stay aware and blessings be with you." Zuri stood, and they all followed. As they passed the opening to the room where Ige played, they could see him sitting on the floor holding the precious Condor tear that Fletch had given him.

"Thank you for your kindness. We wish you joy with your youngling to come," Karia said before she stepped through the door, followed by Juna and Fletch. She looked back, raising her hand in a gesture of friendship, and Zuri returned the gesture.

Chapter 26
Counting Trees

I was back in my room writing in my journal when there was a knock on the door. Aunt Carol called to my room, "Dino! You have visitors."

When I reached the living room, Autumn and Jade were waiting for me inside the door. "Hey, Dino. Do you want to come and see where our dad works? He said he would take us all with him today if we want," Autumn offered.

"Sure. What does your dad do?"

"He's a forestry technician. He works for the Bureau of Land Management," Autumn said.

"Okay, but what does he do?" I asked.

"He does a lot of different things. If you ask him, he would tell you he counts all the trees in the forest." Jade grinned. "Come on. It'll be fun."

The three of us walked outside to where Mr. Linder was sitting in his truck talking to my Uncle Joe and my dad. "Climb on in, kids," he said as he waved us around to the passenger side of the truck. Jade climbed in the front, and Autumn and I got in the back of the cab. Mr. Linder said goodbye to my dad and Uncle Joe and backed his truck down the driveway.

As we drove up the mountain road, I stared out the window and wondered what Karia and Juna might be doing right now.

"I've been thinking about them all morning," Autumn whispered, seeming to read my mind. "I'm sure they are fine."

We continued to drive in silence until we saw a large brown sign that said "Bureau of Land Management, California Division." It directed us down a wide road and into a clearing with a couple of buildings, several trucks, and a couple of Jeeps. Mr. Linder stopped his truck near the main building. We all jumped out, and Jade ran toward the front doors.

As she reached the wooden steps, the door opened, and a man stepped out. "Hey, Jade!" he said, raising his hand to high-five her.

"Hi, Mr. O'Connell," Jade responded and returned his high-five. "Is Melissa here today?" she asked.

"She sure is. She's right inside, packing up some of her gear," Mr. O'Connell said.

Jade ran past him and into the building as we were just reaching the steps.

"Hi, Allen," Autumn's dad said. "Dino, this is Allen O'Connell. He's a smoke jumper. Allen, this is Dino. He is visiting from Illinois."

"Hi, Dino, Autumn! Glad you could come out for a visit," he said.

"What's a smoke jumper?" I asked.

"Well, Dino, we're a group of firefighters who are specially trained to jump out of airplanes or helicopters in remote wooded areas that are too hard for other firefighters to get to," Allen said.

"Wow! That sounds dangerous," I responded.

"Yeah, it is, but that is why we have so much training. You don't want to go out there unless you really know what you are doing and have a great team with you. We're heading out for a training run this afternoon so I've got to go load up the gear, but it was nice to meet you Dino. Have a great time, and maybe we'll see you around. See ya later, Mike. You too, Autumn," he said as he walked past us and toward the trucks.

Mr. Linder held open the door, and Autumn and I walked in. We saw Jade sitting on the floor next to a lady in a jumpsuit like the one Mr. O'Connell was wearing. She was packing a lot of stuff into a bag.

"Hey, guys!" Jade called to us. "This is Melissa. She's a smoke jumper just like I'm gonna be when I grow up."

Melissa looked at Jade and smiled, nudging her a little. "Okay, then help me carry this stuff to the truck," Melissa ordered.

"Copy that," Jade said, standing and picking up a heavy duffel bag.

"Here, take this one." Melissa handed Jade a smaller one and took back the big one. "It was nice to meet you all, but I've gotta get moving. We'll see you around."

Just then a group of others in the same jumpsuit came out of a back room and headed for the door. Melissa jogged toward the door with Jade following close behind.

"Come on, guys. I'll show you my office and we'll get started," Mr. Linder said. We followed him into a small office with two desks. "This is my office, though it's nothing special I'm afraid."

Autumn and I looked at the pictures covering the walls. There were photos of firefighters, forests, and fires.

He shuffled through some papers, placed some on a clipboard, and grabbed a set of keys from his top drawer. "All set, guys. Let's get going."

When we walked out to the parking lot, Jade was watching the caravan of trucks pull out of the parking lot.

"Come on, Jade!" Mr. Linder called to her.

"Coming, Dad!" she called back and skipped over to where we were standing.

We climbed into a khaki green Jeep and pulled out along the mountain road. We drove for a while and turned onto a path that didn't seem wide enough for the Jeep. The branches of the bushes scraped against the sides of the doors until we entered a clearing. Mr. Linder pulled the Jeep to a stop, opened his door, and climbed out. We followed him as he walked around the area looking at different trees and taking notes on his clipboard.

Suddenly we heard voices. We followed Mr. Linder through another path and came upon a group of teens in hiking gear. Their large packs were lying on the ground. "How we doing today?" Mr. Linder asked them.

"Just fine, sir," one of the teens responded.

"This is a pretty remote area. You sure you know where you're headed?" Mr. Linder continued, looking at the ground strewn with beer cans and other assorted garbage.

"Yeah, we're good. We know where we are," another teen answered.

"You know, there is a no-burn order in this area, so no campfires, okay? And make sure you carry out your garbage. You don't want to get fined for leaving it behind," he warned.

The four teens looked at each other. One snickered and was nudged by another. "No, Sir, we won't be setting any fires," the first hiker said, "and we'll take our garbage out, no problem."

"You boys stay out of trouble. Be careful out here and keep you're eyes open. There's a rogue cougar roaming the area. You will invite her in if you leave any food lying around." Mr. Linder slipped his hand into his inside pocket and pulled out a business card. He handed it to one of the hikers. "You got a cell phone on ya?" he asked.

"Yeah," the young man answered.

"If you get into any trouble, just call this number. Someone here will be able to help you out."

"Thanks, man," the teen responded, slipping the card into his back pocket.

Mr. Linder wrote something on his clipboard, and then we headed back to the Jeep. Most of the day was spent doing the same thing all over the mountain: going through the forest checking up on the few people who dared to hike in the remotest regions of the mountain, warning them about the cougar, making sure everything was safe, and of course, counting trees.

We stopped at one point in an even more remote area on the side of the mountain. Mr. Linder had a cooler in the back of the Jeep packed with lunch for us all. While we were eating, we heard the sound of an airplane, and we could see it flying by through the trees. We watched for a while and then saw five specks fall from the plane.

"It's the smoke jumpers!" Jade proclaimed excitedly.

Then we saw the parachutes open and watched as they floated down and disappeared into the forest.

"I'm gonna do that some day!" Jade sighed, longing for the sky.

"You are my little daredevil," Mr. Linder added.

Chapter 27
Qendrim and the Ternion

Karia, Juna, and Fletch reached the rock outcropping atop the cave where the bats made their home. Fletch climbed up on the rock and scaled down the back side with Karia and Juna following close behind. It was very overgrown with vines and plants, definitely not a place that was visited often. Karia and Juna followed closely, holding on tight to the side of the rock face. The three Traegons moved easily across it and reached a small opening that brought them back on solid ground. Fletch continued a short way through the thick, dense underbrush until he came to a break in the trees that looked out over the mountain. There was a small plateau where they all sat down, side by side.

"What do we do now?" Juna asked.

"We wait," Fletch answered.

"What are we waiting for?" Karia asked.

"The rain," Fletch answered and then was silent.

Juna looked all around at the sky. "There is not a cloud in sight, no indication of rain at all. It seems we may have quite a wait," he commented.

In the quiet of their waiting, Karia's mind began to wander. It was then that she realized she had not had one of her fire dreams since they had arrived in California. She began to wonder why and was just going to tell Juna about it when a large shadow flew over them. They instinctively ducked, except for Fletch, of course, who watched and waited in anticipation. A bat landed on the ground in front of them. Karia and Juna stared in silence as it seemed to struggle to crawl. *Such an odd creature,* Karia thought as she watched it make its way slowly across the ground toward them, using its large delicate, papery wings. It was covered in soft fur, and its ears were almost as long as its whole body; they stood straight up on the top of its small head. It crawled with its leathery wings and its tiny hind legs on its belly across the ground. Once it approached us, it worked to upright itself, using its single claw at the top of each large, awkward wing. How strange and beautiful this creature seemed, standing before them. Its face was kind and sweet, like a mouse or rabbit. They remained quiet, watching and waiting. *But for what? How will it communicate?* Karia remembered when Oracle Balstar's raven and the small frog had spoken to her through her thoughts and wondered if it would be like that.

The bat looked slowly and carefully at the three friends, and then a soft, high-pitched squeak came forth. As Karia stared intently, she began to hear its words. "You come in search of something, one familiar and two unfamiliar. Peace and unity are sensed. I am Wayra, guardian to the portal of Traegonia in this region. I will assist you to enter and continue on this journey." She paused.

Karia looked over to Juna and Fletch. She wondered if they were hearing the same thing she was, but they were both just blankly staring at her. "Are you hearing this?" Karia asked, and they both nodded slowly and then returned their gaze to Wayra.

The sky suddenly became dark, and a rumble of thunder could be heard in the distance. The three friends and Wayra looked to the sky. A large, dark cloud rolled in over them.

"The thunder head," Fletch murmured.

"It will be time soon. You must follow my direction. Just over this rocky ledge is a much smaller ledge. You must carefully scale down it. Stand upon the ledge and await your next instruction." With that, and no farewell, Wayra opened her wings and lifted into the air. She circled over them once and plunged over the edge.

Fletch stood. "Come on! We must go now."

The thunder clapped, and a flash of lightning threatened. Karia and Juna stood and obediently followed.

Fletch unfurled a rope he had hanging off his belt and secured it to a root growing in the rocks then tossed it over the side. He looked over the edge and could just barely see the small ledge that Wayra had spoken of. "I'll go first. Karia, you follow, and Juna, you bring up the end. Agreed?"

Karia and Juna nodded. They knelt down by the edge as Fletch began to lower himself over the side. A large cold drop of rain hit Karia on the top of her muzzle, followed by another loud clap of thunder.

"Don't be long!"

Fletch's eyes met Karia's. They were all feeling a bit nervous, as none of them truly had any idea of what was to come. Karia followed, just as Fletch had instructed.

Fletch helped her onto the tiny ledge, and moments later, Juna slid down the rope. Just as Juna was safely on the ledge, and a long, loud rumble of thunder preceded a torrential downpour that lasted only a few minutes. The three of them stood very close together on the ledge, watching the rain batter the plants and water run like a waterfall from the mountain across from them. They were safe and dry.

"This is the Rain Shadow," Fletch stated.

A cool draft came from behind them and the rain abruptly ended. Karia, standing between Fletch and Juna, turned her head to observe an opening form in the rock behind them. She grabbed Fletch and Juna by the arm and stepped into the darkness.

"Welcome," a familiar voice said.

"Their eyes adjusted to the darkness to reveal Wayra hanging upside down from a low overhang. "We are almost there. Watch your step and follow me." She released her hold on the overhang and flew into the darkness.

Dino C. Crisanti

Wayra the Guide

Fletch stepped forward and noticed a rocky stairway that guided them down into a deep cavern. They walked silently, in single file down into the darkness. Every few steps, it seemed as if the next portion of the stairway became more illuminated. It was dark, but then it was also light.

When the steps came to an end, the three of them stopped. Their eyes were drawn to the center of the stone cavern. There they saw an old cloaked Traegon sitting on a carved stone throne with three she-Traegons standing to his side. The old Traegon stood and slowly approached the three friends. "I am Oracle Qendrim. Greetings, my young friends. We are glad you have come to visit," He said kindly.

Although he was probably as old as Oracle Balstar, Oracle Qendrim, moved and spoke with a younger air about him. Fine lines of wisdom could be seen in the hewn wrinkles on his face. Outwardly, he appeared much less stoic than Oracle Balstar, as many laugh lines furrowed at the corners of his upturned mouth. His moss-green eyes reflected the deep roots of his inner knowledge. His cloak, unlike the clothing of Karia and Juna's homeland, was a mix of muted colors of the sunset. He walked with the support of a handsomely carved staff of redwood, adorned with many symbols and burnished to a smooth, shiny finish, quite unlike the walking staffs used by most Traegons that Karia and Juna knew. He turned his gaze to the three she-Traegons standing at his sides. "I wish to introduce you to the Ternion. They are my daughters."

The three she-Traegons were dressed in the colors of the autumn trees, golds, browns, oranges, and reds.

"This is Ljena," he introduced first.

An enchanting she-Traegon stepped forward, curtseyed, and bowed her head. Her skin was much like all Traegons in texture but was much, much lighter in color, almost white. Her feathered hair was a dramatic contrast to her light skin, being a deep, rich brown color nearly black. She said nothing but smiled politely.

Oracle Qendrim continued, "This is Bora."

Dino C. Crisanti

The Ternion

Ljena stepped back, and Bora stepped forward. She was captivating, an absolute contrast to her sister Ljena. Her long, feathered hair was as white as snow, and her skin as dark as a baby black bear. "It is a great honor to meet you," she spoke kindly but with strength and power in her voice.

As Bora stepped back, the third she-Traegon stepped forward. Not waiting for an introduction, she said, "I am Pranvere. It is a joy to make your acquaintance." Pranvere was graceful and refined, likely the eldest of the three. Her appearance was much more customary. Her skin was the same color as Karia's, although her feathered hair was a calico blend of white, black, and tan.

Karia and Juna looked at one another and then back at the four, who were now standing in a group in the center of the large open space beneath the ground. Karia stepped forward and spoke. "I am Karia, and this is my brother Juna and our friend Fletch. We are grateful to be granted the privilege to come before you."

"We are completely aware of who you are. Zuri informed us of your intent to visit. You would not have made it here without our knowledge," "Qundrim said.

"But we came directly from her. How did—"

"That which you ask, you already know," said Qendrim, interrupting her. "We would like to discuss that which you may not yet know, for that is what will quench your thirst for knowledge," he stated in what sounded more like a riddle.

"You have come here seeking something and have also come with something to give," Bora gently pressed.

"Stay with us for a meal or two and let us become more aware of you and you of us," Ljena invited.

"We wish to share more of Traegonia—or more correctly, *our* Traegonia—with you," Pranvere said.

Karia turned to confer with Juna and Fletch with a slight puzzled look on her face.

"Is this not part of the journey, Karia?" Juna said.

"Was it not your dreams that brought us here?" Fletch continued.

She glanced back and forth into the eyes of both of them. She felt completely comfortable and safe with them and trusted their advice and was grateful to have them with her. She turned back to Oracle Qendrim and the Ternion. "We would be honored to stay and visit," Karia announced.

"Ahh, most excellent!" Oracle Qendrim exclaimed. "Bora, tell Samoon to prepare a special meal. Pranvere, call the community to the Garden of Mirth. Ljena, you will escort our guests to the gathering. Following the meal, we shall attend to business. Until then, you are in good hands." Oracle Qendrim stood and departed through an archway in the cavern wall.

Chapter 28
Patience

It was almost dinnertime when Mr. Linder dropped me back at my aunt and uncle's house. When we pulled into the gravel driveway, both my parents, Uncle Joe, and Aunt Carol were sitting on the front porch.

"Thanks, Mr. Linder. I had a great time," I said before I opened the truck door and jumped out.

"You're welcome, Dino. I'm glad you enjoyed yourself," Mr. Linder replied. "You're welcome to come out again before you go back home if you'd like to."

"That would be great," I answered through the open truck window.

"We'll call you later. Do you think they are back yet?" Autumn whispered, leaning out the back window.

"I hope so. Talk to you later," I said as Mr. Linder began to back up and turn around in the driveway.

"See ya, Dino!" Jade waved from the front passenger window.

"Bye!" I hollered. I waved and ran toward the front porch.

"Hi, Dino. Did you have a nice time?" my dad asked.

"I sure did! Mr. Linder sure has an interesting job. I would love to be able to spend my days in the forest and get paid for it too," I added.

"Well, a few more years, and you'll be off to college. You are welcome to stay here if you want to go to college out here," Aunt Carol suggested.

"Whoa! Everyone just wait a minute. We are quite a ways from college. Let's not get ahead of ourselves," Mom snapped.

"Not ready to get rid of him yet, Anna?" Uncle Joe laughed.

"No, not just yet. He's still my baby boy," Mom teased, pinching my cheek.

I rolled my eyes. "I'm not a baby, Mom," I corrected her.

"I think you will always be her baby, so you had better get used to it," Dad said.

"When is dinner?" I asked.

"In about a half-hour," Aunt Carol answered.

"I'm going to go lie down for a little bit. Call me if you need me for anything," I told them and went to my room. I walked into my room, closed the door behind me, and looked around. "Pssst! Anyone here?" I whispered.

There was no answer.

Just then there was a knock on my door. I turned just as my mom was opening the door. She popped her head in. "They're not back yet. I've been checking on and off."

"Did you check outside for them?" I asked.

"No," Mom responded.

"Okay, I'm going to go for a walk and see if I find them." I walked toward the door, but Mom stopped me before I could walk out.

"Don't worry about them. This is their natural environment. They will be fine, and they have friends out there to look out for them," she tried to reassure me.

"Is that what you will tell their mim?" I blurted.

She squinted her eyes at me and whispered, "You are not their mother. Don't go far." She squeezed my arm as I walked past.

I looked around the back yard and walked around the house. I even walked a ways down the path, quietly calling for them. There was nothing. I breathed in deeply, remembering my mom's words. *This is their natural environment...Don't worry...You are not their mother.*

Finally I heard my aunt call, "Dino! Dinnertime!"

"Coming!" I called back.

Aunt Carol made her famous pulled pork and homemade French fries. She is a great cook, and the warm food filled my stomach. Plus, laughing and visiting with my aunt and uncle took my mind off of worrying about Karia and Juna, at least for a little while.

Chapter 29
Ember Augury

Karia and Juna were amazed at the many differences between the California Mountain Traegonia and their own. They stepped through a dimly lit, narrow cave opening and found themselves in a bright garden that seemed to appear out of nowhere. The garden opened to the wide open bright blue sky.

We must be on the top of the mountain! Karia thought.

The garden was busy with many other Traegons, happily milling about. The atmosphere was festive with music, laughing, and much chatter. None of the Traegons seemed to have any concern about being exposed; there was no fear that a human might wander in unannounced.

Karia turned to Ljena. "Why do you not fear the humans finding you here?" she asked.

Ljena smiled. "Here, there is much land, much space. Here, we are virtually unreachable by humans. There are other regions of Traegonia where we must remain more hidden, where we would not be able to be as apparent, but here?" She raised her arms wide. "Here, there are no worries. Here we are free to just...be."

There was a break in the crowd before us, and Oracle Qendrim emerged, accompanied by Bora and Pranvere. "Welcome to the Garden of Mirth! This is one of the seven gardens of our Traegonia. It is much larger than just what you see here. Beyond the buckthorn is a path to six other gardens, each of which has its own purpose, its own energy. You are always welcome to come and use any of the gardens. The only requirement, which pertains only to the Garden of Peace, is that you must enter in silence and remain completely silent within that garden, as it is a garden of contemplation—a place of connection."

Karia remembered her time in the willow garden when she was *charging* and imagined that the peace garden would be used in much the same way.

Oracle Qendrim raised his voice to the crowd. "First, we shall feast in honor of our familiars from another land, another Traegonia."

A cheer came from the fellow community members.

Qendrin lowered his voice and spoke directly to his guests. "Following our meal, we will gather in the Garden of Alliance to further discuss the purpose for your visit." Raising his voice again, Oracle Qendrim called, "Let the feast begin! Our guests, Karia, Juna, and Fletcher shall be served first."

The gathered crowd of festive colorfully dressed Traegons once again parted, revealing a long table, carved of a heavily grained wood and embellished with fine, ornate etchings. The table was filled with more food than Karia and Juna had ever seen in one place. A colorful array of fruits, nuts, small game and almost anything a Traegon might imagine wanting to eat was laid out. Karia, Juna, and Fletch stepped forward and walked toward the table. All eyes were upon them as they made their way through the sea of familiars. Whispers of "Welcome! Wonderful to have you here! Anything you need, let us know," came from the many smiling, friendly faces.

Bora handed each of them a smooth square wooden tray that held a smooth wooden cup in one corner. Karia held the plate with one hand and lifted the cup near her slightly opened mouth. She breathed in the sweet scent, it called to her to taste, so she placed the cup to her mouth and sipped slowly.

"It is honeysuckle nectar," Bora whispered. "There is nothing like it in all of Traegonia."

Dino C. Crisanti

Karia closed her eyes as she sipped and said, "I believe you might be right about that!"

She, Juna, and Fletch filled their trays. Karia looked at Juna's tray. It contained more food than Karia's and Fletch's combined. Karia shot him a disapproving glare.

"What? I do not wish to be rude!" he explained.

They were led through the crowd past a small group of music makers. One he-Traegon tapped soulfully on drums that resembled bongos, while a young she-Traegon played a happy melody on a beautifully carved wooden flute, and another plucked the strings of a hollowed-out burled oak instrument. Frogs and crickets chimed in with their contrasting deep tones and high pitches.

The group continued on to a small circular nook in a corner of the garden. There were grapevines draped all around where they sat. From time to time, Juna would look up, pluck a sweet grape from the vine, and pop it into his mouth. From where they sat, they could see the whole garden and all of the interesting Traegons as they ate, danced, and played games. The small group ate and spoke with others who came to meet the strange familiars. Once they had finished their meal, they sat a little while longer, drinking honeysuckle nectar and talking about their different Traegonias. Many of the Traegons dispersed to different areas of the garden, while others remained and partook in the festivities. Oracle Qendrim could be seen walking slowly toward the path beyond the buckthorn to the remaining six gardens.

"It is time," Pranvere whispered, noticing Qendrim.

Silently they stood and followed toward the same path that led to the six gardens. Once they reached the Garden of Alliance, they stepped through an archway of amber and red columbine and were directed to where Oracle Qendrim was already sitting. Large round-topped mushrooms scattered before Oracle Qendrims' large wooden chair gave each one a place to sit. Karia looked at the others and then glanced around at the serene beauty. They sat in an area surrounded by tall red elderberry bushes' bursting with enormous bunches of deep purple and red berries. Looking up, all could clearly see the vast blue sky spattered with fluffy white clouds. It felt as if they were sitting on the top of the world.

"Karia, come forward and sit here," Oracle Qendrim called, motioning to a large purple velvet pillow that lay on the ground before him and drawing her attention back to the group.

Karia stood, moved slowly to the pillow, and knelt before Qendrim.

"You have made this journey for a purpose. You have felt a need to come before us. Tell me why you have come."

Karia paused for a moment and pondered his question. She hadn't really thought about why she had come—only that things had come to her that ultimately led her to this place. She hadn't intentionally or specifically come to seek out these Traegons, and it was her thoughts and dream that were the catalyst for her journey. Finally she spoke, "Oracle, prior to our journey here, I was having sleep tales that turned to waking visions. These images caused much fear within me. They were not anything I could clearly understand. I spoke with Oracle Balstar in our Traegonia, and he was not able to fully explain to me what these impressions meant. He helped as best he was able but ultimately placed the quest back into my hands. Once we came here with Dino, the human boy from our home, the images ceased. I am not sure why."

"Do you remember the images?" Qendrim questioned.

"I do. I am always able to recall the images when I think on them, but they bring up fear each time I recall them," Karia said.

"Recount for me these images," Qendrim requested.

Karia took a long, deep breath and closed her eyes. A few moments passed before she began to speak as if in a trance. "I hear a crackling sound coming from above where I sleep. I wake to an intense heat, unaware that I am still within my sleep tale. I move to the door, opening it slowly. I begin to ascend the spiral root staircase that leads to the willow garden. I am overcome by a thick, dense smoke. It chokes me and makes it difficult to breathe. I can hardly see. I climb to the top and see an orange glow, flickering, flashing. I cough, but I press on. I call out, and suddenly I realize that I cannot hear my own voice. When I look out through the reddish-orange glow, I can see nothing familiar. Traegonia, my home, is gone. The leaves on the trees are being swallowed by the intense flickering flames as they devour everything they touch. I fall to my knees." Karia paused. "In another vision, I am in the forest again. I hear a deep, fierce, angry growl. I am not able to see the creature that made the sound, but moments later I see creatures of all kinds fleeing the approaching flames. I see them running past me, so many with so much fear. The sounds, the glow, the heat—I see it repeat itself to me even in my waking." Karia's eyes blinked as they slowly opened, glistening with moisture. She looked pleadingly into Qendrim's eyes. "What does it mean? Why does it cause me such sadness and fear?"

Pranvere stepped to Qendrim's side. "My Oracle, could this be the Ember Augury?" she leaned in and whispered into his ear.

Without taking his eyes off of Karia, he spoke aloud, "The Ember Augury would require the appearance of the Ember Rune, which has yet to been seen."

Karia gasped. She reached for her pouch and held it for a moment. She felt at that instant that she was constantly the messenger of misfortune, remembering the Sunbow Prophecy. Although she also remembered that the fate of her people was not unalterable; she, Juna, and Dino were able to direct the course of the outcome. Karia unlatched her pouch and took it into her hands. Qendrim, Pranvere, and the others watched intently. She opened her pouch and turned it upside down, and out dropped the dolphin charm Dino had given to her and the smooth, round, metal object that had come into her possession through Kamara.

Qendrim's eyes grew wide as he stared at the objects lying at Karia's knees. Pranvere gasped and grabbed tightly to the back of Qendrim's chair. Bora and Ljena rushed forward in order to get a better look. Bora grabbed Pranvere's arm to steady her.

Suddenly there was a rustle in the bushes nearby. All eyes were drawn to the disturbance. Out of the bushes fell a thin, awkward-looking Traegon. He scrambled to his feet and looked sheepishly at the group. He wore woven plaid pants with a hole in one knee and a patch on the other. His shirt was wrinkled, and he wore a checkered cloth on his head that matched the patch on his knee. A leather apron was tied around his waist, and a bottle of black liquid hung from it. In one hand he held an unrolled scroll, and in the other a ragged feather tipped at the quill in ink.

Oracle Qendrim shot the Traegon an annoyed look. "Scrival, come here!" his voice boomed.

Scrival hurried to Oracle Qendrim. He apologetically dropped to one knee and bowed his head. Looking up with raised eyebrows, he said in a trembling, weak voice, "Oracle, I did not mean to interrupt."

"But you did. What is it that you are in need of that brings you sneaking through the garden?" Oracle Qendrim demanded.

"Oracle, it is of utmost importance that this meeting be chronicled. The accounts of our past times may hold truths for our future. My sire and grandsire and their sires before them have kept our stories. It is in my blood. It is my duty, my work, and my ardor. I beg of you to allow me to stay. I shall sit quietly to the side and be a bother no more."

Oracle Qendrim looked down at Scrival's pleading, groveling face. "You are just like your sire. Stay, but remain silent!" he demanded.

"I am grateful, Oracle." Scrival smiled and scurried past the others, out of the way.

"Karia, please forgive the disruption and continue when you are ready," Oracle Qendrim said.

The sound of the paper scroll could be heard as Scrival readied himself. Oracle Qendrim glared at him. Scrival held his hand up to say he would not be making any further noises.

Karia looked down at the items lying at her knees. She gathered her thoughts and spoke, "I am heavyhearted, as I can see that why I have come brings with it a dreadful forewarning. I must share with you that I have been in a similar circumstance to one such as this, and what is foretold can be altered. As much as I would rather have not brought this news, I believe my friends and I just might be the key to altering the outcome."

Through the three lines that ran from the sides to the center on the amulet, a bright orange light glowed within. It began to vibrate on the ground. Karia scooted back, as she had not before seen it do such a thing. The strange light became brighter, and every Traegon in attendance stared at it. Suddenly the three sections on the amulet burst open, sending the bright light skyward. They all shaded their eyes.

At that moment, in the wide clearing above their heads, a wind began to blow furiously. It swirled and spun snatching leaves and other debris from the ground and trees. It would have snatched Scrival's scroll if he had not held it tight. They all looked up as the wind blew in a circular motion. They could see the light twisting and spinning within the wind. Energy filled the small space, as static like electricity lifted the feathers and hair upon each Traegon's head until it suddenly and abruptly stopped. The light disappeared into the circular object, and the wind ceased. All that was left behind was a chill in the air and more uncertainty.

Chapter 30
Return to Traegonia

Karia and Juna were still not back when it was time to go to bed. I placed the White Acorn under my pillow, the way my mom told me to earlier. I leaned against my pillow and began to sketch the forest and Mr. Linder.

The next thing I knew, my mom was standing over me. "Come on, Dino. It's time to go."

"Go where?" I asked, opening my eyes.

"They are waiting for us," a soft, small voice beckoned.

I sat up quickly. There, standing on my bed, was Karia and Juna's mim. I stared at her. "Are they back yet?" I asked both of them.

"Not yet," my mom answered "but I am sure they will come back soon."

I got out of bed and stood next to my mom. Alistia was standing on the foot of the bed, and my mom and I were standing beside her.

"Join hands. It has been a long while since I have done this. Let us get there in one piece."

We closed our eyes, and the next thing I knew, we were standing in the willow garden where Karia had taken me before. Once again, we were the size of the Traegons.

"Welcome, Dino, Anna," Sir Antar spoke. "Come near, and let us sit and talk."

Alistia led my mom and me over to where the others were waiting.

Again it seemed so strange seeing the Traegons eye to eye. I still had trouble imagining that I was actually their size, standing in a garden beneath a willow tree in the middle of the forest. Not only that, but this time we had been taken there all the way from California. I looked at my mom, and she too was in awe. She gazed in wonder at the beautiful garden as she walked over to where the others waited.

"Please sit," Oracle Balstar's kind, soft voice invited.

"Thank you," my mother said, sitting on a small stool of tightly woven whips from the willow tree. I sat on the one next to her, and Alistia sat on the other side of her.

"Karia and Juna were unable to join us, I presume?" Sir Antar spoke.

"They went to the Traegonia in California," I responded.

"California?" Madam Calthia questioned.

Master Zoal cleared his throat, drawing the group's attention, and brought himself to his feet. He unrolled a scroll and began to speak. "California is the name given by the humans to a large area of land that borders the vast, deep water where the sun falls into the darkness." He rolled the scroll and reseated himself.

"We are visiting my brother. I was not aware that Karia and Juna are with us until just a day ago, nor was I aware they even knew my son," my mom stated. "As I told Alistia, I do promise to ensure their safety until I am able to return them to her."

"What is it that Karia and Juna are doing in this other Traegonia? What was the purpose of their visiting with you, Dino?" Oracle Balstar asked.

"Sir, the only reason was that Karia and Juna wanted to see the mountains, and we didn't want to be apart. Before we left on our vacation, something had been really bothering Karia."

"We are aware of Karia's sleep tales, although her concerns have been unfounded," Oracle Balstar interrupted.

"Karia didn't feel that way. She still believed there was something important about them. The she-Traegon she met in the forest out there seemed to think there is a reason we are all there too."

"What she-Traegon? Who is this you speak of?" Oracle Balstar interrupted again.

I paused to think. "I think her name was Ka...Ka... Kamara, that was it."

All but my mom, Alistia, and Argus gasped at the same time. I could hear her name ripple among them. Murmurs in low, shocked whispers came from almost everyone in attendance. "Kamara! Kamara is back? No one has seen her in many winters. What could she want?"

"Silence!" Oracle Balstar raised his voice. "Dino, are you sure she said Kamara?"

"Yes," I stammered. "Why is she in danger? Who is Kamara?" I asked, concerned.

"Kamara is an Arcane. She is older than any other known Traegon. It is unknown where she dwells, as she is able to be anywhere at any time. She alone holds the wisdom of the ages. She is the matriarch to all Wayseers and ultimately to all Traegons. When she appears to the Seer, there is change in the wind. She holds power beyond all power of the Oracles. She brings the lessons, the difficult lessons. She is the catalyst to the power of the Seer. Karia is on the verge of learning her true power."

"Why has it been so long since anyone has seen her?" Alistia choked, her eyes wide and filled with concern.

"A Seer becomes fully a Seer only after they become open to their lessons, only when they truly quest for the knowledge and the illumination. Karia is most certainly not even aware that she has come to this point in her training. Does she understand the power of Kamara, Dino?" Oracle Balstar asked.

I swallowed hard. "I know she is aware that Kamara is trying to teach her, but I don't think she really knows who she is."

Master Zoal stood and cleared his throat. "Upon the appearance of the Arcane to the potential Wayseer, there will be great change. The Wayseer will take into her possession an amulet. It is a gift of the ages, a piece meant to guide, protect, and thrust forward the learning.

These things are destined to come to pass. There can be no intentional interference, or the cycle will be broken and the Wayseer in training will slip into the abyss with Kamara for the course of four winters. Be steady, be wary, and be prepared." Master Zoal rolled the scroll and replaced in his sack.

Everyone sat in silence until Madam Shoran spoke. "I think we are all beginning to understand the deep significance of this process for Karia. This knowledge changes everything, so our strategy must be altered."

"Do we send Arbalest, or do we wait patiently for the process to unfold? What are the consequences and risks of both options?" Madam Calthia asked.

Anna placed her arm around Alistia's shoulders. She could feel her trembling. Sire Argus took her hand.

I looked at my mom and Alistia and knew they were worried beyond anything they had experienced before. I stood and began to speak. "I know you all are worried. I know I am young and have less experience than all of you put together, but I also know Juna and I will always watch over Karia. We have met others there, Traegons and humans. It seems like we were meant to meet them, to be there together, for whatever we are supposed to do. These things came to us, and we did not go looking for trouble. Maybe we just need to keep doing what we have been doing and let things happen the way they are supposed to."

"That, young Dino, is a difficult proposition. We lay plans, follow prophecies, and we find ourselves moving in one particular direction. What you suggest is to release control and to wait and to be at peace with that waiting," Sir Antar restated.

Madam Calthia stood "This is something that only a young Traegon and a young human would find effortless. As we grow and age, we find peace and comfort in our well-laid plans. We forget that all is as it should be and that we, too, used to just allow things to move within our lives and our world. This just might be a lesson for all of us as well."

"She is right." Alistia released Argus' hold on her and stepped forward. "These words are true. These are the lessons I have always taught my younglings. It is as it should be, we are each here for a purpose, and when that purpose begins to unfold, it is like dropping a stone into a pond. It creates ripples that extend out beyond our place of comfort. It may not be easy for others around us to accept the movement, but we must trust the direction we choose." Alistia took a deep breath and seemed renewed in strength.

"We are being asked to become like the young and to trust, and in that we will find our strength," Madam Taendia said.

"We may hold wisdom, but we also need to be open to truth and change and not be clouded by our fears," cautioned Sir Gortho.

It seemed that all were coming to an understanding, this which brought enlightenment to each of their thoughts, one at a time.

"I would feel more comfortable if Arbalest were near them," Alistia requested.

"He may go, but he must not interfere with the process. He must live moment to moment with them. You must allow them to take the lead," Oracle Balstar directed. "Is that something you feel you are able to do, Arbalest?"

"I fish and hunt. There is never a plan for those, as you never know what the hunt holds for you. You may find nothing, or you may encounter something much larger than you are expecting. It is within the patience and the trust that we are rewarded. I am fully able to complete this task," Arbalest stated confidently.

"Then you shall leave at sunrise. Go swiftly and safely."

"With this, we shall adjourn. We will come together when we have further information. For now, the best we can offer is positive thoughts and pure light sent to Karia, Juna, and Dino on their quest and to Arbalest on his journey." Oracle Balstar stood, tapped his cane, and turned to leave.

Alistia grabbed my mom's hand and pulled her to follow. "Oracle!" she called after him.

"Yes, Alistia?" Oracle Balstar said, raising an eyebrow and turning to them.

"Thank you for keeping our secret for so long." Alistia and my mom stood side by side before Oracle Balstar.

"You two had a greater purpose than the Sunbow Prophecy, and you have served it well." Oracle Balstar turned and faded into the shadows of the garden.

The madams rushed toward my mom and Alistia. "Stay for a while! We have food and drink. Let us talk and laugh and just be together," Madam Shoran suggested.

Arbalest approached me from behind. "Come, Dino, and sit with the males. We will let the females visit."

And that is what we did. I would look over at my mom from time to time, and it was good to see her laughing and smiling. Again I was reminded that no matter the differences in appearance or culture, and no matter how old we get, sometimes we find true friendship in the most unlikely places.

Chapter 31
Arbalest's Journey

Arbalest Bendbow stepped onto the rocks just outside his maple tree home. The sun had yet to climb into the eastern sky. He stood staring into the darkness, listening carefully. "Ohanzee!" he called in a deep, low voice. Again he stood, quietly waiting and listening.

A muffled *SNAP!* broke through the darkness, and a large hawk landed before Arbalest. "EEEAK!" the high-pitched call announced Ohanzee's arrival.

"Ohanzee, it is good that you have arrived on time. We have a long journey ahead of us." Arbalest drew the reins over Ohanzee's curved, sharp beak. He shook his head and ruffled his feathers.

"Ah, be still, my friend. I know you do not enjoy being reined, but for this excursion, I need to be in control. I would never harness your freedom for any other reason. It is your strength and companionship that I am grateful for and require for this journey.

A *click* and grumbling sound erupted from deep in Ohanzee's gullet, and then he lowered his head, allowing Arbalest to slip the strap over his beak and pull the reins tight. He began to turn his body and lean in toward Arbalest, allowing him to climb onto his strong back. Once Arbalest mounted, Ohanzee gave his strong wings a mighty flap and ascended effortlessly into the air. They flew among the treetops that followed the tranquil boundaries of Traegonia. With a snap of the reins and another strong flap of Ohanzee's wings, they flew off in a westward direction in a silent farewell. Ohanzee flew, climbing higher and higher into the air. The ground became a distant memory. Ohanzee climbed higher still. Suddenly they found themselves in a strong tailwind that pushed them effortlessly on their way.

Arbalest checked the map given to him by Bayalthazar and familiarized himself with the plotted route, this the quickest and most direct route. "Nice job, Ohanzee!" Arbalest exclaimed as he felt the wind push them along on their path.

Chapter 32
Fire!

Morning came, and Karia and Juna still had not returned. I was really getting worried now. I got out of bed and walked to the window. I pulled back the curtains and looked out. The dew on the grass glistened in the early morning sun. I strained my eyes, trying to see into the forest. I was hoping I might be able to see them returning, but they didn't emerge from the forest.

A knock on my door drew my attention away from the window. "Are you awake?" my mom's voice whispered through the slightly open door.

"Yeah," I answered. "They are not back yet," I told her.

"I am sure they are alright. Maybe they have decided to stay with their kind a while longer?" she consoled.

"Yeah, maybe. I just worry, that's all," I said.

"Remember your own words from last night and practice what you preach." She smiled. "Come and have some breakfast. You'll feel better." She turned and waved for me to follow.

As we entered the kitchen, the phone rang, and Aunt Carol answered it. "It's for you, Dino." She smiled, holding out the phone to me.

"Are they back yet?" the voice on the other end questioned.

"No, not yet," I answered.

"Jade and I will be down with the horses in about an hour. We can go out for a ride and see if we can find them, alright?" Autumn said, seeming to have a plan.

"Okay. See you then." I hung up, ate breakfast, and told my mom I would be out for the afternoon.

A little while later, Autumn and Jade came up the drive on Wind and Junebug with Rory trailing behind.

"Autumn and Jade are here. I'm going out!" I yelled as I walked quickly to the front door.

"Be careful and don't be gone too late," my mom said, looking out from the kitchen doorway.

I walked toward the girls. Jade was leaning forward on Junebug. "I see you got a new backpack," she said. "What's in it?" Jade said in a teasing way.

"Food, what else would I have in it." I responded sarcastically, to her teasing.

"Well, alrighty then. We brought food, too, so we should be good," Jade said pulling back on Junebug's reins and turning her around.

I climbed up on Rory's back with ease this time. Autumn smiled at me, and we headed down the driveway. When we reached the road, Jade gave a firm kick to Junebug's sides, and she took off in a trot. Autumn and I followed. We rode like that until we reached the narrow path that would take us to the bat cave. The horses grunted and whinnied and slowed to a walk as they made their way along the path. Finally we reached the clearing where we had first picnicked—the one where Karia, Juna, and I had met Fletcher; it seemed so lonely without our little Traegon friends.

"Hey, Dino, are you okay?" Autumn asked.

Realizing I had zoned out, I looked at her oddly. "I was just thinking about them. When do you think they will come back?" I asked her.

"I wish I knew," she replied.

"Let's take that ride we were gonna take before Dino dropped Karia and Juna off the cliff," Jade joked.

Autumn and I both shot her a look.

"Oh, come on, you guys. I'm kidding. Lighten up. They'll be back soon. Let's just have some fun. It'll take our minds off things," Jade said.

Autumn's face relaxed and she turned to me and said, "She's right, Dino. We can't spend all our time worrying about nothing."

Jade steered Junebug toward the cliffside. I followed Jade, and Autumn fell in behind me. As I reached the spot where my backpack slipped, I took a deep breath.

"Don't try to steer her, Dino. She will follow me. And whatever you do, don't look down," Jade stated, turning to look me in the eye.

I looked Jade in the face and relaxed my reins. My eyes caught sight of the wide expanse of the landscape. It was beautiful with the trees, the mountains, and the huge sky. I could hear the hooves of the horses on the rocky ground and an occasional rock falling off the side. Finally we stepped off the precarious ledge onto more stable ground. The forest was quiet, and the only sounds were the breathing of the horses, the leaves blowing in the breeze, the birds, and a few other forest sounds.

Jade paused for a moment and snapped her reins, directing Junebug toward a grouping of rocks and trees. Jade led us onto another path that took us deeper into the forest.

"I hope you know where you are going," I said, only half-joking.

"Don't you like an adventure once in a while?" she scoffed.

I looked back at Autumn, and she just winked and smiled.

After a while, Autumn called from behind, "How about some lunch?"

"Alright. There's a place up ahead," Jade responded.

A few minutes later, the horses stepped out of the forest into a wide grassy clearing.

"Hold on! Yah!" Jade hollered, snapping her reins.

Junebug whinnied and took off running. Rory followed without any direction from me. Startled, I held on for dear life. We ran through the field.

Just as I was getting my rhythm, Jade stopped Junebug at a large pile of rocks. "This is a good place for a picnic, ya think?"

Rory and Wind slowed to a stop as Jade jumped off of Junebug.

"How about a little warning next time?" I requested.

"Sorry. I was just...adding to the adventure." Jade laughed. "I bet it got your blood pumping though."

"Among other things," I responded, climbing off of Rory.

Autumn laughed. "You don't need to change your pants, do ya?"

"No, I think I'm alright." I laughed too.

I dropped my backpack off my shoulders while Autumn pulled a blanket from her saddlebag and Jade unpacked more food. We laid the blanket next to the rocks and leaned against them while we ate.

"This is a neat place," I told them.

"There are a lot of really neat places on the mountain. You just need to know where to look," Autumn shared.

"Where do you want to go after lunch?" Jade asked.

Suddenly Autumn stood up, distracted. She stepped back away from the rock pile. Her smile dropped, and she looked puzzled and concerned.

"What are you looking at?" I asked her.

Jade jumped up and walked over by her. She, too, looked in the same direction. The look on her face was one of shock. "Fire!" she breathed.

I jumped up and looked too. Sure enough, there was black smoke rising from the treetops in the distance. "Maybe it's just a campfire," I offered.

"Remember what Dad told those teenagers? There is a no-burn order. No one should be burning anything out here right now," Autumn said stoically.

Jade quickly began packing up our lunch. Autumn looked at her, and then she grabbed the blanket, folded it, and shoved it into the saddlebag.

"What should we do?" I asked.

"Get on your horse and follow us." Jade climbed quickly onto Junebug and started heading in the direction of the smoke.

"Shouldn't we go back and get help?" I asked.

"We need to know where it is. It's hard to know how far away it is. It could be on another ridge, for all we know. There are other ways off the mountain. Just stay close," Autumn replied.

Jade snapped her reins, and the horses all trotted toward the direction of the rising smoke.

Chapter 33
Grimalkin

"How are we going to know what we are supposed to do next?" Juna asked as the three friends climbed out of the darkened cave. The sun seemed so bright; they all squinted, waiting for their eyes to adjust.

"We have not had a plan to this point. It seems that each time there is something we should know or do, it comes to us." Karia blinked a few times. "I will go to the forest this night to see if I can speak with Kamara. How long have we been gone?"

Fletch tilted back his head and opened his mouth slightly sniffing the air. "Two nights, I imagine," he answered.

"Dino must be terribly concerned," Karia said.

"He knew where we were going. I am sure he is fine. You will be back tonight," Fletch assured her, assessing the air again.

"What is it? What do you smell?" Juna questioned.

"I am not sure. It is very distant. Smells like...like trouble," he stated as he stared off.

"What do you mean by trouble?" Karia asked.

"If I knew exactly what it was, I would have been more precise. All I am aware of is that something is not right—something is off. Come, let's continue on." Fletch led them into the forest.

They walked for a long time. The cover of the trees and brush offered their eyes a break from the glaring sunlight. There was a sound in the distance that caught their attention, and they all stopped in their tracks.

"Shh!" Karia held out her hand in a gesture for them to not move. "Did you hear that?" she whispered.

Juna whispered back as he reached for his knife, "I heard something moving in the woods."

"I heard it as well," Fletch breathed, slowly sliding an arrow from the quiver slung over his shoulder.

They stood very, very still, and in the moments that followed, they heard nothing more. They continued on with Fletch in the lead, his bow in hand, and Juna bringing up the rear, walking forward then turning backwards, keeping watch for whatever might have made the sound. Karia walked between them both. They walked as quietly as they could, listening carefully. Suddenly they all stopped at the same time, turning and looking into the dense forest.

"I believe whatever it is, it is still following us. I can feel it. The sound stops when we stop. I cannot determine what direction it is coming from though," Karia said, looking from side to side.

The three friends stood back to back, looking off into all directions. They were silent and heard nothing more. Then there was a low growl in the distance.

"Did...did anyone else hear that?" Karia's voice trembled.

"Uh huh," Juna said, taking a defensive stance and pushing Karia in behind him.

"It is not as close as it wishes us to think," Fletch observed.

"Do you know what it is, Fletch?" Juna asked.

"By the sound of its growl, I believe it could be the Grimalkin," Fletch murmured.

"A what?" Karia demanded.

"A feline, a large, old, angry feline," Fletch related.

"A cat? How can you determine it is old, large, and angry just by hearing it growl?" Juna asked.

"Yes a cat, but no common field cat. All Traegons know of her. She is a black shadow cat, not like others. Traegons live peacefully with all creatures of the forest. We only take what we need, as do other creatures. But this Grimalkin is different. She will snatch anything out of the forest just because she can. She has taken Traegons too. She will kill and destroy and then move on. There is no way to reason with a selfish and powerful creature like that. She may be old—or at least she looks it—but she can move with the speed of an arrow. Her eyes are not very good, so I think if we split up, we might be safer."

"Split up?! Have you lost your wits?" Juna snapped.

"No, I am completely serious. She will become confused by the separation of our scents. She will not be able to chase all of us. Once we know who she chooses, the other two can follow. Does that not make more sense?"

"Yes, I understand. Juna, he is right, and he knows his home better than we. We must trust him," Karia urged.

"Alright, I'm in," Juna conceded.

"On my mark, run as quickly as you can in the direction you are facing. Try to remain hidden and unscathed," Fletch said. Then he took a deep breath and wailed, "NOW!"

They each ran in separate directions, followed by the sound of a heavy pounce, hitting the ground hard where they had just been standing. All of them heard it, but none looked back to see who it had chosen. Finally Fletch slowed, he jumped behind a tree, and breathed heavy. He did not hear anyone following him. Juna popped into the hollow of a large fallen tree and peered out, listening carefully. He, too, heard nothing. Juna and Fletch immediately began running back to the spot where they had started from.

Karia could hear the large padded feet running behind her. She darted through the brush, around trees, and over fallen logs. She could hear her own feet making many more steps than the long strides of the Grimalkin behind her, and she knew she had to come up with a plan because she would tire long before the Grimalkin. Ahead she could see a large old tree with vines winding all the way up the trunk. She ran toward it, grabbed the low vines, and scrambled up the tree as fast as she could, circling around to the backside, out of sight. Halfway up, she paused and peeked from behind the large trunk to see if the Grimalkin was coming. She held silently to the tree when she heard a scratching sound below her. She leaned back and looked down. The old Grimalkin may not have been able to see very well, but she still could follow a scent, and she knew Karia was in that tree. She extended her long, curved claws and dug them deep into the bark of the tree. Karia could hear the Grimalkin's low, deep breathing. Karia quickly began to climb further into the tree, but the cat began to climb as well. Karia could hear her claws tearing through the vines and ripping at the bark, whining and growling all the way. Karia found a narrow branch and began to move out on to it. *She is much too heavy to get out here*, Karia thought, walking slowly on the branch and looking back to see the Grimalkin's progress.

When she turned back, she was startled to see another creature sharing the branch with her. Karia screamed, as did the baby bear. The branch began to creak and crack, and then it snapped, sending the two of them tumbling out of the tree toward the ground. Each of them hit several branches on the way down, slowing their fall. The baby bear landed first with a *thud*. The young bear broke Karia's fall and went running, terrified, into the forest.

Karia quickly got to her feet. She turned to run and found herself face to face with the Grimalkin. Her large yellow teeth were the first thing Karia saw, and the stench from her putrid breath almost made Karia gag. Her eyes were milky white, there were patches of fur missing from her body, and a large scar extended from her torn ear to her jaw. She looked as if she had been in more than a few fights that she didn't win. Karia was still and quiet when she realized that the Grimalkin could not see her. Still, with its keen sense of smell, the big cat knew Karia was close. The Grimalkin opened her large, toothy mouth and lunged forward at Karia. Karia tucked and rolled off to the side and under a low bush. She scrambled to get out from under the bush before the cat realized where she had gone. As Karia started running, the Grimalkin reached out its large paw, extended its claws, and caught

Karia by her dress. Karia jumped up and grabbed a low branch. Her dress tore, releasing her from the claws of the Grimalkin. She swung herself around the branch, and as the Grimalkin rose up in a mighty roar, Karia came around and kicked the angry creature hard on the top of its nose. The Grimalkin let out a loud yowl and fell forward to the ground. She rubbed her nose in the dirt and brushed it with her paws. Karia flipped off the branch and landed several feet from the pained cat. Her heart ached for the old beast, but her fear drove her to flee further into the forest.

Fletch and Juna had made their way back to where they had all run from. They followed in the direction Karia had gone. They ran, Juna with his knife in hand and Fletch with his bow at the ready. They listened and ran further. They stopped when they heard a growling whine off in the distance. They looked at each other with fear in their eyes and began to run in the direction of the noise. They came up from behind the Grimalkin; she was still rubbing her nose. From behind her, neither Juna nor Fletch could see what she was doing. To them, it looked as if she was chewing on something, and they thought it was Karia. Juna took a running leap and landed on the back of the large cat. Fletch did a flying somersault and landed on the head of the Grimalkin, pinning her to the ground. Juna raised his knife, ready to plunge it deep into the Grimalkin's back, while Fletch had his arrow poised to go in through the back of cat's head.

Karia couldn't let them do it. She jumped from a nearby tree and screamed, "STOP! Don't hurt her!"

Juna and Fletch were startled to hear Karia's voice, as they were sure the cat was making lunch of her.

"She is old and hungry. She is alone and hunts for what is small and weak. Look at her! Look at how thin she is. The fear she instills is her only defense. Release her and let her live." Karia walked toward the large Grimalkin. The cat blinked her milky white eyes and growled deep in her throat. Karia placed her hand between the ears of the cat and stroked her. Juna and Fletch stood their ground, unsure if the cat

Dino C. Crisanti

Sight Restored

would understand Karia's kind intent. Karia closed her eyes and felt warmth flow from the palms of her hands. It felt strange, tingly. A slow groan, followed by a sigh, came from the Grimalkin as she also closed her eyes. In Karia's mind she thought these words: *Great creature, you deserve peace, health, and life. You deserve a second chance. May your sight return to you so that you may care for yourself. With this gift, you will one day help another. You will always be able to call me a friend.* Karia opened her eyes.

Fletch and Juna were staring at her in disbelief. "Step down," she directed them. They looked at each other, unsure of how they felt about what Karia was asking of them. Karia nodded an assurance. Juna jumped to the ground, still with his knife in hand. Fletch followed, and Karia stepped back.

The large cougar opened her eyes slowly and looked at Karia. To Karia's surprise, her eyes were no longer milky white. They were now crystal blue with a pitch-black pupil. The cougar blinked in an attempt to focus, let out a low growl, shook her head, and looked into Karia's eyes. These words flowed into Karia's thoughts. "The gift you have given me seems undeserved. I have taken what was not mine and more than I needed. I would have taken your life, too, if I had caught you. You had the chance to leave or to let the others destroy me to save you, but you chose a different path—one of kindness and compassion. For this, I am eternally grateful. Never in my miserable life have I been shown compassion, only distain and hatred. What may I give to you in return for this gift you have granted me, other than your freedom, of course?"

Karia stared, filled with compassion, at the awesome creature lying before her. She tried to reconcile for herself if she had truly given the Grimalkin back her sight. She looked at her hands and then looked at Juna and Fletcher. They were still standing off in the distance, ready to defend her at moment's notice. She realized that they had not heard what the Grimalkin had told her. "Put away your weapons," she directed. "She will cause us no harm."

"What are you saying? How can you know this?" Fletcher cried.

Juna remembered that Karia had been able to speak to and understand the frog and other animals. He knew she was telling the truth. "She can understand them," Juna told Fletch as he placed his knife in its sheath.

"She has granted us our freedom," Karia explained.

"*Our* freedom? It is us who have given her freedom. She has caused fear to so many for so long. Why should she be spared?" Fletch let his fear turn to anger.

"Fletcher P. Webenaki, you who cares for so many other creatures, should understand. It has been the fear of her darkness and the pain of her past that have formed her into the creature she had become. Come around her and see for yourself," Karia invited.

Fletch and Juna walked cautiously around to the head of the cougar, where Karia stood and looked at her face. They, too, saw what Karia saw: a beautiful and noble creature whose eyes were now an incredible ice blue.

Fletch looked at Karia. "What have you done? How did you do this?" he asked in amazement.

"I myself am not sure how or why I was able to. All I know is that it was meant to happen. There is a purpose for her sight to return to her," Karia answered.

The cougar made a sound that resembled a purr. "What can I give to you?" she asked Karia once more.

"There is nothing now. One day, though, you will be asked to give, maybe to me or maybe to another. You will have to recognize the request, so be aware in your living. I am grateful for the honor of knowing you and the lessons I have discovered because of you. In a way, that is one gift you have already given," Karia told her.

The Grimalkin stood and looked down upon the three Traegons. "I will be always aware. Thank you."

Karia, Juna, and Fletch looked up at the enormous creature as she towered over them. They looked at her huge paws. "Until we meet again." Karia bowed her head.

The Grimalkin took a step back and gracefully bounded into the forest.

When Karia looked back, Juna and Fletch were staring in amazement. "Well, I suppose we should continue on, if we wish to be back by nightfall," she said. "Which way, Fletch?"

Fletch looked around and started back on their path toward home.

Chapter 34
Lost and Found

I could smell the smoke as we trotted down the overgrown path. I remained quiet, but could feel the nervousness welling up in the pit of my stomach. Autumn pulled Wind up alongside Jade and Junebug, and they slowed to a stop.

"What's going on? Why did we stop?" I asked.

"Listen! We must be getting close," Jade whispered loudly.

We all sat quietly. We could hear the sound of crackling in the distance. Autumn and Jade looked at each other, and then Jade snapped her reins again, guiding Junebug further down the path. The path ended abruptly, but Jade continued into the forest through the dense trees.

"Hey, there isn't a path. Where are we going?" I questioned them.

"We just need to take a closer look. Autumn has a cell phone in her saddlebag for emergencies. As soon as we locate the fire, we can call for help," Jade replied.

The low branches made all of us have to duck down close to the horses' necks. The trees pressed tight as the horses followed one after the other. Rory walked between two trees that were so close that for a moment, my leg was uncomfortably wedged between Rory's heavy body and the rough bark. I could feel a painful scrape on my leg under my jeans. I was busy watching for the branches that seemed to reach down and grab at my hair and clothing when Jade and Autumn stopped. I looked up and through the trees and saw an orange glow. "Okay, now will you call for help?" I asked.

Autumn reached down and opened her saddlebag. She shoved her hand in deep and felt around. She finally pulled out a small cell phone. She opened it and dialed. "Dad, it's me," she spoke into the phone.

I could hear the muffled voice of Mr. Linder as she pulled it away from her ear. "Where are you? There's a fire. You need to get home now!" he demanded.

"I know, Dad. I was just calling to tell you. It is up at the top of Hadderly Ridge. We can't be sure how big it is," Autumn shared.

"Leave the firefighting to the firefighters. Just get your butts off that mountain and get home. Where are you now?" he asked.

"We're on the west side of Hadderly Ridge. We'll turn back now," Autumn told him.

"Move fast. The wind is picking up and could change direction at any time. Please just get out of there," he pleaded.

"Where are you, Dad?" Autumn asked.

"I am leaving the office and heading out to that vicinity now. The smoke-jumping team has just taken off. Call me when you get out of the area. Go NOW!" he said very seriously.

Autumn closed her phone and slid it into her back pocket. "Okay, Jade, lead us out."

Jade turned Junebug around, and we headed back through the dense trees.

"Shouldn't we be at the path by now?" Autumn questioned Jade after we had been riding for a while.

"I think it should be right up through here." Jade rounded a grouping of pine trees and stopped.

"What's wrong?" I asked, noticing the concerned look on her face.

"I think I must have made a wrong turn. The trail should be right here." Jade sounded puzzled.

Autumn looked around, Jade looked around, and then I looked around. I began to feel my nervousness turn to panic. I looked at the two of them, trying not to let on how scared I was.

Finally, Autumn spoke. "Let me see if I can get us out of here. I know Deer Path Road comes up the north side of the ridge. I think if we go this way, we should run right into it. Then we can follow it down."

Autumn pulled on Wind's reins and changed directions. Jade followed, and so did I. It seemed as if we rode for a long time when Wind stopped suddenly.

"What is it, Wind?" Autumn rubbed the side of his wide neck. Wind let out a high-pitched neigh and stomped his hooves on the ground. This unnerved Junebug and Rory, not to mention me. Several birds flew through the trees above our heads, and then there were the sounds of other animals scurrying past us.

"Well, I can tell you one thing," I said.

"What's that?" Jade asked.

"I don't think we should go that way." I pointed in the direction the animals were coming from.

Autumn gave an uncomfortable smirk, turned Wind, and started in the direction the animals were headed. She walked a few steps, and then Autumn gave Wind a good kick and we all took off trotting. We continued for quite a while when we stumbled on a small campsite.

"Is anyone here?" Jade called out.

No one answered.

"Maybe they left," I suggested.

"Yeah, maybe," Autumn replied, as she jumped down from her horse.

"What are you doing?" I hollered. "We're supposed to get out of here."

"Maybe they know the way out. Maybe they don't even know there's a fire coming. We have to warn them if they're still here." Autumn began to walk toward the campsite, and Jade jumped down too. "Hello? Is there anyone here?" Autumn called.

Silence.

"Hello?"

"Everything is still here. They have to be close by," Jade noticed.

Just then two hikers climbed up from the side of a hill. The man was in his early twenties, wearing a white tank top and tan shorts. He had shoulder-length curly brown hair. "Hey, you guys, who are you?" he said in a carefree tone. The woman he was with had long, straight blonde hair that was pulled back into a ponytail. She was slender and wore faded blue jeans and a gray t-shirt. They walked over to their campsite and dropped soft-sided jugs of water onto the ground.

"Hi. I'm Autumn, and this is my sister Jade and our friend Dino," Autumn introduced.

"Well hey, Autumn, Jade, and Dino. I'm Owen, and this is my friend Sam, short for Samantha." As he introduced the two of them, his demeanor was very kind and laidback, so I was sure they weren't aware there was a fire coming.

"We stopped because there is a fire on Hadderly Ridge. We ran across your campsite on our way off the mountain. You should pack up and get out of here too," Autumn told them.

"Really? A fire?" Sam repeated, looking to Owen.

"Really!" Jade repeated.

"We better pack up and hit the road then. How far away is it?" Owen asked.

Autumn looked back over her shoulder. "Close enough. Do you guys have a car, or did you hike all the way in?"

"Our van is about a mile and a half that way." He pointed. "Why? Are you guys lost or something?"

"You're gonna want to get off the mountain soon. The firefighters are coming, but they will go to the fire first. We're on our way out now. We did get turned around a little. If you could point us in the right direction, we would appreciate it," Autumn said.

"Where is the fire now? Do you know which way it is coming from?" Sam asked, looking around nervously.

Autumn and Jade looked up and noticed smoke in the distance. "There! See it?" Jade pointed.

"Come on, Owen. We had better get this packed up and get outta here," Sam insisted.

"If you head in that direction, you will run into a wide path. Turn right on the path, keep going, and you will run into the mountain road. That will take you out. You're gonna be going for a while, so don't worry. Just keep going. You'll find it."

"Thanks. Do you need any help packing up your stuff?" Jade offered.

"No, you guys go on and get off the mountain. We'll be fine. It shouldn't take us long. Thanks for the heads-up though. We really appreciate you stopping to let us know."

"You're welcome. Stay safe," Jade said as she and Autumn turned to walk back to me and the horses. They mounted their horses, and Jade led the way in the direction Owen told them to go.

Chapter 35
Two-Headed Beast

"I smell something!" Karia said, sniffing the air.

"What is it?" Juna questioned.

"I smell it too," Fletch added. "I have smelled this before." He looked at Karia with a look of concern. "Do you recognize it, Karia?"

Karia looked at Fletch, closed her eyes, and sniffed again at the air. In her mind, she was suddenly brought back to her waking vision. She could see the orange glow in the distance and hear the crackling of the embers. Her eyes popped open wide. "FIRE!" she blurted. "It is coming! It is happening...NOW! I have not had a chance to meet with Kamara, so I don't know what we are supposed to do." Panic shook her voice.

Juna stepped in front of Karia and grabbed her shoulders. "Look at me, Karia. I don't know if this is the time or not. All I know is that we need to head out of the forest and make our way back to Dino. He will know what to do."

"Yes, you're right. We need to get back to Dino," Karia agreed, exhaling deeply and trying to calm down. "Fletch, do you know the way?"

"Does Fletcher P. Webenaki know the way? But of course I do! Follow me," he directed.

They moved quickly through the forest, not saying a word. They just walked, listened, and stayed aware. Finally Fletch led them out of the cover of trees into a small clearing. Traegons don't usually go out in the open, but Fletch had a plan. He brought them to a huge rock formation that jutted upward. When they reached it, they stood at the base looking up to the steep, towering growth on the land. "Stay here," he commanded. "I'll be right back." And then he began to climb the side of the rocks.

Karia and Juna watched, wondering what he was doing. "Where are you going?" Karia asked.

"I am going up to see the progression and location of the fire. We must be sure we are not heading straight into it!" he hollered back over his shoulder.

Fletch grunted as he continued. When he finally reached the top, he pulled himself the remainder of the way up onto the flat plateau. He stood and glared at the sky. He looked in all directions until he finally saw a black stream of smoke rising out of the sky. It didn't stretch wide across the land, thankfully, indicating that the fire was not that huge—at least not yet. Fletch turned just in time to see a large bird flying in the distance. He squinted and then pulled a small scoping glass from the pouch on his belt. As he gazed through the scope, he focused on the dark shadow in the sky.

"How far is the fire?" Karia yelled from the base of the rock growth.

Fletch lowered his glass and looked down. "It's a bit hard to tell, but I do know we are heading away from it, which is what I wanted to be sure of!" he shouted back at her. Just as he returned his eyes to the sky, the large bird that was a silhouette in the distance only moments ago was now on top of him. "Hey!" Fletch howled as he threw himself to the ground and then rolled over as the bird swooped past.

"What was that?" Juna hollered, watching the large shadow pass over.

"Fletch, get down from there. It's coming back!" Karia noticed.

Fletch didn't have time to ready his rope, and as he went to jump, unsure of his safety, he was grabbed from behind. "Release me!" he screamed, kicking his feet. He felt himself being pulled further onto the flat of the rocks away from the edge. Fletch struggled to reach his bow and arrows. Suddenly, he was released. He dropped to his knees and scrambled back in a hurry, turning to look up in the sky behind him. The sunlight beamed from behind the head of a great bird, and he had to squint to get a better view of the creature. The head turned from one to two, and Fletch gasped, for he had never seen anything with two heads before. He grabbed his bow, notched an arrow, and readied it, aiming at the heart of the two-headed beast. At that moment, the heads together blocked the sun so Fletch could finally see what it was that stood before him. One of the heads was that of a magnificent golden hawk. When his eyes focused on the second head, what he saw was not another hawk head, but a strong, square-jawed Traegon. Slack jawed with confusion, Fletch forgot he was still holding his readied bow. He let loose the shot, and the arrow stuck deep into the ground, nearly catching his foot.

With the slightest of grins, Arbalest raised one eyebrow.

Snapped out of his daze by the sound, Fletch quickly bent down and snatched the arrow from the ground. Turning red with embarrassment he notched it once again into his bow and then focused his attention back on the newcomer.

"Who are you?" Fletch asked in a strong and protective tone.

"Where did you plan to go if you jumped off the side of this rock?" Arbalest asked calmly.

Fletch looked back toward the edge. "I do not know. I was just trying to get down before I was knocked down. Who are you?" Fletch asked again, lowering his bow slightly.

"I am Arbalest Bendbow, and I have come a long way to find some young Traegons," he explained.

"What are you going to do with these young Traegons?" Fletch asked.

"I am not looking for just *any* young Traegons," said Arbalest, stifling a laugh. "I am looking for two very specific younglings. Their names are Karia and Juna. Have you seen them?"

Dino C. Crisanti

Arbalest and Ohanzee

Fletch's eyes widened. "Hmm. I *may* know of them. What do you want with them?" Fletch stood up taking a protective stance, and raising his bow once again.

"I do not wish to bring harm to them, my friend. Rather, I have come to help them," Arbalest replied. "And may I have your name?"

"My name is Fletcher P. Webenaki," he said proudly. Fletch, stepped cautiously back toward the edge of the rock, his bow still at the ready. "Does the name Arbalest Bendbow sound familiar?" Fletch yelled down.

Karia and Juna looked at each other, shocked to hear that name. "Yes! Why?" Karia called back.

The hawk screeched once, took several steps back, and flapped his large wings. Then the bird snatched Fletch by the back of his shirt and carried him down to the ground where Karia and Juna stood waiting. It deposited Fletch in a crumbled heap. With an effortless leap, Arbalest dismounted the back of Ohanzee.

"Arbalest!" Karia exclaimed excitedly as she ran to him. "What are you doing here?" She was surprised at how happy she was to see him.

"I have been sent by the council. You both seem well," he observed, looking them over.

"We are fine, but..."

"But what, Karia?"

"Are Mim and Sire Argus angry?" she asked timidly.

"I would not say angry as much as concerned." He paused. "Well, to be honest, Sire Argus is more angry than concerned. They would have preferred you to stay in Traegonia, but they understand. Where are you heading to?" Arbalest asked.

"We are making our way back to the home of Dino's aunt and uncle," Karia answered.

"Ohanzee, please summon the assistance of your kind to carry these young ones," Arbalest requested of his trusted feathered companion.

Ohanzee let out a loud, long screech, followed by several short, high-pitched calls and something that resembled the gurgling of a hungry belly. Then he just sat quietly. We all waited attentively to see if anything would happen. Moments later, a large shadow followed by another and one more darkened the ground over and around them. They circled above and then whooshed in for a landing. Standing before them were three very different birds: a hawk; an eagle; and something only Fletch had seen before—a bird Karia, Juna, and Arbalest had never laid eyes on.

"What is that large one?" Juna asked the group in a whisper, pointing to the biggest of the four.

The four birds were cawing and grumbling as they seemed to be getting acquainted.

"I have not seen such a bird in all my days. He is a bit of an odd sort, isn't he?" Arbalest replied. "He somewhat resembles the turkey vulture back home."

"It looks a bit like a turkey, would you say?" Karia added.

"He is not anything like a turkey," Fletch snapped, shooting Karia an icy glare. "He is a great soul, a kind heart, and one of very few. He is Condor." Fletch stepped forward toward the four birds that were still carrying on their conversation in clucks, chirps, and squawks. They all stopped and looked down at Fletch, almost as if he was intruding. "My friend, it is very good to see you. It has been a long time," Fletch spoke.

Condor stepped between the other birds and moved toward Fletch. He towered over Fletch, and cast a darkened shadow over Fletcher when he approached. When he spoke all of the Traegons were able to understand. "You, young Traegon," Condor said, cocking his head back and forth with a jerk, "we met once before. If my memory serves me, I saved you then too," he scowled.

"Yes, great one, and it was my fortune and honor to have met you on that day and on this day as well," Fletch said, in awe of the strong, majestic creature.

Arbalest stepped up. "We would be very obliged if you would aid us in our travels."

"Climb on, and we will take you where you need to go," Condor growled.

Fletch immediately stepped up to Condor, and the large bird crouched so he could climb on. The eagle, who was the next largest of the birds, stepped up to Juna and crouched down. Juna being a bit nervous about his first flight looked back at Karia, who nodded for him to go ahead. Karia turned and the smaller hawk stepped to her side, almost bumping right into her. The hawk bowed her head and crouched down. Karia reached out, gently grabbed onto her neck, and pulled herself into position on the hawk's back. She looked around and saw Arbalest, Juna, and Fletch all mounted upon the others, ready for flight. It was the very first time Karia had flown on the back of a bird, and although she had seen Sire Argus do it many times before, she felt slight trepidation as she sat upon the back of the beautiful creature.

"Show us the way, Fletcher!" Arbalest called out.

Condor stepped forward, opened his mighty wings, and with only one great flap took to the air. The others followed one by one. Juna held tight as everything on the ground grew smaller and smaller. The wind rushed past his ears, and his stomach flipped and flopped like a freshly caught fish. He started to think he much preferred his feet planted firmly on the ground.

Karia was filled with a sense of admiration as the hawk and the others ascended skyward. When they finally climbed above the tallest of the trees, Karia looked down at the beautiful mountains below. The spires of the evergreens seemed to reach to the sky. The other trees crowded together into one green clump, as though there was no separation between them. She took a long, deep breath and closed her eyes as she felt the wind blow silently in her face. It was a feeling she wished she could hold onto forever. Opening her eyes once again, she gazed across the jagged mountains and plush green treetops. In the distance she noticed a dark, ominous slash streaming into the sky from the ground below. She squinted to try and make out what it was.

"What is it Karia? What do you see?" Juna asked, flying an eagle's wing below her.

Dino C. Crisanti

Traegons Take Flight

"I cannot be sure," Karia responded. "Look over there." She pointed for Juna to look. "Do you see that dark...." She hesitated and then finally allowed herself to say what she didn't want to say aloud. Juna looked, too, and at the same time they yelled, "SMOKE!"

"Where? Where do you see smoke?" Fletch asked, circling back to see from Karia's vantage point.

"Over there!" she pointed.

"We must go there and investigate the source," Fletch demanded.

"We should go and find Dino first. He will know what to do," Karia justified.

They both looked to Juna to see who he might agree with. "Do not look to me," he said. "I am merely a companion."

They all then looked to Arbalest. Remembering what the council had stated prior to his departure, he felt uneasy about giving any guidance. "It might be best to seek out the boy first," he conceded.

"Well, then let us be swift about it," Fletch remarked. Pulling gently on the cowl feathers of Condor, he guided the bird into the direction of Dino's aunt and uncle's place.

The other great birds turned and gracefully glided into line and followed.

They arrived at Dino's aunt and uncle's house, circled around to the back of the house, and landed under cover of the nearby forest.

"Wait here!" Karia demanded as she jumped to the ground.

"I am coming with you, Karia," Juna insisted.

Fletch moved to the edge of the tree line and peered out, watching Karia and Juna make their way to the house.

Karia picked up a small stone and threw it toward Dino's window. She waited a few moments, as Juna kept watch. When no one came to the window, she picked up another stone and threw it, but there was still no response. "Juna, he is not answering. He must not be in his room," Karia whispered loudly.

Suddenly they heard the back door slam.

"Someone is coming!" Juna exclaimed. Karia and Juna darted for a bush that stood halfway between the house and the edge of the woods.

They simultaneously slid under it, but not before Dino's mom noticed the movement. She looked back over her shoulder and then walked quickly toward the side of the house. "Karia! Juna! Don't run! I need to talk to you." Anna walked to the bush and ducked in behind, out of sight.

Karia and Juna crawled out from under the bush. "Where is Dino?" Karia and Anna asked in unison.

"Have you seen him?" Anna spouted again at the same exact time.

They all stopped and stared at each other.

"He's...he's not here?" Karia asked right as Anna stated the same thing. "I think there is a fire!" Karia spouted, and again Anna echoed her.

"Stop!" Juna interjected. "I can only understand you both because you are saying the same thing at the same time. Now, Dino's mom, tell us what you know."

Anna took a breath and looked around. "Dino went out with Autumn and Jade this morning. Their father called and told us there is a fire on the mountain at Hadderly Ridge. Once he found out the kids weren't here, he said he would go look for them. They haven't returned, and we're getting worried."

"We saw the smoke. We could not determine the location of the fire, and we decided to come and get Dino before we investigated further," Karia stated. "We have help. We will find them. Do not worry, Dino's mom."

"All I know right now is that the smokejumpers are headed to the ridge. We have no idea just how far it has spread or in which direction it is traveling. Please be careful," Anna said, looking deep into Karia's eyes the way her mim would have if she were there. Anna then stood, brushed off her jeans, and glanced around. She looked down at Karia and Juna and headed back toward the house.

Karia and Juna looked at each other, peered around the bush, and darted toward the forest edge.

"What have you found out?" Fletch said hurriedly.

"They are not here," Karia whispered. "Autumn and Jade are with him. We need to find them. Dino's mim is worried." Karia paused. "They may be in danger."

"The girls are familiar with the mountain and the forest, but they could easily get turned around in a situation such as this," Fletch interjected. "Let us go now. There is no time to waste."

Chapter 36
Round Up

The forest was thick, and the trees created a dense ceiling that blocked our view of the sky. I couldn't tell if we were going in the right direction, and the girls were being so quiet I didn't want to ask. "I don't smell the smoke anymore," I started.

There was no response.

"Hey guys, is there something you're not telling me?"

The horses in front of me stopped. Jade turned and looked at Autumn and then at me. "I think we're lost," she revealed, biting her bottom lip. "We have been riding for a long time, and I still haven't seen the path Owen told us about. I'm sorry, you guys. I...I really did think I could get us out of here. I thought I knew where I was going."

"It's alright. Don't worry, Jade. We'll find our way out. Let me lead for a while," Autumn said, pulling Wind to the front.

"What will the Traegons do? Shouldn't we warn them?" I asked, turning my thoughts to Karia and Juna.

The girls both looked back at me, and Jade said, "I think right now we need to help ourselves before we can help them,"

Autumn led us into a clearing. Finally, out of the cover of the forest, we could see the sky. We could also see the heavy black smoke trailing through the sky. Autumn jumped off of Wind. "We need a plan guys," she said as she walked her horse over near a pile of rocks.

Jade and I jumped off our horses and followed.

"Okay, the smoke looks like it is coming from that direction," Autumn said, looking into the sky.

"Yeah, but watch the way the wind is blowing the smoke. It will also push the fire that way," Jade observed.

"Well, then we should go that way," I said, pointing in the only direction left.

We were all looking up at the sky when Rory let out a wild neigh and stood up on her hind legs. She began backing up, which spooked Wind and Junebug. The three of them made a huge commotion before taking off into the forest.

"Wait! Stop! Come back!" Autumn cried.

"What happened? Why did they run off?" I asked, completely confused.

"Shh! Don't move a muscle," Jade said quietly and slowly, staring at the rocks in front of us. There, at the base of a few smaller rocks, she could see the glistening coppery coils of an angry snake. Its head raised, and its black beady eyes watched our every move, just looking for a reason to strike.

I heard the rattle before I looked down and thought to myself, *You have got to be kidding me! First there's a fire, then our horses take off, and now this?* Then I finished my thought quietly but out loud. "Traegons, we could use a little help here!"

"I think you'll have to say it a little louder than that," Jade said.

Suddenly the snake hissed and slithered forward a little.

"Or maybe not," she said, her eyes growing wide with horror.

"Guys, were gonna need to move soon, or this snake is gonna take one of us out," Autumn said in a heavy whisper.

At that very moment, a huge bird landed on the top of the rocks, distracting the snake. Autumn grabbed both me and Jade and pulled us out of striking distance right in the nick of time. The giant bird spread out his expansive wings, stretched his featherless neck, and let out a deep, loud, guttural growl—a sound I didn't even know birds could make. The snake hissed his disapproval and slid past the rocks toward a pile of dead branches and into the forest. Autumn, Jade, and I stared intimidated by the huge bird, and wondering if we were its new target. Above we noticed several more shadows heading in our direction.

"Let's get out of here!" I yelled, pulling on Autumn's and Jade's arms.

"Wait!" Autumn broke free of my grip. "Those birds do not eat people, at least not live ones. And they never get close like this. Just stay very still, you two, and don't startle him."

"What is that thing?" Jade asked in a muffled whisper.

"I think it's a condor," Autumn answered.

"Really!" Jade said in amazement.

We all paused and stood very still. The others landed on the rocks and ground on either side of the largest bird.

"Dino!" a small familiar voice called. Karia appeared next to one of the smaller birds, and then Juna leapt off of the eagle.

Fletch, in true Fletcher P. Webenaki fashion, made a grand entrance, yelling "Haw!" as he directed Condor to the ground. With what seemed more like a big jump, Condor opened his wings, casting the ground in deep shadow as he gracefully landed.

"Fletch! We have been crazy worried about you!" Autumn ran toward him. As she did, Condor opened his broad wings again, startling her. She stopped and stepped back timidly, turning slightly to her left, and then she noticed Arbalest Bendbow standing beside a large hawk. She squinted and questioned, "Fletch?"

Fletch jumped from Condor's back and landed on the ground beside Arbalest. "No, silly! Here I am!"

Autumn looked confused as she stared at what looked to her like a grown-up Fletch.

"Arbalest?" I questioned as I, too, stepped forward.

"Yes, young Dino. It is I, Arbalest Bendbow," the older he-Traegon confirmed.

"What are you doing here?" I asked.

"I have been sent by the council to assist where I am needed and to ensure all of you get in as little trouble as possible."

"So far, you guys have perfect timing. We could definitely use your help. We got lost trying to get away from the fire, and then a snake scared off our horses. Now, not only are we lost, but our ride is gone too," I explained.

"We'll help you get home," Karia said.

There was a rustle in the brush at the edge of the tree line that caught Arbalest's attention. "Shh! Quiet! There is something moving over there!"

Everyone fell silent, and Arbalest and Fletch reached for their bows as Juna unsheathed his knife.

Suddenly Ige burst forth from the edge of the woods. "Fetch!" he hollered, running toward the group. The birds hopped and squawked, unnerved by the intrusion.

Slowly Zuri emerged behind him. "Ige! Slow down and come back here," she called after him.

Ige ran over and threw his arms around Fletch's waist.

"What are you doing here?" Fletch asked Zuri as she approached.

"We are headed to the Rain Shadow to take shelter. There is great danger coming!" she replied.

"Yes, there's a fire! It is spreading fast. We have to get off the mountain," Jade blurted.

"What about the rest of the Traegons? Shouldn't we help them get to safety?" Autumn added.

"They are all being warned by the Traegonian council. They are being told to take cover underground or to get to the Rain Shadow to take refuge within the caves of Traegonia. Being underground is the safest place for Traegons until the flames subside. Ige and I are going to the cave to meet Bidziil, my mate. He has been on a hunting expedition. Oracle Qendrim has called him and the other hunters back to assist in bringing the community to safety." Zuri, shared. "It is not safe here for any of us. We must keep moving."

"I will take flight and scout our path to safety. Fletch, you come with me. Your knowledge of the area will quicken our pace. The rest of you stay here, and we shall return straight away," Arbalest said.

Fletch was flattered and honored to be chosen to go with Arbalest.

"Juna, you keep watch over the others. The birds will remain here as well," Arbalest directed.

Arbalest and Fletch climbed onto their feathered steeds and took to the air. They circled around once and then disappeared beyond the tree line.

"We will fly toward the blaze to assess the size, threat, and distance. Once we are clear as to what exactly we are up against, we can chart out our escape route," Arbalest informed Fletch.

They flew toward the distant smoke. They stayed low to the treetops in order to get a clear view of the ground, always alert for others in trouble. A distant rumbling proved to be the smoke-jumping plane that had flown above a bit earlier. Fletch turned to see it flying into the smoke. Suddenly a large dark shadow caused Condor to take a quick sideways turn to the right. As they moved out of the way, Fletch saw something completely unfamiliar to him: a human woman floating in the sky carried by a large, oddly shaped canopy of what looked like fabric. Condor and Fletch both turned their heads at the exact moment the woman drifted downward. Their eyes met. The woman blinked hard and shook her head slightly. Fletcher winked at her and saluted her before directing Condor to turn and soar above her, out of sight.

Fletch caught sight of Arbalest and headed in that direction to catch up. Soon they were close enough to see the flames. They could hear the crackling sounds as the fire tore through the forest, gobbling up trees and sending small animals scurrying from their homes in horror. The fire looked to be containable, but it was in an area that was not very accessible to the humans. It would only be a matter of time before the relatively small fire would become completely out of hand. A strong wind gust hit them hard, pushing the strong birds and their riders skyward.

"The wind seems to be picking up!" Fletcher yelled.

"Though I am not from this land, I know this wind does not bode well for us. It will feed this fire and carry it farther and faster," Arbalest stated.

They both looked at each other as they heard a distant rumble that seemed to be getting closer. In the distance, they could see a large, dark plane moving in their direction.

"What sort of birds are these that fly in your skies?" Arbalest questioned.

"They are human made. They use them to move humans around, as well as to assist with putting out fires. A fire-putter-outer is what that one is. We had better change our course and get out of the way NOW!" Fletch hollered, turning Condor away from the path of the plane.

Arbalest followed suit, and the plane flew past them, dropped down, and released a red substance into the trees.

"Will that red mist that the metal bird spat stop the fire?" Arbalest asked as he watched intently.

"No, but it will help. There will be more of them, many more. We had better scout out our path and get back to our friends," Fletch suggested.

The two changed course and headed back to where they had begun. They flew in low, searching for roads as well as the runaway horses. Finally, a break in the treetops revealed a narrow forest road, larger than a path but not by much. They dropped into the trees so they could follow the road and determine how near the others were to it. Parts of the road lined a steep gully that cut deep into the mountain. The trees were dense and at times reclaimed the road, breaking apart the asphalt.

"Wait! I see something!" Fletch called to Arbalest. He turned Condor around and dropped even deeper into the forest, and Arbalest followed.

As they came closer, it was clear that what Fletcher had stumbled upon was a vehicle belonging to a human. It had tumbled off the road and rolled down the embankment. It was perched precariously in a crisscross of twisted and tangled trees, only two of which had any real girth to hold the weight. The front wheels were still spinning slowly.

Condor and Ohanzee landed the road nearby. Arbalest and Fletch dismounted and moved to the edge for a better look. Arbalest removed a rope from his belt and tied it off to a tree that grew beside the road. Fletch was impressed and did the same, and then the two lowered themselves down the side of the gully.

Fletch peered into the shattered window and called to Arbalest, "There is one human male inside! He is not moving!"

Arbalest secured himself and surveyed the vehicle. "It will hold for now, but not for long. We will need other humans to get him out. Climb in and see if you can determine if he has any life left in him."

Fletch swung himself over, caught his foot on the running board, and pulled himself onto the vehicle. As he climbed inside, the twisted metal creaked and groaned. Fletch pulled a rough-edged piece of mirror from a pouch on his hip. He carefully held it under the nose of the man and watched; the mirror steamed slightly. Fletch turned and made his way out of the truck. "He lives!" Fletch called out to Arbalest.

"Good! Then we must go for help." Arbalest tied his rope to the vehicle. "Tie off to the vehicle. It may not be much, but I believe anything will help." With the small Traegon ropes secured to the truck, Arbalest and Fletch climbed back up to the road where their trusty birds waited.

Arbalest and Fletcher flew low along the road under the cover of the trees. As they came around a curve in the road, Fletcher spotted something in the woods. "Whoa!" He called to Condor, who landed on the road. "Take me up there!" Fletch pointed to a large, sturdy branch in a tall tree, and Condor lifted up and landed on it. Fletch peered intently into the woods, and there in the distance he saw Wind, Junebug, and Rory, nonchalantly munching on some leaves.

Arbalest landed on the same branch.

"There!" Fletch pointed. "Those are Autumn's and Jade's horses. If we take them back, they can assist in the rescue of the human."

"Good thinking!" Arbalest commended. "Will you be able to get them to come with us?"

"Let's see…" Fletch climbed off Condor. He knew that if he approached atop the bird, the horses would get spooked and run off again. So, Fletch climbed down the tree and moved stealthily through the forest. Quietly, he climbed up the back of a rotted old tree. "It is I, Fletcher P. Webenaki!" Fletch said, more quietly than he had in the past.

The horses neighed and whinnied and moved back as if they would turn and run at any minute. It was Wind who first recognized Fletch. He shook his head and stomped the ground with his front hooves. Junebug and Rory calmed down and took another look. They, too, recognized Fletch.

"I know where the girls are. Come with us, horses. They need your help," Fletch coaxed. Fletch jumped onto Wind's back and grabbed the reins. He guided Wind out of the woods and back to the road as the other two followed.

Arbalest was waiting patiently on the back of Ohanzee, and Condor waited alongside.

"You will have to guide me from above," Fletch requested.

"Ohanzee and I will fly above the treetops. Ohanzee will call down to Condor, who will then guide you through the forest to the others," Arbalest directed as he and Ohanzee lifted through the trees.

Fletcher looked at Condor, and Condor nodded back at him to indicate that he understood, and then the bird lifted into the trees. Fletcher guided Wind along the road, awaiting direction. Suddenly Condor swooped down and growled his gravely call.

Fletch snapped the reins as best he could, and Wind began to trot with Junebug and Rory following close behind. From time to time, Fletch heard the high-pitched calls from Ohanzee to Condor, who continued to lead them on. Finally, Condor turned off the road and onto a narrow dirt path that appeared to not have been traveled much and definitely not recently. Fletch slowed the horses so they could carefully navigate the rocks and branches that lay as obstacles in the path. Eventually they emerged into the clearing where Karia, Juna, Zuri, Ige, Dino, Jade, and Autumn were waiting. When they saw Fletch on the back of Wind, they all jumped to their feet and cheered.

Autumn ran up to Wind and threw her arms around the horse's neck. "Where did you find them?" she asked.

Arbalest on Ohanzee and Condor landed in the clearing. "There will be time for happy reunions later, my friends," Arbalest interrupted. "There has been an accident. There is a man human in a vehicle that has fallen off the road. He lives, but for how long I cannot be sure,"

Autumn stepped forward and looked into Arbalest's eyes. "What kind of vehicle?" she asked slowly.

"It was difficult to see, as it was bottom side up. I believe it was near the color of the drying leaves," Arbalest tried to describe.

Autumn looked back over her shoulder at Jade. "Come on! Let's go!" She ran toward Wind and without stopping hoisted herself into the saddle.

Fletch slid down Wind's tail and ran to climb aboard Condor. Jade and Dino mounted Junebug and Rory.

"Me want to ride!" Ige pointed to the horses and jumped up and down, tugging on Zuri's arm. Zuri just looked up at the huge creatures, and her eyes grew wide.

"You can both ride with me," Jade offered.

Dino looked at Karia. "Do you want to ride with me?" he offered.

Karia smiled. "Absolutely!"

The hawk that Karia had been riding on came in behind her, picked her up by the back of her vest, and delivered her to Dino. Then she returned and did the same for Zuri and Ige.

"WEEEE!!!" Ige exclaimed.

Juna looked at the majestic golden eagle he had ridden on, and the eagle gazed back at him. It crouched slightly, and Juna hopped on.

"YAH!" Autumn yelled, and in a flurry of activity, the group of would-be rescuers was off.

Chapter 37
Karia's Place

The calls of Ohanzee guided Condor through the forest road, leading the horses to the place where the vehicle had tumbled off the embankment. Jade, Autumn, and Dino, with Karia holding on to his back, jumped off the horses and moved carefully to the edge of the broken road. They stared down at the overturned vehicle.

"That looks like one of the Jeeps from the Forestry Department!" Dino observed.

Autumn and Jade looked at each other. "It sure does," Autumn responded with a sigh and a scared look on her face.

"Let's get the ropes and your cell phone," Jade recommended.

They gathered as much as they could carry from their saddlebags.

"Dino, bring Wind. We're gonna need him," Autumn directed.

Dino brought Wind, and Autumn dropped the ropes and other gear on the ground before she dialed her cell phone. The ringing from the Jeep confirmed their worst fears. "Daddy!" Autumn breathed, and then she began to tremble.

Jade grabbed her shoulders and looked into her eyes. "Come on! We can do this, Autumn. We have to—for Dad."

On the back of his newfound friend, Juna swooped in and grabbed the end of one of the ropes. They flew down, landing very gently on the underneath side of the Jeep. Juna climbed off and slowly made his way to the front bumper of the Jeep. He struggled with the heavy rope and was finally able to wrap it around the bumper. He secured it with a knot that Sire Argus had taught him, one he knew would hold. Fletch followed Juna's lead, grabbing an additional rope and tying off at the rear bumper. Arbalest directed Jade and Dino to tie the opposite ends to the sturdiest trees they could find, while Autumn phoned for help.

"The lines are busy. The fire must be getting worse," Autumn stated.

They were all silent for a moment, and in that silence, they heard a grim sound in the distance—a sort of crackling, crunching, cracking sound.

"Listen!" Jade cried. "The Fire! It's getting closer."

"The Rain Shadow!" Zuri blurted.

"What?" Karia asked.

"If we can get to the Rain Shadow, I think we might be able to bring rain," Zuri suggested.

Jade was tying herself into another rope she had dropped over the side of the embankment. "We're not going anywhere until we rescue our father!" Jade snapped.

"I am not suggesting *we* do, but *I* could go. The hawk could take me," Zuri continued.

"You guys figure it out. I'm going down," Jade said as she stepped to the edge of the road.

Autumn and Dino held tight to the rope as Jade disappeared over the side.

"You shouldn't go alone!" Karia reasoned with Zuri.

"Look, I have lived here all my life, I know my way. I can feel it, if something is not done soon, you will not make it out of the forest." Zuri looked through the trees. "It is closer than you think. All I ask is that you keep Ige here with you. We will be flying much too fast, and I fear he might fall."

Fletch stepped up. "We will keep him safe and bring him to you at the Rain Shadow when we return."

Zuri knelt down beside her youngling. "You're my brave little one.

These are friends, and they will take care of you, but you must be brave and stay out of trouble. Understand?"

"Me stay with Fetch, Yeah!!" Ige jumped up and down, not understanding the seriousness of the situation.

"Yeah, Ige, you can stay with me," Fletch said. Then he looked Zuri square in the eyes. "Be safe. I'm not going to keep him forever." Fletch smiled and gave her a playful wink.

Zuri walked over to the hawk that had carried Karia earlier and he graciously crouched for her to board. In an instant, they were gone through the trees.

Jade was just getting close to the Jeep. She grabbed the fender and pulled herself to the door. "Daddy! Daddy, can you hear me?" she called through the window.

There was no movement.

Autumn, Dino, Arbalest, Karia, Juna, Ige and Fletcher stood at the edge, silently and helplessly waiting and hoping.

Jade pulled at the door, but it was wedged shut. With each pull she could feel the Jeep shake like it might fall at any moment. Although it was tied in, she couldn't be sure how long the ropes would hold, so she began to untie herself from her rope.

"Jade! What are you doing?" Autumn objected.

"I have to get in through the window. I can't with this rope on." She slipped the rope through the door handle so she could retrieve it when she needed it. She carefully climbed in the window of the Jeep and slid over to where her father hung, still strapped in by his seatbelt. She reached up and felt for a pulse. "Daddy? Daddy, can you hear me?" Jade called to him. She patted his cheek. "Please, Daddy, wake up!" Tears welled up in her eyes.

Suddenly, her father opened his eyes and blinked slowly.

"Daddy! He's awake!" she called to the rest of them.

"Jade, wh-what are you...what are you doing here? I told you girls to...to get off the...the ridge," he stammered, trying to hide his pain.

Suddenly the Jeep lurched and slipped, but then it stopped. Jade and her father looked at each other.

"Try the radio!" he said, remembering the Forestry radio in the Jeep.

Jade reached out and turned the knobs on the radio. Static screeched from the speaker. Jade pressed the button on the side of the mic. "Hello? Hello? Is anyone there? Can anyone here me?" She waited, but there was no response. She turned back to her dad. "Are you hurt bad? We are going to get you out of here, but I need to know where you are hurting. I don't want to make it worse by moving you the wrong way."

"My head," he replied. "I hit it pretty hard."

"What about your neck?" Jade asked.

"No, I think my neck is okay."

"I need to release your seatbelt, Dad. You should try to brace yourself so you don't fall," Jade suggested.

Her father grabbed onto the seatbelt close to the seat, creating enough slack for Jade to pop it open. Her father slowly lowered himself onto the roof of the Jeep. That was when he realized he had a much more serious injury. "My leg!" The pain shot through him like a knife, and he groaned and began breathing hard.

"Daddy, are you alright?" Jade urged.

He tried to catch his breath.

"Is everything okay down there?" Autumn cried.

"Yeah, yeah, we're okay!" Jade called back. "Come on, Dad. I have a rope right here. We just need to tie it around you and get you through the window, and Wind will pull you up," she explained.

He started to move to the passenger side of the Jeep, but the shift in weight caused the Jeep to move in a very unsettling way.

Jade poked her head out the window and looked up. She could see Juna and Fletch looking down at her. "I need the rope on the other side!" she called.

Fletch put Ige's hand in Karia's and without hesitation stepped off the edge, sliding down the rope. He landed with a soft *thud* in the underside of the Jeep, grabbed the rope, and brought it to the other window. Jade and her father could hear Fletch's soft footsteps pad across the metal before the rope dropped into the driver's side window. Jade's father looked at her, puzzled.

She quickly grabbed the rope. "Here. Let's tie this around you," she said, pretending not to have heard the footsteps.

Meanwhile, Juna swooped down on the eagle and grabbed Fletch just as Jade's father was pulling himself from the Jeep.

"Daddy!" Autumn cried. "Hold on! We'll have you up in just a minute."

The sweat began to bead on Jade's and her father's foreheads as the flames licked the trees not far from where they were. They looked at each other concerned and Jade said. "We'll be out of here before it gets here," she smiled and hoped she was right.

Autumn and Dino secured the rope to Wind and began to coax him forward. The rope tightened, and Mr. Linder tried to help by pushing himself the remainder of the way out of the Jeep. The pain was nearly unbearable, but he grabbed the side of the Jeep and slowly worked his way toward the embankment. Wind continued to pull as Mr. Linder struggled to climb the side of the embankment with his arms and his one good leg. As he came close to the top, Juna, Karia, Ige, Arbalest, and Fletch hurried to the tree line to get out of sight. Autumn and Dino each grabbed one of Mr. Linder's arms and pulled hard, sliding him up onto the road. Autumn wrapped her arms around her dad and hugged him tight. They then began to untie him so they could send the rope back down to Jade.

That was when they heard it: *SNAP!* Autumn and Dino looked around to see what it was. The Traegons also heard it and peered out of the edge of the forest in panic. Arbalest noticed one of the ropes he and Fletch had used originally to secure the Jeep had snapped and was lying slack at the edge of the embankment. Soon after that, the other one snapped.

"What is that?" Autumn's dad asked.

"Don't worry, Daddy. You just lie here. We need to get Jade." Autumn hurried to the edge of the road and looked over.

Dino noticed the ropes they had tied on were now stretching and beginning to fray from the weight of the Jeep. They could all hear the metal and wood creaking in chorus. "It's gonna go!" Dino gasped.

"Jade, you've gotta get off of there right now. It's gonna fall!" Autumn screamed, throwing her a rope.

Another rope snapped. Jade was hanging out of the Jeep reaching for the rope, but Autumn threw it and missed. Dino tried as well but missed too. Although they risked being seen, Fletch, Juna and Arbalest charged from the forest and called for Ohanzee, Condor, and the eagle. The Jeep slipped further, and Autumn and Dino both began screaming for Jade to get out of it and away from it before it carried her down with the inevitable fall. The last rope snapped, and the Jeep began to slide down the embankment with Jade lying on the underside of it. She screamed as it slipped further, but then the Jeep came to a sudden dead stop, and Jade stopped screaming.

Ohanzee, Condor, and the hawk simultaneously grabbed Jade by her arms and the back of her jean jacket and lifted her off the Jeep, bringing her safely to the road.

Mr. Linder happened to be looking up at that very moment, and he saw his youngest daughter gently placed on the road by three large birds of prey. In all his years in the forest he had never before seen anything as amazing as this. *I must have bumped my head harder than I thought*, he thought to himself, blinking hard.

With a final *snap* of wood and *creak* of metal, the Jeep flipped back and tumbled the rest of the way into the gully far below. The sound drew everyone's attention back to the side of the road.

Standing there beneath where the Jeep once sat was a large mountain lion and a strange she-Traegon with a blackbird on the walking stick she held.

"Kamara!" Karia gasped.

A *crack* of thunder could be heard throughout the forest.

"Who is that?" Fletch asked.

The name was all Arbalest needed to hear; he knew exactly who she was.

Kamara began climbing up the steep embankment with the mountain lion at her side. She moved with ease, considering her age and how crooked she was. Her bird let out an occasional gravely chirp as he tried to maintain his balance atop Kamara's stick. When they came closer, Karia noticed that the mountain lion that was with Kamara had crystal blue eyes. It was the Grimalkin she had encountered in the forest earlier that day!

"This is Kamara," Karia said, introducing her to the other Traegons and extending her hand to assist Kamara as the Grimalkin gently nudged the old she-Traegon to solid ground.

Jade was now kneeling at her father's side. He was lying on his back with his eyes closed, trying to endure the pain in his leg. He let out a loud and agonizing groan that caused the others to look in his direction. Then, with a deep sigh, he passed out.

"Daddy? Daddy!" Jade cried.

Autumn ran to her father's side and knelt across from Jade.

"What's wrong with him?" Jade pleaded.

Autumn leaned down and placed her ear to her father's chest. Then she quickly placed her fingers on his neck. "He's not breathing!" she cried. "Daddy? Daddy! Someone please help!"

Both girls were in tears now, helpless as the fire grew closer.

I wanted so much to help, but there was nothing I could do. I looked to Kamara and asked desperately, "Can you help?"

Kamara cocked her head and looked up at me. "I could, but it is not my place," she responded in her croaking voice.

Karia glared at her. "If you are able, then why do you not help him?" Karia's voice was filled with strength and force. In all of her kindness I had never before heard her speak in such a tone.

"You, young Wayseer, have the power to help him. It is *your* place, not mine!" Kamara demanded.

Karia was surprised by Kamara's words. She glanced over at Mr. Linder and then looked at me with a puzzled look on her face.

"You have to try, Karia," I urged her. "I believe in you."

"Please, Karia! Oh please try!" Jade pleaded, tears streaming down her dirt-smudged face.

Autumn looked to Karia, and her eyes filled with tears as well. "Please," she choked out.

These girls risked their lives to help us, so how could I not do this for them? Karia thought. Then she thought of Sire Argus and how she would feel if she was placed in a similar circumstance. She knew she had to try. Karia ran over to Mr. Linder. She could already feel that strange heat pour into her hands, just as she had with the Grimalkin earlier that day. She rubbed her hands together vigorously, and the tingling sensation began to move up her arms. The feeling was so intense that it seemed to vibrate through her entire body. Autumn and Jade moved to the side to give Karia room to step in. Karia felt the pouch on her hip where she carried the amulet; it began to move and jump. She reached down and placed her hand on the pouch, but the heat in her hand flared, causing her to pull her hand away. She looked at me and reached again to pull the pouch from her hip. She opened it quickly, knowing there was little time left to help. A bright orange light beamed from the open pouch. Karia turned the pouch over and let the Ember Rune roll out. It lay there on the ground with the reddish-orange light seeping through the grooves on the front. The amulet began to vibrate, and the same energy that Karia felt in her hands seemed to envelope her entire body. It shook and then began to roll toward her and finally came to rest at Karia's feet, motionless.

Karia turned her attention back to Mr. Linder. She moved in close and stared for a moment at his pale face. She then climbed onto his chest. She looked to Kamara, who gave her a slight nod. Karia laid her hands side by side over his heart and closed her eyes. She imagined herself being draped in the white light she had first experienced in the willow garden back home. A sense of peace came over her as she saw the white light envelope her and Mr. Linder. She felt warmth streaming from her hands and pouring into him. She could feel her own heart beating; she focused only on the sound of her heart and the feeling of it pounding in her chest. In her mind's eye, there was nothing else in the world but Mr. Linder, herself, and that healing white light.

Unbeknownst to Karia, the Ember Rune began once again to rattle on the ground beside Mr. Linder. The three sections on the amulet burst opened, sending reddish-orange light flooding forth from its center. We all had to shield our eyes from the bright light, except for Kamara. The light created a bubble around Karia and Mr. Linder. The dome of light pulsed and shimmered. To us, what was in actuality only a few seconds seemed much, much longer. Karia had lost track of time as well. A loud clap of thunder came from above.

Suddenly, Mr. Linder took a strong, deep breath and sat straight up. Karia tumbled off of his chest and landed on the ground between his legs. The light that had surrounded them moments before disappeared, and the small amulet rolled to where Karia had fallen. The rest of the Traegons and the animals that had gathered quickly scattered to the cover of the forest edge. Mr. Linder took another deep breath and coughed.

"Daddy!" Jade cried. She wrapped her arms around his neck and hugged him tight.

Autumn moved in closer. "Dad, are you alright?" she asked cautiously.

"What happened? Where...where are we?" he questioned.

"The Jeep went over the side of the road, Dad. Don't you remember?" Autumn asked him.

"Oh! Ugg," he groaned, reaching for his leg and nearly swatting Karia in the process.

Seeing this, I stepped in and grabbed Karia out of the way.

"I feel like I was hit by a truck," he muttered in a groggy voice.

Dino C. Crisanti

Power Comes from Within

I walked to the edge of the road and set Karia down. I could see the flames as they began to engulf the Jeep where it now lay. The crackling and popping of the forest being consumed by the fire was loud and right on our heels.

I ran back to the girls, "We have to get out of here! The fire is here! Look!" I said pointing to the forest.

Chapter 38
Traegon Chain

When Zuri reached the Rain Shadow, Wayra the bat greeted her and took her deep into the cave. She quickly descended the winding stone stairs with Wayra trailing just above her. Oracle Qendrim sat in his large stone chair in the center. The Ternion, his three constants, were by his side, and the cave was filled with Traegons—more in one place than even Zuri had ever seen. They had found their way to the protection of the cave and their community. There, they would wait until they could return to whatever would be left of their homes, if anything at all.

"Oracle!" she said, coming to a stop on one knee, directly before him.

"It is good that you made it, for you will be safe here," Oracle Qendrim said.

"My own safety is not my concern, Oracle. There are others in the forest—the visitors Karia and Juna and our own Fletch, as well as my youngling, Ige. Their human friends are there too. We cannot just wait for the fire to burn itself out or for the humans to bring it to an end. This time, we Traegons must take action," Zuri explained.

"These fires happen, Zuri. It is the way the Earth clears the old and makes way for the new," Qendrim said.

"But you know this one is different from the others. This could cause so much more destruction and devastation not only to the homes

— 224 —

of the Traegons and the animals, but to so many humans as well. There must be something we can do. We must take some responsibility upon ourselves…for a greater purpose," Zuri pleaded.

"Zuri!" a warm deep voice called from off in the distance within the cave.

Zuri looked around, and her eyes caught movement from a high stone balcony deep in the back of the cave. It was her mate, Bidziil. She left her place before Oracle Qendrim and ran toward the dark-haired, strongly built Traegon. His defined bare arms caught her at the bottom of the stairs. His rugged tunic made of coarse animal skins stitched together with sinew was stained and weathered from his hunting excursion. Leather gauntlets and shin guards bore the symbols of their clan. The two had been apart for quite some time.

Bidziil stepped back and looked down at Zuri's large, round belly. "She grows strong like her mim." He smiled, placing his hand upon her midsection, and returning his gaze to her eyes.

"It is so, my love." She smiled back.

"Where is our young warrior, Ige?" Bidziil questioned, looking around.

"He has remained with Fletcher. I had to return here. Come," she said, taking Bidziil's hand and leading him back to Oracle Qendrim. "I must explain later."

They returned to where Qendrim and the Ternion waited.

"Forgive my momentary departure," said Zuri. "I haven't much more time. I must return to the others. Is there not a way to conjure the rains to extinguish the blaze?" Zuri asked, getting right to the point.

"It is not usual, nor is it our place to call forth the elements to do our bidding," Qendrim stated.

"Was it not fate that started this fire? Who are we to stop it?" Ljena interjected.

Pranvere stepped forward. "Zuri is correct, Oracle. This is different. The appearance of the Ember Rune makes it so. Its presence calls to our individual and communal prowess, to find within ourselves our abilities, talents, and excellence. In the name of the Ember Rune, I believe it is appropriate to take action, to embrace our own strength and power to bring about the change necessary for the greatest good of all creatures."

"I concur!" Bora piped in.

"Agreed," Ljena conceded.

Oracle Qendrim looked at his three daughters, then to his community who stood silently, watching and listening. "Do you, as a community and a whole, agree to what is being presented here?" Qendrim bellowed.

The large crowd of Traegons erupted with a loud, "AYE!"

Qendrim returned his gaze to Zuri; her eyes beckoned his consent to assist. "It is my duty to listen to my community. We shall utilize our powers to intercede for the greatest good," Qendrim proclaimed. "Are there any suggestions among us to stop such a formidable, destructive force as these consumptive flames?"

Bidziil placed his hand on Zuri's back as she looked to him, her strong hunter and provider. His thought was of what he and his pack of hunters might be able to do to stop the blaze, but for all of their strength and cunning, he could not think of a way. The crowd buzzed as a blend of thoughts and ideas poured into the cave, but there was no truly workable, feasible suggestion.

Suddenly, from behind a crowd of onlookers, the thin, awkward, lanky Traegon they had seen first in the garden stepped before the group. He pushed his way through the crowd carrying in his arms several scrolls, so many that a few dropped to the stone floor as he approached. His face was kind, and the glint in his eye told of an enigmatical knowing. He stood before Oracle Qendrim and dropped the scrolls into a pile on the rough stone floor. "My name is Scrival." He bowed his head in respect to Qendrim and the Ternion.

"We know who you are, Scrival. What do you bring forth?" Qendrim questioned with a bit of doubt and annoyance in his voice.

Dino C. Crisanti

Guidance from the Past

"I do believe I may have the answer you seek," he began with a knowing smile. "We, as a community, hold a strong bond to each other, to the Earth, and to all of creation. It is innate. I have it, you have it," he said, pointing to Zuri and Bidziil, "we all have it." He waved his long arms, gesturing to all who stood present. "This is why it is so hard for us to just look the other way when one is in distress. I have spent my life, as did my sire and his sire before him, studying our history. We have kept logs and scrolls filled with the past. We have watched, listened, inquired, and explored our kind. I believe I know how we can stop the spread of this devastating blaze."

"You do?" Zuri looked at the thin, slight Traegon standing near her broad, strong mate.

It was as if Bora could see what Zuri was thinking. "It is not always power in strength that can defend. Power comes in all shapes and sizes." Bora stepped off the platform where Qendrim and her sisters stood. She approached Scrival, looked into his eyes, and smiled. I believe you do have something to share."

Scrival gave a nervous smile. He reached down and fumbled through the pile of scrolls on the floor at his feet. "Ah, here it is." He picked up the one he was looking for and unrolled it. He cleared his throat and read, "The power lies in the masses, attuned to common awareness, locked within the grasp of one another. The manifestation of the notion is certain." He looked up from the scroll, pleased with what he had read.

"What does it mean? What are we supposed to do?" Ljena asked.

Pranvere stepped from the platform and stood next to Bora. "I understand!" she announced.

"You see?" Pranvere said excitedly. "Together we can cause this change!"

Qendrim stood before the community, knowing that even those that did not understand would now receive awareness. "Take the hand of the one next to you. Everyone must be linked, for we must create an unbroken chain within these walls. We haven't much time."

As each Traegon took the hand of another, the chain began to grow. It wove throughout the cave, from the floor through the balcony, every Traegon joined hands.

Oracle Qendrim continued, "Our thoughts will be of the life-giving rains. We will call to the spirits of the thunderhead. Focus! See the clouds moving in over our mountain home. See the sky open in a heavy cloudburst and the rains fall to Earth. See the flames extinguished and our land returned to us, alive and green and flourishing. See it, and it shall be."

Qendrim held out his hands: Pranvere took one, and Ljena took the other. Bora took Pranvere's other hand, and then Scrival's. Zuri held tightly to Bidziil's hand and graciously took Scrival's other hand. One by one, hands were joined, and soon the chain was complete.

"Now close your eyes. Focus, concentrate, and believe that you as an individual and we as a whole have the ability to bring the rains, to change the Ember Augury!" Qendrim directed, and all did as they were told.

Chapter 39
Help

M r. Linder was emotionally and physically drained from the day's events. He had no more strength to help himself. All he wanted to do was close his eyes and sleep.

I tried to hold Wind still while Jade and Autumn attempted to lift their father, but the horse insisted on stepping nervously from side to side.

Arbalest stepped out from the shade of the trees and motioned for Ohanzee. He climbed onto his hawk and directed him to take flight. As he passed over Wind, Arbalest jumped off and landed on the saddle. "Go help the girls, and I will steady the horse," Arbalest told me.

I wondered how he was going to keep the horse still if I was having trouble, and the horse was a hundred times the size of him at least, but I have learned not to question the abilities of the Traegons. I stepped away from the front of the horse and walked over to Jade and Autumn.

Arbalest removed two pieces of tattered fabric and a leather strap from a pouch on his hip. He used the fabric to cover Wind's eyes. Immediately, the stubborn and agitated horse began to calm down. As he strapped the fabric on temporarily, another loud and long clap of thunder rang through the forest. Rain began to fall, lightly at first and quickly increased to a steady shower. Wind became startled by the thunder and began to shift direction on the road. Arbalest held tight and leaned into his ear. No one could hear what he said, but whatever it was, it calmed him down.

Autumn, Jade, and I struggled to move their father. We had finally managed to prop him up on his knees when we heard a rumble in the distance. We glanced up to the narrow mountain road just in time to see an old, loud van coming around the curve.

"Lay him back down," I said before I ran to the road. I waved my arms in an attempt to get them to stop.

As the van came closer, it slowed down and finally stopped. The two campers we had seen earlier climbed out of it. "Hey ,you guys! We thought you'd be long gone by now," Owen said, coming around the front of the van.

"Please! We need your help!" Autumn called from the ground behind her horse Wind.

Sam then noticed Mr. Linder lying on the ground. "Oh, my gosh! What happened here?" she shrieked, running to the girls.

"Please help! This is our dad. He works for the Bureau of Land Management, and his Jeep skidded of the road. We need to get him to a hospital. Please, will you help us?" Jade pleaded.

"Owen, quick! Pull the van over here!" Sam called to him.

Arbalest was still hanging on Wind's neck, but Sam and Owen didn't seem to notice. He whispered again in Wind's ear, and he proceeded to move out of the way toward the forest edge and the other two horses.

Owen pulled the van up and opened the side door. He shoved their camping equipment out of the way to make room for Mr. Linder in the back. Then Owen and Sam carefully began to lift Mr. Linder into the van.

"Be careful. His leg is broken," Jade said, stepping up to help.

"You riding with us?" Owen asked.

Jade looked at Autumn and me.

"Just go on. We will be fine," Autumn replied to Jade's questioning look.

"Yeah, I'm coming." They loaded Mr. Linder into the car, and Jade looked at Autumn and me and gave each of us a hug. "Be safe, you guys. I'll tell them where you are."

"We'll be fine. Just get Dad to a hospital quick," Autumn told her.

Jade climbed in the back of the van, and Sam shut the door. "As soon as we get signal on our cell, we'll get help to you. Be careful," Sam said. Owen and Sam climbed into their van and drove off down the mountain road.

Autumn and I watched the van until it was out of sight, and then we turned to see Karia, Juna, Fletch, and Ige emerge from the edge of the forest. Arbalest was now sitting in the saddle on the back of Wind. Ohanzee, Condor, and the eagle were perched on the branches of a large tree above.

"Where is Kamara?" I questioned.

We all looked around, but Kamara and the Grimalkin were nowhere to be seen.

"She does that," Karia said with a shrug.

Another clap of thunder roared through the forest, followed by several low rumbles. We looked up to see the fire climbing the embankment toward the road.

"The fire! I almost forgot about it," I said. "Come on. Let's get out of here." I ran over to Rory. Karia was standing in front of her, holding Ige's hand. "You can ride with me," I said, reaching down and picking them both up. I placed them on the front of the saddle and climbed on myself.

"Who is riding with me?" Autumn questioned.

Ohanzee flew down to the ground and landed near Arbalest. "I shall fly above and guide our way," he stated.

Condor swooped down and landed before Fletch. He turned and crouched down, and Fletch quickly climbed on.

Juna looked to the eagle with some regret and waved to him. "I'll ride with Autumn. Your service has been much appreciated. Many thanks!"

The eagle let out a mighty screech and took flight into the woods.

Autumn bent down and picked up Juna. She swung him onto her back just as she had always done with Fletch. Juna held tight as she hurried over to Junebug and pulled the reins over her head, then returned and mounted Wind. Autumn gave Wind a jab with her heels and hollered "Yah!"

We galloped up the road in the same direction as the van and away from the fire. It was still raining steadily, and we were all very wet in no time at all. Thunder clapped again, and the lightning seemed to tear open the sky, letting out what seemed like all of the rain it could hold. We tried to stay to the side of the road to be shielded some by the massive trees.

Chapter 40
Power vs. Strength

Somewhere deep in a cave, the chain of Traegons urged on the rain, and it was working! Zuri brought her hands together, linking Bidziil and Scrival and never breaking the chain. Oracle Qendrim did the same with Pranvere and Ljena. Oracle Qendrim and Zuri ascended the curved stone staircase toward the Rain Shadow entrance. Wayra followed above, silently flying ahead. When they reached the opening to the outside world, they pushed aside the overgrowth and stepped onto the ledge. The ledge was dry as a bone, as it should have been, for this was the Rain Shadow. But out beyond the Rain Shadow, the skies gave way to a storm that equaled no other they could remember. The rain came down in sheets. A deluge poured down the sides of the mountain, and although there was no more lightning, the thunder continued to rumble and clap. Smoke coiled and drifted into the air in the distance as the flames were extinguished.

Zuri looked to Oracle Qendrim. "I must go and find my youngling," she said, rubbing her hard, round belly.

"You are a true warrior, Zuri. I do not know of too many she-Traegons who would have done what you chose to do, especially in your condition," Oracle Qendrim praised.

"It is my calling, Oracle, which is why I chose Bidziil as my mate. We are strong Traegons and will make other strong Traegons, warriors to protect our community. But I must say I have been humbled by the

Dino C. Crisanti

Oracle Quenrim, Zuri and Bidziil at
the Rain Shadow

words and actions of Scrival. I have never seen him before, but I am glad to now have the honor of knowing him," Zuri shared.

"Sometimes in our darkest hour, our light will come from the most unlikely places. Scrival will be seen much more often within the community. He will now find the place where he can utilize his knowledge, and we will create a place to store all the knowledge he and his fore sires have gathered. Besides, I think Bora has taken a liking to him." Oracle Qendrim smiled.

Wayra opened her wings and gave two big flaps, then Bidziil stepped through the cave entrance and onto the ledge. "Wayra, fly down and tell the clan their actions have been successful. Tell them it is time to celebrate. I think a feast is in order. Tell them we have succeeded in calling the rains to put an end the Ember Augury! I shall be down soon," Oracle Qendrim directed.

Wayra obediently disappeared into the darkness of the cave to go bear the message to the Traegon community.

"Go on, you two. Find your youngling and bring him back for our feast, along with the familiars, if they wish to join us." Qendrim placed his hands on Zuri and Bidziil's shoulders. "It is in the face of adversity that we have choice. We can choose to do nothing or we can attempt to change the course laid before us. It is when many come together for a purpose that serves the greatest good of all. That is the Augury, the opportunity to seize a moment of despair and create a new beginning." With that, and nary a farewell, Qendrim turned and disappeared into the cave.

"Wait here, "Bidziil told Zuri, and he began to scale the rough mountain wall. As he reached the plateau, his eagle Gui and the hawk that had brought Zuri to the Rain Shadow, flew down to meet him. Bidziil watched as Zuri's hawk flew down, allowing her to climb on from the ledge in the Rain Shadow. Zuri and Bidziil took flight toward where she had left the others.

The rain was steady, and it beat heavily down upon them as they flew through the sky. Although rain is sometimes bothersome to humans, it is just a natural part of the Traegons' world. They are never bothered by foul weather, though it does make bird travel slightly more challenging.

They flew low, skimming the tops of the trees, and then climbed higher into the sky before arriving at the gully where the Jeep had slid off the road. When they arrived, the others were already gone. They could smell the smoldering remains of the wet, burnt forest, but there was no sign of fire. The rains seemed to be doing their part in dousing the flames.

"This is a good sign," Zuri said, climbing off the hawk after landing on the road. "They must have gotten him out and are headed to safety."

"This looks to have been a most grave and serious accident. I hope all are well," Bidziil stated as he peered over the edge at the burned out wreckage. He continued to walk along the road side, searching for any tracks to indicate the direction they might have traveled. "Here!" he called back to Zuri, who was searching in another area. "They must have gone that way." Bidziil pointed down the road in the direction the horses had gone. "I have found fresh hoof prints. Many have been washed away by the rains, but I see none going in any other direction"

"Excellent!" Zuri responded. "Let us fly above the trees in search of them.

They walked back to where their hawk and eagle stood preening their wet plumage, perched on a fallen log. They mounted their feathered companions and flew above the tree line into the stony gray, cloud-filled sky. Black smoke permeated the air as the rain continued to douse the remaining flames, leaving smoldering embers behind. Bidziil looked back in the direction of the billowing smoke.

"What is it, Bidziil?" Zuri asked.

"I wish to see the extent of the destruction, left in the wake of the blaze. I do wonder how far it extends," Bidziil told her.

"There will be time for that later. We must find Ige now and bring him home," she reminded him.

Chapter 41
Smoke Jumpers

The smoke-jumping team was heading out of the area they had been dropped in. They hiked out to the rendezvous point where Mr. Linder was scheduled to meet them and another team so he could bring them down out of the mountain. When they reached the road and found that Mr. Linder was not there waiting, they radioed the base.

"Mel to base. Come in base. Over." Her voice echoed through the other team radios.

"This is base. Come in, Mel. Over," she heard back from the dispatcher.

"Hey, Lee, Mike isn't here. Any word on where he is? Over," Melissa told the man on the other end of the radio.

"We lost radio contact with him earlier. We were hoping it was just a glitch in the reception. We were trying to track his path up the mountain, but were shorthanded. Everyone was already dropped by the time we realized he might have a problem. We'll send in a chopper to pull you out. There is a ridge just west of you. I marked it on your GPS coordinates and sent it to you. Radio when you get there. The chopper will be close. Over."

"Copy that. We'll call you when we reach the ridge. Over and out." Melissa put her radio into its holster on her belt and removed her GPS. She looked at Allen and the other two jumpers. "What do you think happened to Mike?" She sounded concerned.

"I don't know, but I don't want to leave this mountain with him still up here somewhere," Allen stated.

"We have no idea where he could be, and you know as well as I do that this mountain is too big to search on foot. Let's get back to base, grab a Jeep and some fresh gear, and then we can search," Rich, one of the jumpers from the other team, reasoned.

"Rich is right, guys. We can't just head out blindly and unprepared. What good would we be if we found him then?" agreed Matt, another jumper.

"You're right. Let's get to the chopper." Melissa brushed the rain off of the protective screen on her GPS, revealing the blinking light of the next rendezvous point. "Come on...this way," She said, leading the team into the forest.

They were sheltered from the majority of the rain as they hiked through the colossal trees of the forest. Once they stepped out onto the ridge, it was clear that the rain had not even begun to let up. They could see the helicopter in the distance heading in their direction.

"I wish every fire could end with a heavy rainstorm like this one." Rich said, half-jokingly.

"I know. What a blessing this storm was. It's weird though."

"What?" asked Allen.

"I checked the weather data today, and there was nothing on the radar to indicate a rainstorm, nothing at all," Melissa added.

The chopper flew in high enough above the ridge to maintain a safe distance from the mountainside. A cable with a harness on the end was lowered from the hovering chopper. One by one, each of the jumpers hooked themselves to the cable and were reeled up. The two teams shook off their wet clothing, took their seats, and placed their protective earphones on their heads.

"Any word on Mike Linder?" Allen asked the pilot, nearly shouting.

"No. We sent a couple of teams out, but they aren't back yet. Don't worry. They are planning on sending everyone they've got to look for him," the pilot responded.

"Yeah, that's what we're planning," Matt remarked.

The team sat quietly watching out the windows as the helicopter headed back toward base. Melissa and the others desperately scanned the massive mountainside as the chopper flew past, wondering where down there their friend might be.

Chapter 42
Rescue

Owen drove carefully down the slick, winding mountain road. The steady rain had evolved into a torrential downpour, making it extremely difficult to see. Mr. Linder slept in the back of the van with Jade watching his chest raise and lower with his shallow breathing. Sam sat at the edge of her seat just trying to see the road in front of them. Finally, Owen spotted a widened area in the road where he could pull over.

"Why are we stopping?" Jade cried.

"The rain is coming down too hard. We need to wait for it to let up some. I can't see, and I definitely don't want to drive us all off the side of this mountain," Owen explained.

"I don't know how much longer we have. We have to get him to a hospital soon. Pleeeease, Owen! Please, we have to go," Jade begged.

A moment later, they heard the sound of the helicopter. Jade pushed open the van door and jumped out into the pouring rain. "It's the Forestry helicopter!" Jade screamed through the pouring rain. She ran around to the other side of the van where she would be more visible. She began jumping up and down, waving her arms and screaming at the top of her lungs. "Over here! Over here! Help us!" She continued making more and more noise, and so did the rain.

"I don't think they will be able to see you, Jade," Owen said, lowering his window.

"Then help me!" she pleaded of the two of them.

Sam jumped out of the van first. She handed Jade a bright yellow rain poncho and put one on herself. Then she followed Jade, jumping and hollering. Finally, Owen got out too. The rain hit him hard in the face, forcing him to close his eyes until he got his poncho on and pulled the hood up. The three of them hollered and flailed their arms, trying to catch the attention of whoever was in the helicopter.

Melissa noticed something on the side of the mountain. "Wait!" she blurted. "Go back around. I think I saw something."

"Where?" Allen asked, looking out the window.

"Over there, on the mountainside. I saw a flash of something yellow."

The team members looked from all sides as the chopper made its way back to where Melissa thought she saw the unusual flash of yellow. As the helicopter came in close to the mountain, the team sprang into action, realizing there were three people who appeared to be in trouble. Melissa grabbed their helmets and harnesses and began to put them on. Allen handed her a first aid pack, which he helped her put on her back. Matt and Rich manned the pulley system, ready to lower Melissa. The pilot radioed base and told them they were making a rescue detour. The helicopter hovered near the three people in yellow plastic rain ponchos. Allen slid open the door on the side of the helicopter. Mel stood ready to drop out the door. Just then, one of the people pushed back the hood of her poncho, revealing her face.

Melissa recognized her immediately from her spot at the edge of the helicopter. "Oh my God! That's Jade Linder, Mike's Daughter!"

Matt checked her harness hook up and said. "All ready!"

Melissa climbed out onto the running board and lowered herself into the air. The wind from the rainstorm pushed her unsteadily as Rich lowered her down. She reached the ground and unhooked the harness from the cable.

Jade ran to her and hugged her tight. "It's my dad!" Jade yelled through the pouring rain and the noise of the helicopter. "He's hurt bad. We have him in the back of the van."

Melissa radioed to the pilot what she was told and hurried to the van. She slipped off the first aid pack and climbed in the back of the van. "Mike? Mike, can you hear me? It's me, Mel." She leaned down to listen to his breathing and placed her fingers on the side of his neck feeling for a pulse. "We need to get him out of here now," Melissa said, looking into Jade's eyes. Melissa reached for her radio. "I need the rescue basket stat. He's in bad shape. We need to get him out of here now!!" was all the team heard.

Allen strapped on a harness and was lowered down immediately, followed by the rescue basket. Melissa attempted to stabilize Mike as best she could when Allen came around the side of the van with the rescue basket. Melissa, Allen, Owen, and Sam helped to gently place Mr. Linder into the rescue basket and carried him to the waiting chopper. The cables were swinging furiously. Allen reached for them several times, but missed. The helicopter struggled to keep still in the storm. From out of nowhere, a hawk and an eagle flew in low, grabbing the cable and bringing it safely within reach of the rescuers. Jade looked up and smiled when she saw the faces of Zuri and another Traegon peeking out from behind the heads of the large birds. Then they were gone. Melissa looked at Allen as he stood dumbfounded at what just happened, as did Owen and Sam. Allen shrugged and then hooked the cable to the basket and guided it as it was raised to the chopper.

"There is only room for one more," the pilot's voice came over the radio.

"Allen, you go. I will get Jade back to her mom and meet you at the hospital, okay?" Mel suggested.

"Are you sure?" he asked.

"Yeah, Allen, go, take care of Mike. I will stay with Jade and make sure these folks get out of here safely. Radio our coordinates to base, and I'll stay in touch," Melissa ordered. "That is, if these nice people don't mind driving us the rest of the way out."

"No problem. We've got you covered," Owen said with a smile.

As Allen was being pulled up to the helicopter, the rain began to let up.

"Nice!" quipped Sam sarcastically, looking into the sky as the clouds began to lighten a bit. "Isn't that always the way it goes?"

"Come on. Let's get off this mountain before it starts pouring again," Owen added.

The four climbed into the van and headed on down the mountain road.

Chapter 43
The Way Back

Autumn and I pulled the horses off to the side of the road just before the edge of the driveway. We climbed down off of Rory and Wind.

"Alright, guys, this is where you have to get off," I told them as I helped Karia and Ige off Rory.

Autumn grabbed Juna and set him on the ground next to them. Condor and Ohanzee swooped in and landed nearby.

With his hands on his hips and a dramatic flair, Fletch proclaimed, "We made it!"

Arbalest covered his face with his hand and shook his head.

It was time for Condor to bid farewell, as his assistance was no longer needed. Ohanzee stayed, though, since he had come originally with Arbalest. Fletch stepped before Condor and looked up into the eyes of his large feathered comrade. "I thank you, my friend. Your service, although greatly appreciated, is no longer needed. Should there ever come a time when I can be of aid to you, all that is necessary is a call, as I am forever your friend and eternally beholden."

Condor bowed his head and gave a deep grunt. He opened his expansive and powerful wings, and with one mighty flap, he rose off the ground and disappeared beyond the tree line. We all looked on in reverence at the amazing, incredible creature.

I finally broke the silence. "You guys go to the forest outside my bedroom window and wait for us there. I will be out in a while with some food and hopefully some news of where the others are."

"Alright, Dino. We will be there when you call." Karia spoke softly, showing the weariness of the day's events. "Let us go and rest," she said to the others, taking Ige's hand and leading him slowly toward the forest edge.

I climbed back on Rory. Autumn handed me Junebug's reins and climbed onto Wind. We began up the long, winding driveway. When we rounded the last curve in the drive, we could see my aunt and uncle's house. I felt so glad to be back, and once the adrenaline wore off, I, too, began to feel exhausted.

"Dino!!!" My mom burst through the front door, followed by Autumn's mom, Miriam.

"Autumn!!" Mrs. Linder cried, running toward us.

I climbed off of Rory and Autumn off of Wind as we were both grabbed and hugged tightly by our mothers.

"You two are soaked!" Aunt Carol announced. "Joe, would you and Jack tie up the horses while we take the kids in?"

My dad stepped up to where my mom was still hugging me tight. "You had us really worried, son." He pulled my arm, and my mom let go. He turned me toward him and gave me a strong hug.

"Come on. Let's get you kids in some dry clothes," Aunt Carol pressed.

"Aren't you going to ask where Jade is?" Autumn questioned.

"She is safe," Mrs. Linder responded, "and your dad is on his way to the hospital. As soon as Jade gets here, we will be heading over there ourselves."

"How do you know all of this?" Autumn asked.

"The Forestry helicopter bringing in the smoke-jumping team ran across them on their way back. They picked up your dad and are taking him to the hospital. Jade and Melissa, one of the smokejumpers, are coming back with a couple who were giving them a ride." Autumn's mom explained.

Autumn and I looked at each other and simultaneously said, "Owen and Sam."

"Who are they?" my mom asked, placing a towel over my shoulders as we sat at the kitchen table.

"A nice couple who offered to drive Mr. Linder off the mountain," I replied. "Is he going to be okay?" I asked.

Mrs. Linder placed a towel around Autumn's shoulders. "I spoke to Mr. O'Connell. He said he's hurt pretty bad, but he thinks he'll be alright."

Aunt Carol placed two steaming cups of hot chocolate on the table in front of Autumn and me.

"We are going to want to hear the whole story once you get settled," my dad informed me, entering the kitchen with Uncle Joe.

I smiled at him. "You got it, Dad," I replied. "It's quite a story. They ought to write a book about it," I said with a smile.

The doorbell rang after a bit, and we all sprang out of our seats and ran into the living room. Aunt Carol pulled open the door revealing Jade, Melissa, Owen, and Sam. Jade ran into her mother's arms.

"Come in!" Aunt Carol invited the others.

Melissa, Owen, and Sam stepped into the foyer.

"Can I get you anything? Some hot chocolate? Coffee? Anything?" she offered them.

"Thank you, but I'll have to take a pass. The team has already sent a Jeep to pick me up. I just wanted to make sure Jade got back safely," Melissa replied.

Just then the rumble of the Forestry Jeep could be heard coming up the driveway.

"That's my ride! I'll see you later, Jade. Don't get lost in the woods anymore, okay?" She winked and smiled.

Jade ran up to her and gave her a big hug.

"Bye, Autumn! Nice meeting you, Dino! Thanks for the lift Owen, Sam."

Autumn and I both waved and smiled, and Melissa turned and bounced down the porch steps to the waiting Jeep.

"How about you two?" Aunt Carol asked Owen and Sam.

"Thanks, but we're going to hit the road. Have you heard anything about the fire?" Sam asked.

"The rain took care of it," Uncle Joe piped in. "Amazing, if you ask me. Out of nowhere we got that huge storm and almost record rainfall—at just the perfect time."

Jade glanced at Autumn and me. We knew it was amazing, but we also knew it wasn't just a fluke.

"Cool. Well, it was nice to meet everyone. Maybe we'll see you next time we come up to the mountain," Owen remarked.

"You're welcome here anytime," Aunt Carol said.

Mrs. Linder stepped up and reached for both their hands. "I don't know how to thank you for all you did to help my husband and my children."

"They helped us first, ma'am. We were just returning the favor. We're just glad we could help and that everything is gonna be alright," Sam added. "It was nice to meet you all. Bye!" Sam and Owen stepped out the door, walked to their van, and drove away.

"Girls, I have a bag of clean, dry clothes here. Get changed, and then we will get on to the hospital." Mrs. Linder handed the bag to Autumn.

"You guys can use my room," I said, leading them down the hall and showing them the way.

Jade and Autumn changed. Jade was shoving a wad of wet clothes into the bag when Autumn called to her. "Hey, look at this!"

"You shouldn't be doing that!" Jade reprimanded her sister for thumbing through my journal that she found lying on the floor next to my open suitcase.

"Look at these drawings," she pointed out.

"Wow! Those are awesome," Jade commented.

"Come on, girls! I want to get to the hospital before it gets too late. I want to know how your dad is doing," their mom called from the kitchen. "Thanks, Carol, for everything," she said making her way to the door.

"I am just glad everything worked out alright. Give Mike our best. Tell him we hope he gets well soon," Aunt Carol remarked.

Autumn and Jade came out of the bedroom and met their mom at the door. "We'll call you later, Dino," Autumn said with a smile.

"I'll be here," I responded.

Chapter 44
Calm After the Storm

When Karia, Juna, Fletch, Arbalest, and Ige reached the area of the forest not far from Dino's window, they found a spot under a large fir tree. Karia and Juna gathered several stones that would serve as seats. While Arbalest and Fletch searched for dry pine needles, dead leaves, or anything that would suffice as kindling, Ige played quietly with a small spider that hung gently from a pine bough.

Arbalest returned carrying a bundle of pine needles and placed them in a pile on the ground. He dropped his quiver on the ground beside him and began to dig through it. He pulled a small pouch from within and opened it, removing a piece of handcrafted hammered steel and a piece of flint. He then removed a clump of dried fine straw. He placed the straw atop the pine needles and picked up the steel and stone. He cracked them together several times until a spark dropped into the straw. Guardedly, he picked up the straw, cupping it gently in his strong Traegon hands, and carefully blew into it. A thin stream of smoke rose from his hands and glided gracefully around his long muzzle. He took a breath and gently blew again, and poufs of small fire erupted in the small clump of dried straw. He cautiously placed the straw onto the pine needles and continued to blow life into the tiny flames.

Fletch came around the base of the tree with additional kindling and set it beside Arbalest and the fire. "Very impressive!" Fletch gushed.

Dino C. Crisanti

Arbalest looked sideways at Fletch, and Fletch watched him with a smile, completely engrossed in what he was doing.

"Where did you get that fire starter kit?" Fletch continued, picking up the hammered steel and looking closely at it.

Arbalest took a handful of the dried leaves that Fletch had brought and dropped them into the flames. The fire flared and popped as it became hotter and began to burn into the needles, and the sap sizzled. Karia and Juna had been sitting on the stones placed around the fire, and they watched Arbalest carefully. The popping sound caught Ige's attention, and he walked over and sat next to Karia.

Arbalest glanced at the young Traegons that were gathered around him. Arbalest didn't have any younglings of his own, but the time he had spent guiding and protecting Karia and Juna in the past had helped him to understand the important role he served to these younglings. He looked at Fletch again and finally answered, "An Unpuzzler friend of mine back in our Traegonia made these implements for me. He is quite the contriver. He has dreamed, fashioned, and forged many items that have served to make Traegon life easier."

The fire popped again, drawing all attention back to it.

"It is burning strong now. Let us rest from our long day of adventures." Arbalest stood and dropped his fur cloak to the ground; it lay partially over one of the stones. He sat with his back to the stone and closed his eyes.

Ige scampered over to where Arbalest rested and knelt down on the edge of the cloak. He stared attentively at Arbalest while the rest followed Arbalest's lead and made themselves comfortable. A few moments passed, and Arbalest, sensing that he was being watched, opened one eye to find Ige staring at him. Ige dug into a small pouch on his hip and pulled out a small, pale amber colored stone that was almost translucent. He held it in the palm of his hand for Arbalest to see. "Want to see?" Ige asked secretively. He scooted in closer to Arbalest, who now opened both eyes and was looking kindly at the pine cone-sized Traegon.

"It a Conor tear," he revealed.

"Condor, Ige," Fletch corrected.

"Yup, yup that's what I said. Condor!" Ige whispered. "My friend Fetch, gived it to me. He a great explorer," Ige stated.

Arbalest opened his hand, and Ige dropped the stone into it. Arbalest looked at it very carefully. He raised his eyes to see Karia, Juna, and Fletch staring at him. "This is a fine gift. It is clear that the Traegon who acquired it must be a skilled tracker and explorer. I am impressed," Arbalest raved, handing the stone gently back to Ige.

Fletch retuned a sheepish grin to Arbalest as Ige dropped the stone into his pouch and ran over to Fletch, giving him a great big hug and sliding down next to him. He found a comfortable position tucked safely under Fletch's arm.

Arbalest returned a proud smile and a wink back to Fletch.

They rested a while in silence, and then they heard a strange call come from above. "Bereek!" The call was loud and high pitched. "Bereek! Bereek!" the call came again.

Suddenly Ige sat straight up and returned with a call of his own. "BEEK, BEEK!" He paused and then repeated, "BEEK, BEEK!"

The movement of the branches and leaves surrounding them let them know something was coming. Again the call came, only it was much closer this time. "Bereek! Bereek!"

Ige called back once more, "BEEK, BEEK!"

The branches on the fir tree they sat beneath rustled, showering them lightly with pine needles as two shadows appeared above. The group listened carefully and silently, except for Ige, who seemed to get more and more excited by the moment. A hawk and an eagle landed at the edge of the lowest boughs of the fir tree, and two Traegons dismounted. Ige stood quickly and ran to his mim. Standing behind her was a strong-looking he-Traegon who none had seen before except for Fletch. After hugging his mim, Ige turned and was hoisted easily up in the arms of the other. The three stepped under the tree and joined the group.

Fletch stood. "All of you know Zuri, and this is her mate Bidziil," he introduced.

Arbalest stood and bowed in a respectful greeting, Zuri and Bidziil returned his gesture.

Zuri turned her attention to Fletch. "I am grateful for the good care and safekeeping of Ige, Fletch. You are and have been as a brother to me. I am forever in your debt."

"I would do anything for you and your families, Zuri, for you have been as a family to me." Fletch smiled as Ige cast funny faces in his direction, and everyone laughed.

"Please sit," Arbalest suggested.

"We appreciate the invitation," Bidziil agreed, setting Ige on the ground and helping Zuri to sit on a nearby rock.

There was a short silence, and then Zuri said, "Oracle Qendrim wishes your presence at a celebration this night. There will be music, merriment, and much to eat, as well as the good company of many Traegons you still have yet to meet," Zuri continued.

Karia glanced around at Arbalest and Juna with an uneasy look in her eyes.

"All are welcome," Zuri reassured, noticing Karia's trepidation.

At that moment, the back door to Dino's aunt and uncle's house was heard slamming shut. All went instantly silent, and a moment passed before Karia heard Dino's voice.

"Karia! Juna! Are you near?" Dino called in a loud whisper.

They could hear him coming closer, and Karia jumped up and headed in the direction of his voice.

As I crawled under the low-hanging boughs of the fir tree, the branches moved, disturbed by my back and head brushing each as I moved.

I sat under the pine tree with a small group of Traegons, most of whom I already knew and one they introduced as Bidziil. I felt oddly large beside them, which was a strange feeling. I smiled awkwardly. "Hi!" I blurted, which seemed to break the uncomfortable silence.

The others smiled back at me.

"Am I interrupting something?" I asked. "I just wanted to bring you something to eat." I dropped my backpack onto the ground and unzipped it. I pulled out some fresh bread and roast beef that my Aunt Carol had made for dinner. I also opened a foil packet with some carrots and potatoes. "Sorry it took me so long. I told them I would clean up after dinner so I could get this stuff without them noticing." The smell drifted out as I opened each package I brought.

"Oooh, that does smell very good," Karia shared.

"There should be enough for all of you," I said, knowing their appetites were nothing compared to mine.

I laid out some napkins I had torn into Traegon-sized pieces, and then they each took turns helping themselves. They filled their napkins, returned to their seats, and began to eat.

"Zuri?" Karia spoke, swallowing a piece of bread. "The gathering you spoke of earlier...do you think it would be permitted for Dino, Autumn, and Jade to join us? They have been as much a part of this journey as we have," Karia reasoned.

I listened, not understanding what they were talking about, but curious nonetheless.

"I will have to speak to Oracle Qendrim first. We have not allowed any humans into our mountain boundaries. Still, many have been aware of Fletcher's acquaintance with Autumn and Jade for some time now. They are considered trustworthy among the Traegons, I can assure you of that." Zuri continued, "I am not sure how they would make such a trip into the mountain though, due to their considerable size."

"I think I know a way," Karia said with growing excitement. "Back in our home, we use something called summoning when we have brought Dino into the boundaries of our Traegonia. I believe this would be possible here as well," Karia explained.

Zuri looked at Karia for a long time. Her eyes showed that she sympathized with Karia and her desire to share all of these experiences with me. "I shall speak to Oracle Qendrim. Prepare your plan to bring them in, for I believe I shall be able to convince him." She smiled at Karia.

Fletch seemed as excited as Karia and Juna. The mood lightened, and they continued to eat.

I heard the back door to my aunt's house open, and then my mother's call. "Dino! It's time to come in."

"I have to go," I told them as I pulled myself to my knees.

"Dino, I will visit you tonight, and then we can go and get Autumn and Jade. Place the White Acorn under your pillow. Don't forget," Karia directed before I crawled away.

"I'll remember, and I will see you tonight," I told her as I turned and crawled out from under the fir tree. I stood up, stretched, brushed off my clothes, and then headed back to the house.

I lay in my bedroom and drew in my journal. *The Traegons here are so similar to the ones back home, but so different, too,* I thought. I finished the picture of Fletch and started one of Zuri and Ige, and I thought about how many more there were. *The world is huge, and if Traegons live anywhere there is land…Wow! They could be everywhere!*

The phone rang around eight thirty. The sun had just set, leaving streaks of pinks and golds in its wake. "Dino! It's Autumn. She wants to talk to you," Aunt Carol called from the other room.

I stood and walked into the kitchen, where she handed me the phone. She gave me a funny smile and returned to the living room, where my parents and uncle were watching TV.

"Hello?" I said into the phone.

"Hey, Dino, it's me, Autumn." Her voice was soft and kind.

"How's your dad?" I asked.

"It was pretty scary at first, but they say he is going to be fine. My mom is going to drop us off over by your aunt and uncle's. Then she is going to pick up a few things from our house and go back to the hospital to stay overnight," she stated.

"That's perfect," I blurted.

"Why? What do you mean?" Autumn asked, sounding a bit confused.

"There is a celebration in Traegonia tonight, and we have been invited," I whispered, peeking around the doorway to make sure no one was listening.

"Where?" a shocked voice came back through the receiver.

"Traegonia, in the mountains. Karia will come and get us tonight."

There was silence on the other end.

"Have you ever been in their world?" I whispered slowly.

A simple "No" was all that came back. "I don't know if I understand what you are talking about, but you can explain it when we get there." Autumn sounded distracted. "I have to go. See you soon." And then there was a *click*.

Mrs. Linder dropped Autumn and Jade off around ten o'clock. My aunt made up the couches in the living room for them to sleep on.

"What were you talking about earlier?" Autumn asked as my aunt left the room.

Jade and Autumn leaned in close, and I whispered, "We have been invited to Traegonia. There is a celebration, and they asked us to come."

"But how?" Jade asked simply.

"That is hard to explain. Just go to sleep as usual, and Karia and I will come and get you. You just have to see how it works for yourself. But remember, you can never tell anyone. Understand?" I told them.

Just then my aunt returned with a three glasses of milk and a plate of cookies. "To bed as soon as you are finished. If you girls need anything, I'll be in the room down the hall, to the left," she said, reaching down and plumping Jade's pillow.

"Okay. Thanks for letting us stay tonight," Autumn added.

"Anytime. Sleep well," Aunt Carol said, turning and heading to her room.

We ate the cookies and stared at the TV. I sometimes caught Autumn and Jade looking at me as if they wanted to ask more questions about the celebration, but I knew they wouldn't believe me even if I told them. For all I knew, they wouldn't believe it even after it happened.

We finished the plate of cookies, and I got up to take the empty plate to the kitchen. "Goodnight. See you later." I smiled, dropped the plate off in the kitchen, and went to my room. I fell asleep immediately, even though I was excited about what was yet to come.

Chapter 45
Celebration

I awoke to Karia standing on the bed next to me, pushing hard against my cheek.

"Come now, Dino. It is time." She pushed again, harder this time, trying to rouse the sleepiness out of me.

We tiptoed into the living room. I shook Autumn by the shoulder, and Karia climbed up and woke Jade the same way she had stirred me. Jade rolled over on the narrow couch, knocking Karia to the floor with a *thud*. The noise woke Jade up the rest of the way.

I placed my finger to my lips, indicating for all to be quiet, hoping the *thud* hadn't woken anyone else. "Come on. Follow us," I whispered, standing and turning back toward my room.

Karia scurried along ahead of me, and Autumn and Jade followed quietly.

"Now what?" Jade asked once we were all in my room.

"Sit in the center of the room." I moved first and sat down, Autumn and Jade followed, and Karia stood in the center of the three of us.

"Close your eyes and do not open them until I tell you. Now, let us hold hands, and whatever you do, don't let go," Karia instructed.

Jade and Autumn looked nervously at each other and then at me. We held hands and closed our eyes.

Karia sat silently, and her breathing slowed. She listened to only the beating of her heart. *Ba-bum, ba-bum, ba-bum.* She felt herself slowly being pulled backwards. She held tightly to Dino's and Jade's hands. Suddenly she felt forcibly tugged out of this world. *Falling...floating...*

The next thing I remember, I heard Karia's voice. "Alright, you may open your eyes now."

I opened my eyes and looked across from me. Jade was staring back at me with an amazed look in her eyes. I looked to my right and saw Autumn; she was looking around at the garden and all of the Traegonian community, who were standing around with looks of wonder on their faces. To my left sat Karia. Instantly, just as it was a year before when she had brought me to her world, I once again found myself the same size as her. Now Jade, Autumn, and I stood face to face with the sea of Traegons. The crowd erupted in applause. Apparently, summoning was not something they saw very often.

Oracle Qendrim approached with Pranvere, Bora, and Ljena at his side. "Excellent! Quite an extraordinary feat for a young Traegon," he said to Karia. "You are in training, I presume?"

Karia nodded. "I am. I believe, as I mentioned before, that this is a part of the connectedness of all things related to my path."

Her words were wise. As witnesses to her journey, I and Juna have found ourselves on our own paths as well.

Fletch, Juna, and Arbalest stepped up to greet us, and it was comforting to see others we knew. Fletch moved to where Autumn and Jade stood. Now face to face for the first time, the girls gazed in amazement at his strong features, his squared jaw with the one protruding tooth, his smooth, rounded muzzle that drew their eyes to his deep green ones. Within his twinkling eyes was the spark of his kind and playful spirit, but also his brave and honorable manner. Jade reached out and gently touched the end of what would be his nose. His skin was smooth with deep groves that resembled the bark of trees or certain kinds of rock.

He allowed her the moment and then reached out and took hold of her arm. "May I escort you ladies to the celebration this eve'?" he asked with a slight bow.

Autumn and Jade giggled, and Autumn gave a slight curtsey in return. "That would be grand." She paused as she and Jade each took hold at the crook of his bent arm. "Always the gentleman...uh, I mean gentle Traegon."

Karia winked at me, and following Fletch's lead, I extended my arm to her. She took it graciously. We looked at each other for just a moment and then turned toward the crowd.

In a tone meant for all to hear, Oracle Qendrim spoke, "We bid you welcome, young friends, Dino, Autumn, and Jade. We are and have been aware of your fondness for nature and the creatures that dwell in forest homes. Given this kindness and understanding, we invite you to partake in our feast and to join in our celebration of the end of the Ember Augury."

Oracle Qendrim and Pranvere stepped to one side and Bora and Ljena to the other, revealing a table filled with food. I was pleasantly surprised to find that there were so many different fruits and vegetables laid out alongside the traditional beetles, grubs, and other insects that made up the Traegonian diet.

Karia and I took a few steps forward, and Fletch, Autumn, and Jade fell in behind. Pranvere stepped up before Arbalest and Ljena before Juna. Nervously, Juna followed Arbalest's example from the corner of his eye, and they each gave a half-bow toward the she-Traegons offering their bent arms to their escorts. Pranvere and Ljena, with a slight curtsey, accepted the offer and took hold of their arms. Scrival was already standing beside Bora. He looked at her with a sheepish sideways grin and held out his arm. Bora smiled, slipped her arm into his, and followed the procession to the table.

Above the din of the crowd, the loud, strong voice of Oracle Qendrim announced, "Let the celebration begin!" and with that the sound of flutes, drums, and wind chimes filled the air. Music and merriment filled the garden.

We sat with Oracle Qendrim and the others. Many Traegons of all ages filed past where we sat within a cove of feathery pink yarrow.

They each introduced themselves, asked questions, or just wished to meet the humans and hear parts of our tale firsthand.

Karia stood and walked back toward the food table.

Fletch watched and then slipped from between Jade and Autumn and followed. "Still hungry, Karia?"

Karia hadn't seen him come up from behind. "Oh, Fletcher, you startled me." She playfully swatted him. "No, but I am fascinated by the many colorful foods your clan eats. Do you know much about them?" They reached the table, heavily laden with food. Karia recognized some of the vegetables that grew naturally back home. There were many odd and exotic-looking fruits, and she questioned Fletch about them. "Do you know of these?" she asked, gesturing toward chunks of pale, off-white cubes set inside a deep purple bowl that looked itself to be some kind of food.

"The bowl is actually part of the plant, but it is not to be eaten," Fletch explained. "The outside is quite bitter."

Autumn stepped in from behind and reached over to take one of the cubes in question and popped it into her mouth. Karia looked at her with a raised eyebrow as she chewed, so Autumn explained, "It is called eggplant. It can be made many different ways, but this is the first time I have had it prepared this way. Do you know what it is seasoned with?" Autumn asked, directing her question to Fletch.

I walked up behind Autumn during her conversation. "You may not want to know the answer to that question," I whispered into her ear. "Would you like to take a walk?" I asked her.

She looked at me and smiled. "Sure," she said, popping another cube of eggplant in her mouth. She grabbed a few more and followed me away from the table.

Just as we walked away, a short, round Traegon in a white apron with a white cloth tied around his head scurried out of a clump of bushes toward Karia and Fletch. "You are inquiring of the morsels we have arranged for the celebration?" He looked up at them. "Do pardon my directness. I am Samoon, the lead preparer of meals, morsels, and fare for our Traegonian clan."

Dino C. Crisanti

A Feast To Share

"Yes, Samoon, I was appreciating the wondrous variety you have prepared. I am sure my mim and the rest of our clan would greatly enjoy many of these delicious fruits. Your land produces such a bounty! If it is not asking too much, could you perhaps share the knowledge to grow such foodstuffs?" Karia requested.

Samoon smiled up at her, pleased at his own accomplishment and glad it was so appreciated by one who had traveled so far. He was also excited to share something else with her. He twisted his apron around his plump middle, revealing several hand carved spoons, forks, and many pouches tied to his belt. Some of the pouches were tied directly to his belt, while other, even smaller pouches were tied to these pouches. He moved them around in an effort to find what it was he was looking for.

Karia looked at Fletch, smiled, and then looked back at Samoon.

He finally said, "Ah! Here it is." He untied a green leather pouch, and after repositioning his apron, he turned to Karia and held it out to her. "These are for you to take back with you to your home."

Karia reached out her hand and gladly accepted the gift. "Thank you, Samoon, but what is in the pouch?" she asked.

"These are the seeds of some of the fruits and vegetables that line this table. If you plant them when the ground becomes warm, you should have a harvest to take you through your winter," he told her.

"How do you know about where I come from?" she asked.

"Word travels quickly in Traegonia." He smiled. "I am glad you are enjoying what I have created, and I hope you enjoy sharing it with your community." He turned and retreated back into the bushes where he had come from.

Autumn and I walked through the garden. We were approached several times by other Traegons who wanted to meet us and see us up close, and then we moved on. We talked and looked at the trees, bushes, and flowers that grew in the garden. We couldn't help but notice how large everything seemed. It was all very strange, yet wonderful at the same time. We saw Jade and Juna playing a game with a small group of

Dino C. Crisanti

Samoon Preparer of Meals, Morsels and Fare

Traegon younglings, including Ige. They were laughing and having the time of their lives. Even though Autumn and Jade had known Fletch for several years and knew that more of them existed, this experience was more than either of them could have ever imagined. Autumn and I went back to where the games were taking place and joined in. We laughed, we smiled, we joked, and we celebrated under the stars, late into the night.

Chapter 46
Three Have Seen

I heard the shower turn on in the bathroom outside my room. I rolled over and looked at the alarm clock on the bedside table. It was glowing with a digital red 9:18. I sat up and glanced around my room. When I leaned over my bed and looked down, I found Karia and Juna sleeping soundly in the open suitcase on the floor beside the bed. I rubbed my eyes as memories of the night before flashed through my mind. I couldn't help but wonder if it was real. I slid out of my bed and slipped on my house slippers. I quietly opened my bedroom door and peered out. I could hear my mom, dad, Aunt Carol, and Uncle Joe talking in the kitchen. I walked quietly down the hall and heard the shower behind the closed door of the bathroom. *I wonder who is in there?* I thought. When I reached the end of the hall, I had a clear view into the living room. I saw one of the girls sitting on the couch but couldn't make out which one. I ducked past the kitchen and into the living room. When I got closer, I could tell it was Autumn. I came around the corner of the couch and plopped down on the far end from her. We both just stared at each other.

"Morning." She smiled.

"Morning," I replied.

Again, there was silence.

I just had to know for sure, so I blurted. "Do you remember where we went last night?"

Autumn smiled, relieved. "I am so glad you asked," she sighed. "Traegonia, right?"

"What?" I looked at her like she was nuts.

Her face dropped, and I felt like a jerk.

"I'm just kidding. Yeah, Traegonia! It was amazing, wasn't it?"

She slid to the edge of the couch and leaned in. "Absolutely!" she whispered. "Is it like that back home?"

"No. It's different but still just as amazing," I replied.

"How do they do that? You know...get us there?" she asked me.

"I still don't understand how they do a lot of the things they do, and most of the time I don't even bother asking, anymore." I whispered back.

"Hi, you two!" My mother came into the living room. "I didn't even know you were up yet, Dino. Would you two like some breakfast? We have cereal, yogurt, and banana muffins," she offered, just as Jade came into the room.

Her hair was wet and combed straight, and she was carrying her things. "Morning!" she said as she made her way to her bag that was sitting on the couch. She sat down and shot a look to Autumn and one to me. Autumn smiled and nodded. Jade's eyes grew wide as if to say *"Really?"* I nodded too.

"I don't know what's up with you three, but if you want something to eat, I suggest you come into the kitchen." Mom turned with a grin and walked back into the kitchen.

"So, it's true, isn't it?" Jade blurted in an excited whisper. "I knew it! I knew it wasn't just a dream."

The phone rang, startling us. We all jumped and then laughed.

"Girls, your mom will be here at eleven!" Aunt Carol called from the kitchen.

Autumn quickly gathered her things. "I'd better get in the shower before Mom gets here." She hurried toward the bathroom.

I looked at Jade.

"I just knew it," she whispered, and then she got up and started for the kitchen. She glanced back. "You comin'?"

Unable to resist any kind of muffin even after my Traegonian feast the night before, I followed.

The girls left with their mom shortly after eleven.

My mom turned to me. "It sure has been an exciting vacation, huh?" She smiled.

I smiled back. "It sure has."

"Well, you need to get your things packed. Our flight leaves tomorrow afternoon," she said. "Your dad and Uncle Joe are going fishing today. If you want to go with them, I'm sure they would love to have you along."

"We're leaving already? It seems like we just got here," I moaned.

"It's been a week, and there are others waiting for our return," she reminded me.

I knew she was talking about Karia and Juna. I also knew that their mim and Sire Argus missed them and were anxiously waiting for them to come home. "I'm gonna stick around here today," I told her.

"Suit yourself," she said, walking back toward the kitchen. "We'll be out on the back deck if you want to join us."

I heard the back screen door clap shut. I looked toward my room, remembering Karia and Juna, and I returned to the kitchen for a muffin and some dry cereal.

Balancing the food in one hand, I turned the knob to my room and slowly opened the door. "Hey, guys. It's just me," I forewarned.

Karia and Juna scurried out from under the bed and climbed up the side.

"Ooh, I am so glad you remembered. I am feeling very hungry on this morning." Juna admitted, eyeing the food in my hand.

I pushed the door closed with my foot and brought the food to the bed. I gave them each a napkin and set the plate with the muffin in the center and the bowl of dry cereal next to it. I reached over to break apart the muffin when Juna interjected, "No, let me." He stood up and sliced the muffin down the middle with his long, curved knife.

Karia looked at him and then at me. She smiled and shook her head. Juna was so different now, than he was when I'd first met them. He has really come out of his shell. In a way, I guess we all have. He pried small pieces of the muffin apart for him and Karia and flipped a Cheerio into the air from the tip of his knife, catching it perfectly in his mouth.

"We are leaving tomorrow, to go home," I told them.

Karia looked at me and then glanced back at Juna as he caught another Cheerio on his tongue. "It seems as though we just arrived," she said turning back to me.

"Yeah, I know," I agreed. "When the girls come back from visiting their dad in the hospital, we can go and say goodbye," I suggested.

"I would like to take a walk alone this day, if you do not mind," she told us.

I looked at Juna, who was now working on skewering pieces of muffin. "I am sure that will be fine. Just try and stay out of trouble and don't be gone too long," I advised feeling like my mother as the words came out of my mouth.

"I will remain close," she confirmed. Karia stood and began to get her things together.

"Are you going now?" I asked.

"Yes, if that is alright," she responded.

Juna slowed his pace, gobbling down the food I brought.

Karia climbed onto the desk below the window and looked at me. "Will you let me down now?" she requested.

I walked to the window and pulled off the screen. "My parents and my aunt and uncle are sitting on the deck out back, so stay out of sight," I informed her.

"I will," she replied.

I lowered her out the window and waited for the tug on the blanket. I saw her run from the side of the house to the tree line as I pulled the blanket back in through the window. She turned and held her hand out to me and then disappeared into the woods.

Chapter 47
The Ember Rune

Karia walked for a while through the forest. She listened to the birds singing and chirping high up in the trees. She noticed a couple squirrels playing on the branches in the streams of sunlight that made it through the full, leafy trees. *It is so beautiful here,* she thought, and it made her miss home that much more. She ducked under a low-hanging branch and stumbled upon a rambling creek that ran through the forest floor. She moved in closer, *I wonder if this is the creek where I saw Kamara last,* she thought to herself. She walked along the edge of the creek, until she ran across a large rock. She couldn't be sure but she thought it might be the place. She sat on the rock and gazed at the water. She closed her eyes and just listened. The soothing sound of the water bubbling over the smooth rocks sent a feeling of pure calm over her. She took a deep breath and opened her eyes. She looked at the strong, large trees that grew along the creek and noticed fallen logs and old dry leaves strewn in piles on the forest floor. Beetles, ants, and spiders were all going about their daily chores, and butterflies of every color and pattern fluttered and floated in the cool forest air, landing occasionally on a rock or leaf in the sunlight to warm their wings. Dragonflies darted back and forth through the branches in what looked to be a game of tag. Bees fed quietly on the mountain bells that grew wild. The tiny purple and white flowers offered a scattering of delicate natural beauty to the brown and decaying leaves. Everything worked together in this circle of nature, and she was a part of it. She closed her eyes again and allowed the thought of what the fire could have done to creep into her mind. It was not what she wanted to think about in such a beautiful place, though, so she shook her head and pushed the dark thoughts away. This time, when she opened her eyes, sitting on a rock not far from her was Kamara.

"Your work here is done. You shall be free of the images that haunted you prior to your arrival. This is just another step of your journey, my youngling. Your future will be sprinkled with teachings, advice, guidance, and truth. It will always be yours to sort through, to choose from and to live. Some will be trivial lessons, and others will require something from you, but all are important and will amass you much wisdom. You have assembled a strong team and will continue to build allies. These are your gifts, Karia. Be strong, be aware, and remember to believe in yourself and those around you. That will be your greatest strength—a tool and a weapon unsurpassed by any other." Her gravelly voice brought forth much wisdom and clarity.

Karia felt the pouch on her hip that contained the shiny trinket which she had carried since the day she had first met Kamara. She untied the pouch, opened it, and removed the amulet. She held it in the palm of her hand, revealing the markings that seemed to be now more deeply etched into its face. "These markings?" Karia glanced from the amulet up to Kamara, who was looking peacefully at her. "What do they mean?"

Kamara paused, and a crooked smile appeared across her aged face. "Those are the marks of your journey, my dear, the lessons that have etched themselves into your knowledge. They will serve to remind you of what you can do because of what you already have done. The etchings will appear faintly at first, and as they etch themselves into your heart, mind, and will, they will show deeper and stronger. They will become Bind Runes."

"Bind Runes?" Karia questioned.

Dino C. Crisanti

Kamara and the Ember Rune

"They are the markings on the amulet—the ones that have represented the Ember Rune, but the amulet is much more than that. It is a time piece, a guide, a piece of protection, an energy amplifier, as you now well know, and it can and will do much more than that. It is a part of you, and as you grow, so shall it," Kamara shared.

"How will I know what the markings represent, if I am not able to read them?" Karia pleaded as she began to struggle with all of the information facing her.

"Look again to the light, Karia," Kamara directed her. "When you become flooded with thoughts, choices or decisions, allow your mind the peace of the light, the air and the Earth.

Karia looked up toward the streams of sunlight as Kamara spoke. A butterfly floated and circled in the air above her head. Almost immediately, she felt peacefulness come over her.

"Not all is meant to be revealed all at once. Piece by piece, bit by bit, your questions and their answers will come into the light. This is as much about the journey as it is about the destination, if not more. Take joy in the labor, and it will not seem as work. The journey is life, a puzzle to solve, every moment a gift." Kamara waved her free hand in the air while her other hand held the gnarled walking stick with her blackbird perched atop. "Every experience, youngling, no matter how ordinary, has the potential to hold the extraordinary. You just have to look to see it." The crooked smile on her leathery face grew a bit. "The markings...you wish to know their meaning, true?"

Karia had become so engrossed in Kamara's words that she almost forgot what she really wanted to know. "Oh yes, the markings. Please tell me what they mean." Karia looked down at the amulet.

"They are three." Kamara paused. "The single symbol is made up of three separate symbols, and each symbol holds several meanings. Let us approach each as one and how it applies to this step of your journey. The first, the arrowhead that points to the horizon. This one represents fire, the first element of your journey. As Oracle Balstar stated, fire can hold in itself many meanings. The ones that pertain most closely to your journey are wisdom, insight, and enlightenment. The fire brought a problem, and insight brought the solution, which in turn has brought enlightenment. The second symbol, the straight staff that has two short lines, one at the top and one at the bottom, reaching out in opposite directions, represents change—the confrontation of fears and the resulting transformation. Within this journey, you have been faced with images and situations that have raised fears within you, yet you have faced them, coming to a resolution for yourself and others. This has brought change in you as well as change in others. Can you see how this has come to pass?" She looked closely at Karia to see if she understood.

"Yes. I see how each of these things has happened within this journey. It is uncanny, but is becoming very clear. Please continue," Karia requested.

Kamara nodded. "The final symbol is a straight staff with two lines that reach out directly across from each other, outward toward the sky. This symbol is that of protection, a shield. This is the one that comes up when you feel the urge to shelter or protect yourself or others, as well as the symbol you may use to shield yourself in dangerous situations." Kamara paused to let Karia think on what she had revealed.

Karia recalled how she felt when Juna and Fletch were set to destroy the Grimalkin or when Mr. Linder needed her help. Her thoughts were brought back to the present as Kamara began to speak again.

"Bound together, these symbols give you strength to call the power from within and to bring it into your awareness." Kamara leaned on her stick in a sign of conclusion.

Karia felt for a moment a heaviness coming over her again. At that very moment, the butterfly that had been floating playfully above her landed upon the end of her long, slender muzzle. It gracefully fluttered its wings and floated up into the forest. Karia's eyes watched as it magically disappeared, as if carrying off her many concerns. Karia's eyes returned to where Kamara stood. The crooked smile was etched seemingly permanent upon her crooked, slightly squared muzzle.

"It is time for me to bid you farewell—not forever but for now. You have done well, youngling." The fireflies and fairies that usually only show themselves at night returned to escort Kamara back to wherever she had come from. In a moment, she was gone.

Karia felt energized and joyful. She looked down at the amulet she held in her hand, and within the groves of each of the etched symbols, a fiery glow of red and orange emanated and then turned to deepest black. Karia slipped the amulet back into the pouch and secured it on her hip. She took one last look around that beautiful place in the forest and turned to return to her friends. Feeling light and carefree, she skipped happily through the forest.

All the while, from a safe and hidden distance, Arbalest kept a guarded watch over her.

Juna and I were sitting under a tree as I drew in my journal, when Karia bounced out of the woods. She almost forgot to look for others and stepped back cautiously. When she noticed it was only us and no one else was around, she continued out of the woods in our direction.

"I am starving!" she announced.

Juna and I could clearly see there was something different about her. She no longer seemed weighted down with worry. She seemed playful and lighthearted, and it was good to see her that way. Her whimsical spirit had returned and seemed to rub off on both Juna and me.

"You seem happy!" I observed.

"I feel wonderful!" she echoed. "Is there anything to eat?" she asked.

"Stay here. I'll be right back." I jumped up and ran to the kitchen to get her something to eat.

My mom and Aunt Carol were sitting in the kitchen when I popped in.

"Looking for something?" Aunt Carol asked.

"Is there any granola left from breakfast?" I asked.

Aunt Carol stood and went to the pantry. She pulled out a plastic container and handed it to me. "Autumn called while you were outside," she said with a grin that embarrassed me for some reason.

"Oh. How is Mr. Linder? Is he doing any better?" I asked

"Much better. She said they will be back around four and will come down with the horses for one final ride before you leave tomorrow."

"Great. What time is it now?" I asked.

"It's 2:20," My mom interjected, looking at her watch as I poured some granola into a baggie.

I turned to look at the two of them. "Thanks for having us this week, Aunt Carol. I've really had a great time." I smiled at my mom, grabbed a muffin that was sitting on a plate on the counter, and ran back out to the yard.

Karia and Juna were waiting patiently. I set the food on my closed journal, and Karia started right in. I had not seen her eat like that in what felt like a long time. Juna joined in as well, and Karia and I stared at him.

"What?" Juna said.

"We know!" Karia and I said in unison. "You do not wish to be impolite."

Chapter 48
No Sappy Goodbyes

My aunt made dinner early so I could spend as much time with Autumn and Jade as possible on my last day in California. It was almost four thirty when I heard the horses coming up the gravel driveway. I ran to my room and grabbed my backpack. "See you later!" I called as I hopped down the front steps.

"Hey, Dino!" Jade called. "We have a surprise for you."

"What is it?" I asked.

"You'll just have to wait and see." Autumn smiled.

I could tell they were excited, whatever it was. I climbed onto Rory and waved to Mom, Dad, Uncle Joe, and Aunt Carol as we headed down the driveway. "See ya later!" I hollered.

"Have fun, but don't be too late!" my mom called back. "And don't get lost this time!"

We turned left at the bottom of the driveway and pulled to the side. I jumped off of Rory and called for Karia and Juna. They appeared a few feet ahead of us.

"This is our last ride. You two ready?" I called as I approached them on foot.

"Sure, but can I ride with Jade this time?" Juna requested.

"Definitely!" Jade exclaimed.

I held out my arm, Juna climbed on, and I passed him off to Jade. He settled himself on the saddle in front of her. I picked up

Karia, and held her up to climb onto Rory, and then climbed on myself.

We walked the horses down the road until we came to the path we always took into the forest. Jade led this time and guided us to the clearing and the rock where the bat cave was hidden. We dismounted the horses and tied them off to a couple of trees.

Within a few moments, Arbalest swooped in and landed on Ohanzee.

"Fletch! Are you near?" Autumn called.

As he had in the past, from out of nowhere, Fletcher zipped out of the forest as quick as the wind. Standing on a rock that jutted out just above the cave entrance, he announced himself. "Fletcher P. Web—" Before he could finish his cocky and ridiculously unnecessary introduction, Fletch tumbled off the rock, popping back up and quickly brushing himself off as if nothing had happened. He ran over to where we were standing.

Juna snorted with laughter. "Well done, Fletch!"

Fletch smiled and shot Juna a wink.

I didn't want to say goodbye, but there was so much I did want to say. We sat down in a circle on the ground. "I had such a great time this week," I started. "Thanks for taking me out, showing me around, and hanging out. And I can't even begin to thank you for helping save Karia and Juna. I am forever grateful to you." I continued to blither on. "This has been one of the most awesome weeks of my life, next to meeting Karia and Juna."

"Don't get sappy on us," Jade joked.

"I'm trying not to, but I want you to know this stuff," I justified.

Autumn turned, looking me directly in the eyes. Her blue eyes smiled at me. "We know what you mean, and believe me we know how you feel because we feel the same. If you hadn't come here, we probably wouldn't have ever had the chance to see Traegonia. We're really glad we got to meet you two also." She looked at Karia and Juna. "We can't begin to thank you for helping our dad the way you did."

Jade became teary eyed thinking about that day. "Thank you," was all she could say before she had to choke back tears.

"Alright, alright. So we are all grateful, truly grateful. Let's not allow this to become a sad moment," Fletch jumped in, attempting to lighten the mood.

"I just have to tell you all that I believe this was more than a chance meeting for all of us. This is and has been as it was meant to be. We are bonded by friendship, and that will always keep us connected," Karia stated wisely.

Fletch jumped to his feet and approached Karia. He knelt on one knee and took her hand. "I completely agree. I to believe we were meant to meet and will probably meet again." he leaned over and ever so slowly kissed her hand.

We all stared in disbelief when Jade piped in. "Now, that is definitely not a sappy goodbye." Fletch and Karia blushed and we all laughed.

"Fletcher!" Arbalest called, drawing Fletches attention. "I have something I wish to give to you."

Fletch bowed slightly to Karia, released her hand and turned to Arbalest.

"You have strong determination and confidence. You will become all that you aspire to be, I have no doubt." Arbalest reached out to Fletch holding a small pouch. "This is the fire starter kit you saw me use. It now belongs to you. Use it wisely."

Fletch took the pouch. He looked at it and then at Arbalest. "If I were to follow in the shadow of any other, it would be yours." Fletch said humbly as Arbalest placed his strong hand on Fletch's shoulder.

Sitting back in the circle, we continued to reminisce about all that had happened over the last week, and before long, the sun began to drop into the horizon.

"Wait, it's almost time!" Jade squealed. "Come on! Come over here."

"Time for what?" I asked.

"The surprise!" Autumn answered.

We all got up and followed her to a spot just outside the mouth of the cave.

She quickly lay down on her back and looked into the sky. "Come on, you guys! Hurry!"

We all did exactly as she did. Autumn, Jade, Karia, Juna, Fletch, Arbalest, and myself laid side by side staring into the sky, watching as the stars began to twinkle. Suddenly there was an echo of a distant rumble. I couldn't quite make out where it was coming from. Then, a swirling blast of blackness poured from the mouth of the cave. The sound was thunderous and magnificent, so loud and powerful it sent chills through my whole body. Every Townsend long-eared bat flooded out of the cave on its way to find food. It was amazing—almost as amazing as my new friends.

Arbalest returned home with Ohanzee that night. We made it back the next evening with no mishaps this time on the plane. Karia and Juna were glad to see mim and Sire Argus and didn't face any serious consequences for leaving unannounced. It would be a long time before we would see Autumn and Jade again, but we kept in touch by writing and phoning. They mentioned that the rogue cougar that had been terrorizing the area had not been seen and had not caused any more trouble. I shared this with Karia and Juna, and Karia was pleased with the news. Traegons have their own way of communicating over the distance, although we helped where we could. I had left an envelope at my aunt and uncle's house for Autumn and Jade. Inside were two drawings, one of them with Fletch at the celebration in Traegonia and one of Karia and Juna.

I think my mom keeps in touch with mim, but she doesn't share that with me. I see her in the yard a lot, feeding the animals, planting lots of flowers, and just enjoying being surrounded by the forest. Karia, Juna, and I continue to spend many days together. We play, we live, we learn...but most of all, we believe!

CPSIA information can be obtained at www.ICGtesting.com
Printed in the USA
LVOW082031220911

247484LV00001B/5/P

9 781432 777180